FORGOTTEN
FOLKTALES RETOLD

virago

VIRAGO

These stories were first published by Audible on the podcast *Hag*, released 2019
Published in Great Britain in this edition in 2020 by Virago Press

1 3 5 7 9 10 8 6 4 2

Typeset in Caslon by M Rules
Printed and bound in Great Britain by Clays Ltd, Elcograf S.p.A.

Papers used by Virago are from well-managed forests
and other responsible sources.

Virago Press
An imprint of
Little, Brown Book Group
Carmelite House
50 Victoria Embankment
London EC4Y 0DZ

An Hachette UK Company
www.hachette.co.uk

www.virago.co.uk

CONTENTS

PREFACE

Professor Carolyne Larrington

E very British child knows about the Little Mermaid, Beauty and the Beast, Snow White and Red Riding Hood. But which of them could tell of the malicious cunning of Tom Tit Tot, or the unsettling Small-Toothed Dog, the tragic Great Silkie of Sule Skerry or the lost, alien Green Children of Woolpit?

The hundreds of traditional tales that make up the rich story-hoard of the British Isles are strangely forgotten. Why do they not play a central role in our imagination in the same way as the Grimm tales, or Perrault's Cinderella, or Hans Christian Andersen's stories? Our British and Irish folktale heritage slipped away from us during the late eighteenth and early nineteenth centuries, during those years in which traditional story transitioned from the oral to the printed. While European collectors were busying themselves in capturing, writing down, popularising and sanitising their stories – or, like Hans Christian Andersen, composing brand new stories in a folk idiom – the antiquarian and folklore enthusiasts in these islands were lagging behind. Continental stories were quickly translated into English and adapted to make them suitable for children. They offered clear morals: warnings about the big bad wolves in the forest and the meanness of stepmothers; the hope that help may be forthcoming from unexpected quarters, that little deeds of kindness will be rewarded, and the suspicion that pitfalls will lie ahead when some supernatural creature seems to be promising you something for nothing.

The systematic collection of British folktales only got underway later in the nineteenth century, an activity that was rapidly incorporated into antiquarian study of a rapidly vanishing pre-industrial past. In those years there was a powerful impetus to track down and rescue the indigenous stock of traditional tales before industrialisation and urbanisation caused them to fade away entirely. For, or so it was believed, the old generations of traditional storytellers lay buried deep in quiet country churchyards and their grandchildren had migrated to the city, where they were now devouring cheap novels and penny dreadfuls and the old tales would be lost in the urban noise and bustle. The great county-by-county collection projects got underway in the second half of the nineteenth century and in the early decades of the twentieth, yet, perhaps surprisingly, this work is still going on in the present day. Researchers are still occupied in capturing traditional tales from some of the remoter parts of the British Isles and from the Gypsy, Traveller, Fairground and Roma communities and adding to the lore already archived. And, importantly, at least since the end of the Second World War, the nation's diverse ethnic minority communities too have begun to share their own stories, ones that may originate and be rooted in locations that range far across the globe, but which share many essential themes – love, loss, value, courage – with their native counterparts. Just as – back in the twelfth century – the Breton figure of the tragic werewolf, cruelly betrayed by his wife and – in the nineteenth century – Bram Stoker's Eastern European version of the suavely charming vampire have both migrated into and lodged themselves firmly within our story-world, so international figures such as Anansi, Haruman, Coyote, Monkey, the *hulda*, the fox-woman and the Japanese *kappa* have found their way across the oceans and into our twenty-first-century consciousness.

Those stories so assiduously collected in the nineteenth century were sometimes taken down in dark, unsettling detail, and were read with alarm, threatening the pieties of Victorian family life and social order. The strange desires, troublingly alluring figures and odd remnants of popular belief, recast as superstition, that many of them preserved could not be made decent for the ordinary reader and they were left in obscurity. Still other tales were sentimentalised or prettified for the nursery. Thus, despite the efforts of popularisers such as Andrew Lang, the editor of the Blue, Lilac and various-coloured Fairy Books, it seems now as if very many of the wonderful stories that constitute the British folktale heritage have been long submerged. Yet their shapes can be glimpsed now and again, here and there, like underwater reefs of glinting beauty and dangerous mystery, lurking just below the surface in the work of many fantasy writers, from Alan Garner and Terry Pratchett to Philip Pullman, from Sylvia Townsend Warner and Susannah Clarke to Ben Aaronovitch. Literary novelists too have found inspiration in our folk-tradition: Max Porter's recent *Lanny*, Sarah Hall's treatment of *Mrs Fox*, and the many books of Helen Oyeyemi, to name just a few. Indeed, the last fifty years have seen a remarkable upsurge of interest in Britain's traditional imaginary. Old stories and motifs have been repurposed to underpin much contemporary fiction, built into new worlds where they gleam like a gloriously strange thread that runs through popular and literary writing alike. For we live in deeply unsettling times, when interest in the timeless, the local and the hitherto unseen has been suddenly and extraordinarily renewed. The Covid-19 pandemic, limiting us for so long to walk only in our own locales, brought to many a new appreciation of how spring, nevertheless, was burgeoning all around. People suddenly found themselves reconnecting emotionally with the natural world, joyfully noticing bursting buds, heady scents of blossom and loud, unabashed birdsong in hedgerows, copses, parks and gardens. So too memory and imagination were kindled into fresh and vivid life as people roamed through places underwritten by history and tradition, reminded of fairies, house-elves, river deities, dwarfs, witches and werewolves whose existences cast a sidelong light across the country's green spaces.

There is, nonetheless, a huge hinterland of unexplored folktale preserved from all across the British Isles, stories that are familiar only to experts, those people who preserve the old stories of their own regions, and enthusiastic amateurs – *amateur* here in its original sense of one who loves something for its own sake. I came to love many such local tales told to me in my childhood in North Yorkshire: of the helpful, healing Hob, the scary boggart – whom we'll meet later in this book – and the hideous Black Dog. Later, as a scholar interested in myths, legends and tales of every kind, I sought them out afresh; indeed, my first book-length publication was *The Feminist* (later reprinted as *The Women's*) *Companion to Mythology*. In recent years I've been increasingly intrigued and delighted by the turn towards folklore in English novels and stories. For nowadays, if we think about the patterning of traditional tales at all, it's probably through the ubiquitous framework of the superhero movie with its endless variations on the familiar plotline, forever pitching the good, if flawed, man against various embodiments of total evil. And, notably, it *is* men who are usually charged with saving humanity, even if they are sometimes assisted by a feisty female sidekick; it's a hero pattern that, thanks to theorists such as Joseph Campbell and his influential *The Hero with a Thousand Faces*, is an all too familiar one. But our traditional tales are neither so simplistic nor so predictable. They give generous space to the subaltern voice: to the powerless, to the poor, to girls and wives, even to animals, all those creatures who need to find ways not only to survive in this difficult world, but to live well in it, despite the dark forces ranged against them. These stories compel, seizing our attention with their strangeness while at the same time speaking clearly to shared themes of human existence. They explore huge questions: of love and loss, and of the conditions under which we do our everyday work and how we might thrive in it. They patrol the shadowy borderlands between life and death and they tease out our hopes and fears for our children. They demand we consider issues such as migration, asking who belongs here, who can make a home here, who can find the strength to begin all over again in a strange new land – and who might have been here for much longer than you think. Folktales pick fights about disability and aging, about women and men, and, crucially, they hold out to us the environments in which we live – our much-loved British countryside – and show how it might slip through our fingers.

Our time-honoured stories grew within different regional cultures across the British Isles that were entirely oral. Thus, their forms tend to be spare and stripped down, freeing different storytellers to expand and elaborate to their listening audiences. Differing nuances and meaning, new details and varying explanations would have been added each time the tales were performed – just as nowadays a good reader aloud will vary her emphasis and intonation, energising and breathing life into the words on the page. Folktales often have very familiar plots – the same narrative patterns recur widely across the British Isles – and so their earlier audiences would always know – or guess – how the tale would end. For them, the intriguing questions would be: *how* does the story arrive at that end? *How* will it be told? What sly asides, jokes or judgments will the storyteller bring to the performance? The traditional tales lost some of this intimate dimension when they were captured in print, imprisoned within a cage of words. In a return to those old storytelling practices, *Hag*, the collection of stories contained in this book, was first conceived as a podcast series. For podcast technology quite beautifully allows the recapture and reproduction of some of those original oral features; there's an intimate voice speaking directly in your ear, telling the tale just to you, while modern sound-design allows really vivid aural effects to be incorporated into the story's sound-world.

Disenchantment, the vanishing of the supernatural marvellous from the workaday world, is a defining feature of modernity, or so the sociologist Max Weber argued. The Victorians indeed feared that the coming of the railway, the factories belching out their dark smoke, the greedy cities with their noise and dirt, gobbling up the pastures and woodlands of older England, would drive the fairies and other spirits away – and perhaps extinguish them altogether. With the ascendancy of technology and science, the victory of reason, superstition and foolishness would be banished. Yet, despite the ringing rhetoric of progress and modernisation, many aspects of the non-rational – in particular, religion – survived. The new technology was indeed harnessed to support the hypothesis that unseen things were moving around us; the microscope revealed teeming life in drops of water, and photography purported to capture spirit beings moving in the darkness of the séance. Heroes of old, King Arthur and Sir Galahad stepped forward to serve as symbols for the British Empire and the British officer in global conflicts; during and after the Second World War, writers, such as J. R. R. Tolkien, turned towards fantasy once again. This turn in some ways looked very much like a nostalgia for what had perhaps never existed, akin to the Victorian mourning for the fairy realm, but in fact medievalist and folkloric fantasy has always been about the present as much as the past. For the world we live in is, of course, not disenchanted at all. Many things move within it that we cannot comprehend satisfactorily through the application of reason nor fit into the logic of our systems and paradigms. Human existence so often calls for exploration through the imagination, through metaphors, images, narratives that give shape to emotions and conditions, to our sense of being and our struggles to survive and thrive. The supernatural and inexplicable, the selkie, the boggart, the mermaid, the Green Children and the fairies return then, tapping into a powerful sense of continuity from past into present and onwards into the future.

For our everyday is not a disenchanted place, however loudly our commuter trains rattle along their tracks or however tall the tower blocks stand in the place where the trees once grew. In her disquieting work 'Glitches', the poet Sarah Hesketh has named what is missed when our attention remains directed downwards to our phones on those tedious daily journeys. Beside the train tracks, if we would only turn to look, we could glimpse 'faces forcing / their way out of the stone, quick bodies etched in gold'; these are 'the residents of the edgelands made flesh'. The modern world still holds on to its magic, its weirdnesses, and spookiness, if we can attune ourselves to the enchantments that lurk in the quotidian. So these new stories aim to make listeners and readers take their normal daily environment just a little less for granted, urging you to notice, even seek out, the strange and quirky, keeping an eye open for those flashes of the ancient and the otherworldly as you go about your business.

Each of the authors in this collection was given a different traditional tale as a prompt for her re-imagining, stories that stemmed from very different parts of the British Isles. Nevertheless, these localities were places that each writer knows well, often as their current or childhood homes. Those original stories are no longer than a couple of pages at most; some indeed are only a paragraph or a few verses long, but each author spins a brand-new tale out of the raw stuff she was given, sparkling, fresh iterations that transpose these universal themes into contemporary life. Although the source tales deal with topics that are always already modern, always relevant, their traditional trappings can seem old-fashioned and quaint, dulling their urgent voices and blunting their impact. But in this new collection, shorn of their three-legged stools and horses and carts, their shiny gold coins and soldiers' muskets, they are set directly in dialogue with the modern.

When I was first tasked with choosing a single set of narratives to represent the many different regions of the British Isles, I had a whole treasury of tales to choose from. At that time I didn't know that the authors who would take up these tales and shape them into new creative works would all be women – some women of colour and queer women – each of whom would bring her own lived insights and experiences to the stories I'd picked out, selected just because I liked them and because I thought them a little different from those more familiar tales that we share with our European cousins. While there are lots of tales about selkie (seal) women, all following much the same pattern, I chose a very short ballad from Shetland that tells of a selkie man and his predatory habits. I've always been rather fond of the quite funny Yorkshire tale of the boggart, a kind of low-level poltergeist that is annoying rather than sinister and the phlegmatic resignation of the farmer that it plagues. Finding a story for London – which has urban myths and legends a-plenty, but not traditional folktales as such – was more difficult. London was (and is) a melting pot to which people brought their own tales as they migrated from rural areas, but these weren't London stories exactly, rooted as they were in the fields, forests and moorlands of the shires. In the end, I found an account of a strange happening in Tavistock Square, an instance of murderous sibling rivalry. Finding a tale from the Midlands also presented a challenge but, as the great cities expanded outwards they incorporated ancient manor houses and their parkland, wild forests and mysterious lakes into their suburbs; some of the wild then is brought into the heart of the new city. Wales has a plethora of stories about the Tylwyth Teg, the Welsh fairies whose activities may help or hinder the humans they encounter and whose rules must be followed to the letter. Mermaids are often glimpsed amid the crashing waves off the Cornish coast and their siren song is heard by fishermen looking for a spectacular catch. In Somerset, the piskies form strong views about human behaviour and how it might affect powerless humans and animals, as well as vexing the piskies themselves. East Anglia is particularly rich in lore: two medieval chronicles yield separate inexplicable accounts of a bright green boy and girl, who material-ise one hot August day at the edge of a Suffolk cornfield. Norfolk breeds bold young women and importunate ghosts while Black

Shuck, the spectral and terrifying Black Dog, roams freely across both counties.

As the original stories came into being as spoken creations, some of the new tales also have a very marked narrator's voice. In Eimear McBride's 'The Tale of Kathleen', the teller has strong views about the world in which Kathleen's tragedy played out, and how that might relate to the Ireland of today. Other stories have narrators who are telling their own tales, stories in which we come to trust – or wonderingly distrust – the experiences they share with us. Daisy Johnson's disturbing story, 'A Retelling', begins self-referentially with the writer's task, commissioned to retell the tale of the Green Children, but it takes us on a compelling journey into strange, hidden places, bringing the wild and uncanny back into the city. Kirsty Logan's tale, 'Between Sea and Sky', is narrated, in part, by an outsider, a woman who is trying to make a place for herself within a community with a secret, but who ends up harbouring a secret of her own. Many of the other tales are first-person narratives: Emma Glass's story, 'The Dampness is Spreading' and Naomi Booth's 'Sour Hall' all give distinctive voices to speakers who are trying to process trauma, only to find that trauma emerging in ways that speak very clearly to women's unique experience of childbearing. Pregnancy, miscarriage and birth transform bodies and alter souls, bringing blood, pain and terror, as well as joy. As Liv Little's 'The Sisters' transposes a tale about two brothers duelling for the love of one woman into a searing story of two rivalrous sisters, we hear voices speaking in Caribbean English, bringing rich cadence to that towering fairy-tale figure: the hostile mother ready to banish her own child.

Mahsuda Snaith and Natasha Carthew take different approaches to voice; their third-person narratives relate tales that take place in the distant past – or an apocalyptic very near future. Mahsuda's 'The Panther's Tale' draws on her own Bengali folk heritage to bring a blaze of vivid jewel-like colour to what was originally just a little anecdote about how a Midlands aristocratic family got their coat of arms and motto. Natasha Carthew's 'Droll of the Mermaid' shares its title with her source story (a 'droll' is an entertaining tale in Cornish dialect), and we hear in it both the musicality and muscularity of the narrative voice and the distinctive speech of Lowan and his family.

Two new stories were commissioned from Irenosen Okojie and Imogen Hermes Gowar for this printed version of the *Hag* collection; they will soon be available as podcasts, for they too have been re-engineered back into the direct and intimate context of the spoken tale. Irenosen was assigned the rousing Norfolk tale of 'The Dauntless Girl', who is afraid of nothing – neither the gloomy bone house in the local church at dead of night, nor her master's persistent dead mother. Dared to fetch a skull out of the ossuary at midnight, the girl succeeds triumphantly, and when approached to deal with a ghost, she declares that this particular service demands an increase in her wages. In her story, 'Rosheen', Irenosen takes up the themes of exploitative labour and extraordinary courage; descent into a haunted space of the dead enables this truly undaunted young woman to understand her family's history. Imogen's Somerset tale 'A Holloway' cleverly transposes the original story's drunken, tyrannical father and his ponies into a familiar modern context. Told from a young girl's perspective, a point of view that holds in tension the possibilities of the supernatural with a wrenching realisation of deep-seated fear and trauma, the tale transports us into the heart of Exmoor and its ancient powers, melding a glorious summer landscape with the dynamics of a troubled family.

Many of the stories in *Hag* are in dialogue with 'folk-horror' or the 'new weird', a cultural trend that emerged in the 1970s in films such as *The Wicker Man* and is still being revived today with hit films like 2019's *Midsommar*. The past re-emerges into the present – or is revealed never quite to have gone away – violently and disruptively; the contemporary characters do not necessarily understand what they are dealing with or how to combat the forces that have been aroused. But with new understanding comes also hope, closure, determination in the face of trauma and pain. Each *Hag* story has a woman either at its heart or close to it; women's friendships and their enmities, their power to give birth and to deal death, to harm and to heal thread their way through the narratives.

Lastly, a word about the title. *Hag* is a very old word in English; its earliest form, *hægtesse*, is found in the tenth-century Old English 'Metrical Charms' where it invokes a fierce, supernatural female who shoots dangerous disease-bearing missiles at hapless humans. For me, and I think for all the writers featured here, the Hag is a powerful figure indeed. In one early and widespread traditional story, found first in Ireland and then across Great Britain in the medieval period, a knight finds himself in deep trouble. Either he, or his beloved king, will be slain if he cannot discover the answer to the trickiest of all tricky questions (as Sigmund Freud would acknowledge, centuries later): 'what do women want?' He searches for a year and a day, interviewing women of every rank; in one poem he is able to compile a whole pamphlet full of all the different answers he has been given. But none seems totally convincing, and he is plunged into despair. Quite by chance he encounters a hag, an ugly, old woman – often with quite monstrous features: bristles, tusks, bleared eyes and a gaping mouth – who tells him that she knows the right answer. And, if he will marry her, she will divulge it. The hag's answer does indeed satisfy all the women who hear it, and the knight is off the hook – except he must now marry this hideous, elderly and low-born woman. With varying degrees of reluctance, he goes through the ceremony. Once they are in bed together she explains that there's a choice: he can have her fair by night and foul by day, or vice versa (or, in Chaucer's version, beautiful and faithless or ugly and faithful). But the knight has learned from the hag's answer – that what women want is to be given agency to decide things for themselves – and he hands the choice back to her. And she chooses to be lovely all the time – as, of course, you would. The curse placed on her by her stepmother is lifted and she is restored to beauty, and marital happiness with a husband who recognises her selfhood and right to choose her own mode of being.

The Hag that presides over this book is not a victim of stepmotherly enchantment, but she certainly knows a thing or two about the ways in which the world can appear and the hidden forces that pulse below the everyday surface. She knows about transpositions and transformations, about the very old and the sparklingly new. And she offers true insight into that eternal question: what it is that women want. For there is nothing like a Hag-tale for crystallising what is really important – and timeless – in women's existence, for teaching us valuable truths about love and desire, about courage and persistence; how we feel about our parents and our children; how we relate to our immediate communities, and how much we should believe – and conform to – what they are telling us.

A RETELLING

Daisy Johnson

Based on
The Green Children of Woolpit
SUFFOLK

ONE

Beneath the dirt there is not enough air to breathe for long. I can feel everything that moves and grows and threshes and dies and is eaten and lives again and dies and is buried. I am buried too but the earth is moving and there are seams of light and I take in a breath big enough for a lifetime.

TWO

I have been asked to write a retelling of 'The Green Children of Woolpit' and so, when I go back to my parents' for Christmas, we pay a visit to the village. It rains on the drive and there are fights over what music to play in the car. Mum won't listen to Christmas music and my sister won't listen to anything else. We settle on an old audiobook which we used to hear when we were children and which has somehow resurfaced again. It is Roald Dahl's *Revolting Rhymes* which are retellings of fairy tales in which Cinderella flashes her knickers and Little Red Riding Hood slaughters the wolf and wears its fur as a coat. This is fitting enough so no one complains. We drive past places that we used to come to when we were younger. We smell Bury St Edmunds before we see it – the stench of the sugar beet factory which you can see from the road. After that we don't recognise any of the signs. My sister's boyfriend has come along for the ride and he asks me about the myth. He's a GP-in-training and is helpful to have around. I tell him the bits of it I can remember from the email and he is particularly interested in the colour of the children's skin when they first appeared: green. 'Anaemia,' he says, 'I'm certain.' We come off the motorway. There are caravan parks and dirty horses tied up on roundabouts and signs for closed farmer's markets and dead-end roads and not many people around. The village is small, we drive from one end of it to the other in hardly any time. It is still raining and our plan – to walk around soaking in the feel of the place, to drive afterwards to the nearby wood said to be haunted by The Babes in the Wood – is foiled. We park outside a church and nervously check the service times by the gate. We are heathens and reprobates and we don't want to interrupt something we don't understand; but the church is empty. We slop up and down the aisles in our wellies and water-proofs, examining the carvings on the ends of the pews which seem to depict animals merged with one another: dogs with the wings of birds, pigs with bodies that do not belong to them. Even the angels above our heads have their hands clasped around their faces as if sighting something over our shoulders, their mouths open and wailing.

It's called Woolpit, I tell them, because of the pits they used to have to catch wolves. Stone pits with stakes at the bottom called 'wolfpits', sometimes with a rope so that mice and frogs could climb out again.

My sister doesn't believe me. Mum has found a leaflet for something called the Lady's Well which I'd seen on Wikipedia and which isn't far from the church. We decide to try to find a cup of tea before attempting to hunt it down. There is a shop which advertises tea and cake but is only selling knick-knacks: Christmas decorations, soft hats and scarves, key rings and jewel-lery. But outside the shop is the village sign which I take a photo of: two children with green-tinged skin and a wolf. We set off to find the Lady's Well. I tell them the story as we go, as far as I can remember it.

'One day,' I say, 'two children appeared in Woolpit. No one

could understand the language they were speaking and they had green skin. Eventually they managed to explain that they had been looking after their sheep in a land with no sun and no moon and had heard church bells. Following the sound of the bells they had found themselves in the village.'

'This way,' my sister says. We are on the main road that comes in and out of the village and there are more cars than there had been before. We stumble along the verge and I shout the rest of the story back to them.

'They wouldn't eat anything except for beans.'

'What sort of beans?'

'I'm not sure. And eventually the boy got sick and died. But the girl grew up and got married and moved to King's Lynn, I think. Apparently she was a bit wild.'

'Slut,' my sister said. 'It's over there.'

There is a gate into a wooded area that runs beside the road. The Lady's Well is apparently somewhere in the moat. We stomp around with the photo on our phones, calling to one another. The earth is soft and my boots sink in almost to the calves. The moat runs beneath the trees, here and there filled with murky water, here and there overcome with brambles and the roots of holly. The sound of the cars passing is cut off, as if they never were. I wait to feel something mystical, an oddity in my blood or bones. I am vulnerable to superstitions and fairy tales, the pockets of weirdness smattering the land. When I was young I became obsessed with washing my hands, certain something would happen if I did the job badly. Often the reality of horror films or books or the nightmares I had as a child would melt into the world and I would find it difficult to tell the difference, to remember which was real and which wasn't. Perhaps this is the state all children live in. I am not a liar but sometimes I would find myself lying about things I had seen or heard and then, later, I would almost come to believe my own lie, become caught up in it.

There is a tree rooted into the bank of the moat with dirty ribbons tied to the branches and crumpled bits of paper half buried in the dirt at the foot of the trunk. I can hear the others calling to one another on the far side of the moat but I cannot see the flash of their colourful coats or their faces peering back at me. I get out my phone and look up the well again. There is a website with blurry photos and spelling mistakes that describes the well as having been a sacred place which people journeyed to visit and the water of which was said to cure eye problems. I put the phone in my pocket and catch sight of something beneath the tangle of ivy and fallen tree branches. It is a metal grate and, when I move around, I find that the entrance of the well is there, a concrete opening into the side of the moat, a sludge of water and mud puddles. I call the others over and we stand looking down at it and then take turns to have photos taken standing on top of the grate. The others get into the shallow water and kick around, calling on good fortune, but I drop to my knees and dunk both hands in up to the wrist and then touch my hands to my face.

THREE

Everyone comes down with flu and Christmas is subdued. My sister keeps saying it was water from the Lady's Well that did it and I tell her I'll put her in the story if she doesn't watch out. We drink Lemsip rather than bubbly wine and no one much feels like turkey. There are fights over who gets the sofa by the fire, whose turn it is to make tea, who had the last dose of Night Nurse. In the end we eat defrosted veggie chicken nuggets from the freezer and beans on toast with cheese, and watch back to back episodes of old Agatha Christie series. No one wants to play Articulate or Trivial Pursuit or even really open the presents under the tree. I keep thinking about how I'm going to write the story, what I'll change about it or keep the same. Some of the reports on the myth say that the children were probably Flemish or escaped servants. My dad says that it sounds like they were kidnapped and kept in an underground cave or cellar and that's why there was no sun or moon. Everyone in the family has an opinion about the story and I wonder if I've somehow ruined it by getting them involved, somehow broken the retelling so that it won't spin out right on the page. My sister thinks I should put a refugee slant on it, a story for our modern times, an allegory. I do a crossword with my brother and the words we get right are: *wood, blood, night*. We decide to try to write the story with random words we can find from the dictionary. It's a game we've played since we were children and though I want to tell them that it's not the same with this story – the one I've been asked to write for an audio-book publisher – I don't want to start the sort of fight that normally happens at Christmas. My grandmother is the most ill so she gets to hold the Concise English dictionary and the rest of us use our phones. We go around the room yelling out words which my mum writes down on a piece of paper. The story goes like this:

Mastoid, nonagenarian, segment, seel, strangle, onanism, once, frog, hazardous, muslin, particular, temperature, unusual, visible, visitant, wad, weir, Lazarus, diarist, disappear, brackish, and, anatomy, brick, dread.

Dread, I think, *that's right*. But the others are yelling so loud about what the words all mean put together that way and in relation to the story that I forget the thought. Some of us are feeling better so we open a bottle of wine and play Articulate and eat almost all of the cheese board that was supposed to come after the turkey which is still in its roasting tray on the side. I am on a team with my sister and at times we work together well, know all the same references; at other times we fight and get only one card right and then get angry and blame each other. She huffs at me when

I don't guess her Napoleon and flicks the card across the table at me – my hands raising to smack it down – and I feel a sharp pain in my left eye.

'Shit,' she says.

I fumble up out of my seat, clamping my hand over my eye and glaring at her out of the other. Never mind, Mum says. I go to the bathroom and fill my hands with water and force my eye open and hold it beneath the water. It feels as if there is something in there, irritating it, moving around harshly as I blink. I fill my hands with water again and flood my eye, trying to dislodge it. I can hear them continuing to play in the other room, and also the sound of Dad and Gran watching a film on television, the rattle of words merging together into odd sentences. I straighten up and look into the mirror over the sink. The vision through my left eye is red-tinged, as if I am pressing my fists hard against it, and the red blot obscures part of my face in the mirror so that – just for a moment – the face behind seems different from the way I know my own to be; different enough that I feel a shock of panic in my belly. I sit on the sofa and watch the end of the film through my one good eye. My sister seems to know I am annoyed and draws me a picture of the Green Children of Woolpit the way she imagines them. They look like aliens with skinny, fidgeting arms and oversized mossy-coloured heads and eyes as big as car wheels. One of them has a dead wolf slung over their shoulders and the other is carrying a brown briefcase in one hand.

'Nice,' I say.

FOUR

Back in the city I do not see friends or go to the cinema or walk around the frosty parks. My flat windows grow foggy and damp with condensation, the coffee maker is on through the night and I take up smoking in a way I haven't done since I was a teenager, huffing out into the icy mornings, dropping the sizzling butts into my empty tea cups. Inherent in retelling is – at first – destruction. Breaking down from the inside out. Suggested is respect but what is really there is vengeance, violence, retribution, the allure of denigration. There are Post-it notes and printouts and scrawled edits stuck up all over the walls and in a follow-me trail across the floor. I run out of all food besides baked beans which I heat up in the microwave and eat from the bowl with a spoon, swallowing through the pockets of cold. I run out, even, of cigarettes but do not feel able to go to the shop to get more. My skin feels raw, sensitive to changes in temperature or the sun through the thin curtains. My eye troubles me some, occasionally smarting or throwing red veins of light across the page I am reading. I write a first sentence and then begin again, scrawl out, delete, move some pages around on the floor. I cannot find an angle, a hook or a way in. My head is full of all of the ideas my family bandied around – the story made from the dictionary words randomly chosen, the drawing my sister had done. I tug the duvet on to the sofa and bury myself. The dreams are fraught, catastrophic: houses crumbling, foundations sinking into mould-soft earth, splintering and flooding. There is a sound running through, constant, metronomic. I am trying to get away from it but all the doors are open behind me and I am waking up and the sound is still there. I check in the kitchen and the bathroom, stick my head into the bedroom. As I move out towards the front door the letterbox flaps one final time and then is still. I stand at the end of the hall, listening. I have been in the apartment for nearly a year and though it is noisy and contracts around other people's smells and worries there has never been any trouble, any knock and runs or arguments over bins or car parking. I wait for the letterbox to flap again and imagine, then, how I will stride over and throw the door open and the tone of my voice and the way I will move my hands. But the letterbox is unmoving, and after a while I decide that, of course, it had been a dream which had lingered the way they often did when I was a teenager and really I needed to feed myself and have a shower and go for a walk and break out from the story I had been trying, so hard, to break into.

I walk to the corner shop and buy milk, bread, cigarettes, satsumas, coffee and some more beans. I take the long way home, down to the bottom of the road and into the small park with the dried-up pond and bins overflowing with poo bags. I try to ring my parents to check in but there is no answer on either of their phones and the texts I send remain unread. There is something about being outside after spending all week in the flat that gives the city a tilt, like looking at it with my head to one side, or over my shoulder. The air smells different, almost damp, the way the fens used to do when we were children and would dig or make strange hidy-holes from fallen branches. Once we had gone out in an enormous freeze and I had fallen through the ice and then run dripping home and not told my parents what had happened – the crinkling sound of the sheet giving way, the shock of cold, the alternative line of sight in which it had been my younger sister or brother on the ice and they had fallen and not come up again. I hadn't told them what I'd seen beneath the water: colours and things growing. I got used to not telling them these stories.

The park is nearly empty and I sit on a bench even though it is cold. There are buildings all around, shutting off the sky into slices and scissors of space, leaving no room. When I look at them from the corner of my eye I think that they appear almost leafy, as if overcome by wilderness, and I think that I have lived with this story too long, too intensely, and that when I am finally finished with it, it will have taken something from me, a sliced away part to keep as it goes.

I am unwilling to go back to the flat and decide I will drop off the shopping and pick up my laptop and go to work in a café or perhaps the local library which is noisy but has big tables and sockets. Someone has scattered rock salt on the stairs for the ice and it grits under my shoes as I go. At the door I cannot find the key and drop to my knees to dig in the bag, shunting aside the shopping. My head is at the height of the letterbox and when I look up, key in hand, I see that there is something on the metal, around the rim and on, also, the flap. I scrape at it with my finger and it flakes away, green coloured, mossy to the touch. I put the key in the door and go inside and close it behind me. My pulse has sped up and my throat feels full, as if with cotton wool. It means nothing, of course, but it does not feel like nothing. I have forgotten about going to the café or the library, about the goodness of being outside after so long indoors. I lock the door and check the windows and make coffee in the kitchen and drink it standing up, fingers clamped around the handle, something buzzing and repeating and swarming in me.

FIVE

I am woken in the night by something, although to begin with I do not know what it is. There are the shadows of tree branches all across the ceiling of my room and the air smells sulphurous, my hands damp with the water from the Lady's Well. Something is banging and banging and banging. I drop out of bed and on to all fours. The panic is not there yet although I can taste the beginning of it, acidic, bubbling on my tongue. I do not turn the lights on or look for my phone. There is a silhouette in the glass of the front door, a figure with hand raised, growing larger as they bring it against the wood. *I am dreaming*, I think, and so open the door without hesitation and only when the door is open and she has pushed past me, mouth cracked wide, knuckles raw, do I think: *I am not dreaming, this is not a dream*. I am shouting and she is too, both of us screaming wordlessly. She is coatless in the cold, bare armed and shoeless, long fingered, her hair streaked with grey, her eyes round as buttons. I go towards her thinking, perhaps, to touch her calmingly or to take her and move her forcibly towards the door and she lashes out with both fists; something hard in one of her hands strikes my face and draws a seam of dark from the corner of my left eye down across me, a clunk as my knees connect hard with the tiled floor. Everything moves in and out of focus: something sticky on my face and on my fingers, the floor very cold, the sound of movement in the rooms around me which have their own pulse, a staticky heartbeat which gives me a headache.

When I come to properly the flat is very quiet. I hitch myself up using the wall. My knees are black and blue and there is pain over my eye, blood on my hands. I peer into the kitchen and the sitting room, the bedroom. There is light beneath the bathroom door, the sound of water moving. I nudge the door open with my foot. She is in the bath, clothes on, hair matted to the bony shape of her skull, elbows jutting over the edge of the tub, the floor covered in shampoo and conditioner bottles, bars of soap, the bath-mat chucked to one side, toilet roll unspooled. I expect her to panic when she sees me but she only looks carefully up at me and then does something complicated with her hands, fingers twisting in the air, thumb popping loosely in the socket.

'What do you want?'

She blinks, turns her hands, signing perhaps. Deaf, then, or mute. I am not afraid of her, though perhaps I should be. Her body is aging and frail looking, only her hands have any strength. She clicks her tongue at me, gestures up to my face. In the mirror my fringe is clotted with blood, my lip bulbous and bruised, my cheeks and neck stained with red. I fill the sink and hand the water up, let it drop ruby coloured back down, rinse and repeat, probe wincingly at the sore spot on the top of my head.

'That wasn't necessary,' I say to her, but she is under the water, face submerged, hair ballooning, hands clamped around the edge of the bath.

In the kitchen I make tea and toast, heat up some beans in the microwave, butter the toast and put it and the beans on to two plates, then take them in to her.

'Is there someone I can call?' I say, but she doesn't answer, prods at the toast and then scrapes the beans off and eats only them, dropping the toast to the floor, ignoring the tea. I eat ravenously, pick her toast up and eat that too. Nothing has ever really happened to me. I fell through the ice as a child but was in no danger; I had a minor car accident when I was a teenage driver; I almost fell in love but never quite made it. I write rather than live, of course. I look at her skin for a greenish tinge and then feel ridiculous. I go into the other room and bring back a notepad and pen, give it to her. She holds it and eyes me.

'Who can I call?' I ask, and point to the paper.

She draws her knees out of the water and rests the pad on them, begins to draw something, one hand curled around so I cannot see. When she is done she holds it up. She has drawn two figures, hand in hand, long haired. She points to one and then to herself and then taps at the second figure.

'Who is it?' I ask, and she grows agitated, lips drawn back from her teeth, the pen snapping between her fingers. 'Okay,' I say, 'Okay, okay. We can go look for them.'

I lend her a coat and some old trainers. She looks more normal then, her hair drying to frizz, her hands carving through the air, making marks and images which I cannot interpret. It is late, early really, but I ring my parents, seeking advice, and again the phones go straight to voicemail. They have disappeared before, emailed from Tenerife where they had gone without telling us, 'a little trip' they said. Sometimes when we were children we'd find that one or other of them had wandered away from the trolley in the supermarket, taken their bag with them, left us skidding up and down the aisles with our shoes in our hands, clambering on to the shelves and hiding.

I lock the flat behind us. At times it seems unclear who is leading and who following. I wonder if she belongs to someone in the building and we stomp up and down the corridors for a while, occasionally pausing outside doors and then moving on. We go out on to the road. The street lamps are clogged with dirt and all the trees on the road are pushing up the pavements, roots like octopus under the stone. She seems uninterested now we're outside, arms hanging from the coat as if she doesn't quite know how to wear it, the toes of the trainers scuffing on the ground. I walk her up to the corner, near the bus stop, hoping to jog a memory or, simply, to walk into someone out looking for her. Even at this time there are people about: a Domino's pizza delivery man sitting in the front of his Polo and talking on his phone, a runner in a fluorescent jacket who has to go around us into the road, a couple of people coming home from nights out with their bare legs flashing, luminescent. At some point she takes my hand. Her fingers are dry and brittle like sticks and she holds on tightly but doesn't seem worried or anxious. We walk around a few of the side streets and then down to the park. Occasionally I say: 'Do you recognise anything?' and she moves her hands in the air or shrugs or smiles and we move on. I think: *I should call the police.* But I know that I won't. I don't know why but I understand that is not something I will do.

SIX

I'd had a boyfriend for a bit although it had never really worked. He had reddish hair and a strong Welsh accent, a family he didn't much talk about, a job at a school as a PE teacher. We met online – I was trying that out – and used to go to the cinema and then to Pizza Hut for the deals, the unlimited ice cream whipped from the machine. I know that he found me curious and that perhaps there wasn't more than that. I did not find him particularly curious although I found the notion of a relationship confusing, at times incomprehensible. Once he came in while I was in the bath and sat on the toilet and talked to me while he defecated and I was undone by that, by the openness with which he bared his humanity at me like an angry sandwich board. He always said, from the first time he met them, that I didn't look anything like my parents or siblings. I think he knew it annoyed me because he said it a lot, sometimes even said it to them. He said that I was different from them in other ways and when I asked what he meant he said only, a little sulky, lots of things. I'd never been with anyone before him and my parents had never much talked about the things they must have presumed we were learning about at school. There was a whole litany of things I did not know, did not – it turned out – much care to know. He got enjoyment out of it and that pleased me, at the beginning, and it was not painful, but, still, I did not much understand it. I knew that was an absence in me and I did not tell him or anyone else that I didn't care for it. Found it, at times, humorous or interesting the way animals mating on television are interesting: my own body thrown into relief, his tight-jawed face and widening eyes, the instruments I had never much thought of before that moment. And when he ended it I was not surprised.

It was he who had put the thought in my head that I did not belong. All those times he told me I didn't look or act like my family, the small jabs and side glances. It was true. At dinner with my family I eyed their soft features, their rounded bodies and dewy eyes, their hairless limbs and secretive smiles, the way they laughed in the same way, the rolling walk they all shared. I was not like that but I couldn't find the words to ask or comment and I knew that even if I did I wouldn't want to know what they had said. That they had found me, that they had adopted me, that I was an illegitimate love child. Or none of the above.

SEVEN

I keep trying to work on the retelling but it is stubborn and won't come out right; the angle is wrong or the words are. I have forgotten how to write something where the original is trapped like a shard beneath the skin of the new version. I have forgotten how to write at all. At times I think perhaps she has something to do with it. I make up the sofa for her but she does not, really, seem to sleep. In the night I hear her ferreting around or there is the sound of the bath running and then sloshing as she gets in, stays in for what feels like hours. She seems content here and, strangely, I am content for her to stay for the moment. In the mornings I sit in bed and try to write and at some point she will appear in the doorway and move her hands through the air and I will get up and make us bowls of beans which we eat on the sofa with the TV on. She likes the television. Sometimes she sits so close to it I think she'll blind herself with all the colours. Afterwards we often go out and walk around again. It is not, any more, that I think someone will find her, only that, rather, we have fallen into a routine – comfortable, easy to continue. We walk to the park and around, pausing to look into the browning fountain, the mountain of coins at the bottom, the rusting water feature. She does not like dogs, does something with her face if they come too close, cheeks puffed up, teeth bared. Sometimes we walk to the chip shop and I get a carton, walk home trying to convince her to try one. She moves her hands disgustedly, pushes the chips away. I eat them but the taste is off, the texture is wrong.

Communication is still an issue. We run at parallels on this and it is often difficult to find a middle point at which to exist and to explain or ask her things. I find myself chatting mindlessly, the words spilling out and sometimes, looking over, I see that she is doing the same with her hands, the fingers twisting in the air, her wrists rolling. We sit with the pad of paper and she draws an image and then I do as well, badly. Often I cannot understand the things she draws any more than the words she makes with her hands and – looking at her – I see that she feels the same way about my spiky drawings of my family or the dog we had when we were younger or the books I have read.

More and more I am certain she is the girl from the story. Older, and not the way she was in my head but, all the same, somehow created by my writing about her, somehow found or brought back or convinced into life. Madness: yes, of course. Except that she does something to the flat just by being there. It changes and shifts and retracts around her. A small colony of mushrooms starts growing from the corner of the sitting room, sprouting from the soggy carpet. The water from the tap sometimes comes out algae tinged or swarms with tadpoles which we gather up and leave in saucepans to grow. In the nights there is the crackle and bark of trees moving in the wind, the scowling call of an owl, the rustle of small things hiding. She has long baths that use all the hot water and leave the whole flat foggy and damp, the walls wet to the touch. I find coils of her hair in piles everywhere, as if she is somehow marking her territory, stretching her reach.

In the night I wake and my forearm is itching and itching. I drag my fingernails across it – still mostly asleep – and feel something come loose, flake away. Sleep is empty as a well and I am on a swing rocking through it. In the morning in the mirror there is a patch of dry skin – almost scaly – on my arm, tinged green and smelling a little like old churches and sulphurous water.

EIGHT

It is impossible to stay here. She eats four tins of beans a day and gets angry with me when I do not understand her. I find carefully broken tea cups in a row on the edge of the bath and I know that she is losing patience with whatever is going on here. What is going on here? I write the beginning of the retelling and she is in a particularly bad mood that day, swinging her arms around, smearing beans on to the screen of the television. It is impossible to stay here and there is only one other place we can go. I pack up the car and she seems happier than she has been for days, smiling a radiant smile and stroking my arm and twisting her hands through the air in sentences I am certain mean: yes, this is the right thing to do. I think maybe I am beginning to understand her more. I have a tent in the back of the car and a couple of sleeping bags I haven't used for years. I wish I was more prepared – not only with the things I owned but with the person I am, the way I am made, the things that I know. I do not know how to make a fire or purify water or tell direction by the stars. I put the address into the satnav and we trickle out of the city, the river coursing away past us, the rattle of trains, the barrage of buses and taxis and then slowly everything receding and she fiddling with the radio and then opening the window and sticking her whole head out.

I had thought that maybe we would stop off at my parents' but the closer we get the more I am convinced it is not a good idea. I change the address in the satnav and stop off for coffee and a snack at a service station. In the dirty bathroom mirror I look almost as wild as she does: unwashed hair, dirty clothes. My left eye is still red and sore, a little swollen around the edge. The patch of greening skin on my forearm has grown a little. I get a pen out of my bag and draw a loose circle around it so I can measure the changes. There is a small girl watching me from beside the hand dryers, hair in bunches, some sort of unicorn under her arm. I smile at her and she looks frightened. I open my mouth to say something, to comment on the unicorn perhaps, but there are no words waiting for me to use them, no logic which I can fall into. I stutter and stammer and a woman who must be her mother comes out of a cubicle and glares at me.

It gets dark quickly: days are short, the motorway is busy. She climbs into the back seat and lies out flat and I see her hands twisting in my driver's mirror. I am blinded by headlights coming the other way, the cat's-eyes clunk beneath the wheels; words for the retelling I have not yet written seem to pass across the windscreen but never quite find purchase. I pull over into a layby and push my chair back and try to sleep but even sleep cannot hold on and after a while I start driving away and she lets out a little croon as if she agrees with this turn of events. The roads are empty and we speed on. The satnav has turned off but I know where I am going. I know where I'm going now. We cut off the motorway and on to smaller roads, tiny lanes, muddy fields, trees hanging over the car. I can see her watchful face in the driver's mirror, her wide eyes on the road. I have an issue with what is happening here. I have a problem with the way things are going. I drive and drive and at some point – still dark but a sort of crease of light coming from the horizon – we are in Woolpit: the familiar sign, the spire of the church rising up like a kraken into the sky. I hitch the tent out of the boot and give her the sleeping bags and we walk along the centre of the road towards the forested area where the Lady's Well is. She wanders off and I pitch the tent, squinting in the low light, forcing the poles through the plastic holders, hunting for the pegs. I do not know what we are supposed to do now we are here. She has still not come back and I think that maybe this is it: I have brought her here and that is enough, she has gone now. But I cannot leave so I get into the tent and pull the sleeping bags over me and I lie still listening to the nothing outside, the long stream of silence.

I fall asleep and I dream the story of 'The Green Children of Woolpit'. It is in my words, the sentences have my inflection, the commas are positioned the way I would position them. In the dream it is clear to me that I am, of course, taking something from her. Her silence is not organic and she has come back to grasp the story bodily from my hands. In the dream I try to speak but I am wordless. It is not that I cannot make sounds – I can and do – but that I do not know the words, I do not own them the way I once did. I am struggling with something, tangled up with it, its forceful limbs wrapped around mine and – coming out slowly – I realise that it is the tent which has sagged in the night and got caught up on my clothes and hair and skin. She is standing over me watching and I clamp my hands over my mouth thinking that she might reach in and pull out the words and drag them away. But she only shrugs and makes a hand gesture and moves off into the greening light.

NINE

We spend all day looking for something I do not know how to find. The village has an air of abandonment to it. The opening times on the pub sign says it should be open but it is shadowy when I press my face to the window, all the chairs piled on to the tables, no one in sight. Even the little shop we'd visited last time is locked up, the parasols out front folded away. I am certain that the well is the beginning and so we traipse around the forest, drop our hands into the water, clamber over fallen trees, peer down into rabbit holes.

'You came from underground,' I tell her, and she twirls her hands at me and then turns away. 'Do you recognise this?' I say, but she doesn't answer.

My eye is bothering me, aching and occasionally fogging over so that the woods and my hands held in front of me are partially obscured, misty with white. On a whim I crouch by the well where the water comes out of the ground and scoop handfuls up, lowering my head into my hands and forcing my eye open into the silty liquid. There is relief and then the fog seems to spread across to my other eye, the pain rising up so that it is, for a moment, unbearable. I ball my hands and press them into my eyes and the water drips from my fingers and on to my skin and then someone is prising my hands away, and looking up I see that it is her and I know her. Not only from the last few days but always. I have always known her. The picture she drew when I first met her – her and someone else holding hands – was of me. She moves her hands and I understand, finally, what she is saying and I crouch next to her on the ground and we start to dig.

TEN

We dig for a long time. The earth is soft to begin with and then gets harder. I break open my hands on rocks and the earth is the colour of blood, I wipe my fingers across my face and the dirt tastes familiar, like somewhere I have always known. She digs steadily next to me, occasionally tapping me on the hand to make me go faster, sometimes smiling or resting her head on my shoulder. There are burrows beneath the earth which collapse as we come upon them, the bones of animals, insects which go scattering away beneath our fingers, the roots of the grass and plants. The ground opens up beneath us. The hole is big enough that, crouched down, we cannot see out of it. She hisses and we keep digging, weary now but continuing, throwing the dirt over our shoulders like dogs. Gradually the animal burrows become so many they are almost cave-like and the earth gives way on its own, small landslides coating us in dirt and water. There is a gap the size of two humans lying down.

ELEVEN

I crawl into the gap in the earth. I lie there waiting for her to come and lie down but – after a moment – I feel her begin to shovel the dirt back on top of me. The dirt falls on to my face, into my mouth and nose and ears, on to my hands and feet, on to my belly and legs. There is a part of me that says: *no no no no no*, but the rest lies still and thinks about the story of the children who lived somewhere

with no sun or moon and who heard the church bells ringing so
went to find them. And a part of me knows that this is not the
first time I have been here, under the ground, in the dirt, in the
town of Woolpit. The dirt falls on to my face and into my mouth.

TWELVE

Beneath the dirt there is not enough air to breathe for long. I can
feel everything that moves and grows and threshes and dies and is
eaten and lives again and dies and is buried. I am buried too but
the earth is moving and there are seams of light and I take in a
breath big enough for a lifetime.

SOUR HALL

Naomi Booth

Based on
Ay, We're Flittin'
YORKSHIRE

An old butter churn, the wood waxy and black; a cattle shed with great gaps in the roof; and a vicious white horse called Mary: these are the things that we inherit along with the house.

George isn't one for superstitions or bad omens. She says we'll start again and make the farm ours. She says we'll make something better of it than her father ever did.

She's hired a box van and we sit high up in the cab either side of Shaun, our extra muscle. We drive the steep, narrow road up the valley side, judder across a cattle-grid and then we're on to the long road that slices across the moor-tops. Our turning is an obscure wooden sign at knee-height: *Sour Hall Farm*, it reads, the words mouldered with rot. This road isn't tarmacked, and cobbles and building rubble fill the worst of the pits in an attempt to make it passable. The van bounces then grounds, a horrible sound of metal on rock. George hits the accelerator, grinds us over the bump.

'Steady on, Georgie,' Shaun says. 'I paid the deposit on this van for you, you know.'

It is late summer. The sky over the farm is hazed with brightness, the hills around us drenched in gold.

George pulls up the van alongside the house, behind the old Land Rover she's bought off eBay. She jumps down from the cab, runs to open the passenger door for me.

'What do you think?' she says.

I've only visited once before. Sour Hall passed to George last year, but we waited for the weather to turn to make a start on the building work. The front of the house has been painted and fettled: gutters fixed, window frames repaired, the old stonework coated with adhesive to stop the wind and the rain driving in through the winter – even through a foot of wall, water had turned the plasterwork inside black with mould. Above the door the numbers *1684* are scored in deep, though George says the house has burned down at least twice in its history so that stone might be the only thing left that old.

'It looks smart,' I say. 'It looks dead smart.'

Inside, George has been relentless. When we first visited, the house was dark and cluttered and smelled of teabags and manure. She's gutted it. She shows me the new kitchen, the new bathroom, the bedrooms that have been replastered, rewired and freshly painted. She shows me the old utility room, which is now a work-space where she'll process orders. Each room is clean and bright and smells of volatile chemicals. Nothing of her parents remains.

'I'm going to start on the boxes,' Shaun shouts through to us.

'Let me show you the shed,' George says, and she's practically dancing me back outside. This is her real pride. This is where most of the money's gone – the EU development grant that she won to restore the dairy. She hadn't seen her parents for more than twenty years before her mother and then her father went in quick succession. But her father left all of the information she needed in shoe-boxes on the kitchen table: bills, letters of sale, old adver-tisements – evidence of Sour Hall farm serving the Calder Valley since the seventeenth century. He left her this, and the paperwork for the grant, ready to be completed. But George isn't grateful. She has no fond memories, she says, of him nor of the old farm. It's ours now, not his. It's our work that will make it a success: we've nowt to be grateful for.

We walk into the milking shed together. The roof has been patched up – no raw scraps of sky above us now. The wooden beams have been repaired, light new oak patching into the old timbers, which are black from the fire that put George's father finally out of business. There are pens for the cows, who'll need to stay in during the winter months when the grass is poor and the weather would perish the fat and the milk from them. There is hay baled out and waiting for milking time, and already a hint of the warm, green smell of their urine, of the soft, green cud at their lips.

'Come see the new dairy,' George says.

The room at the far end of the barn, a dingy old shed, has been completely refurbished: it is white now and forensically clean. It houses steel vats and steel storage containers and steel fridges for the milk.

A cold current in here, prickling across my skin. 'Fridges on?' I ask.

George smiles. Dimples in the reddish flesh of her cheeks; she looks as though she's already a farmer. 'Not yet,' she says. 'You'll get used to the moors, Ash, and that east wind.' And she shows me the electronic churn and the sachets of blue and white mould cultures and the gleaming surfaces where she'll knead salt into the fresh butter.

It's on the way out that I spot it, the one old thing that George has kept: the ancient butter churn that we found out here when we first visited. An old, blackened anomaly, squatting in the corner of the dairy. George sees me looking: 'You need some wood in the environment,' she says. 'Something old and damp to stop the air from drying out.' She looks around the room then as though searching for snags, for something left undone. 'I'll need to keep the bacterial levels consistent. It's a delicate business, you know,' she adds, as she closes the door behind us. 'You won't need to come in here, Ashleigh, once we get going.'

We spend the afternoon shifting furniture and boxes inside the house. Then we sit out on the grass with Shaun and he rolls a ciggie and George vapes, making big icing-sugar clouds on the air. Even now, even at the deepest, warmest point of summer, the wind is wild and we clutch our jackets around us.

'You girls really going to be all right out here?' Shaun says. He doesn't look at us: he trains his eyes out on the moorland horizon. 'There's rural crime, you know, plenty of it. Lads out after cattle and cars and equipment.'

George gives me a look. 'Ta for the tip, Shaun. I've never been to the countryside before, I didn't grow up out here or owt, so that's reet useful.'

'Just saying,' Shaun says. 'You could do with a gun, George. Or some dogs at the very least.'

Shaun grinds his cig into the ground. He needs to get the van back to Manchester. Once he's gone, George and I put on jumpers and sit outside until the hills darken and the colour burns out of the sky.

'I'll dig us a fire pit,' George says. 'I'll dig it tomorrow.' She kisses my fingers until they're warm.

I feel it before I hear it: a sharp bang that cracks through the bones of my spine.

'Ashleigh, love,' George says, laughing, cupping her warm hand to the nape of my neck. 'You jumped a mile. It's just a gate somewhere, caught in the wind. There's nowt up here can hurt us.'

The cows arrive a week later, one by one. The transporter can't make it up the steep, narrow road to Sour Hall, so George borrows a horse-box from a couple who farm across the valley, brings the Friesians up one at a time. Unloading each one is an act of devotion for her. She stands in the field at the bottom of the ramp, lowing. The very first one refuses to budge. George mounts the box, pats the cow's thick neck as though she's a dog, murmurs something into her whiskered ear. Then she leads her down, shoulder to shoulder, and the cow trots out into the field, lifting her muzzle, braying at us. She stalks around the perimeter, begins to run along it.

'What's she doing?' I say. 'I thought cows were docile.'

'She's after the others,' George says. 'They don't like to be alone. Let's get them shifted quick as we can.'

After the Friesians we take delivery of the Ayrshires and then the Red Poll. All of them dairy cattle. All of them big, solid creatures. They've muscled flanks but their hips protrude like coat-hangers as they walk. We'll milk them twice a day with the shiny new equipment, the clusters in various shapes and sizes that fasten to the cows, cool steel sucking at their warm tissue. George will make organic cheese and organic cheese custards and raw, fermented butters for fancy restaurants in Manchester. She'll sell in the local farm markets too. She has grand plans for an online shop, for contracts with Morrisons and the local Co-op. The cows will calve each year, and we'll keep some of the females to slowly grow the herd.

'What about bull calves?' I ask. 'What will you do with bull calves?'

George is taking her boots off. She's just come in from checking on the pregnant cow, Vera, and on the dairy where our first vat of milk is fermenting. 'I've been thinking,' she says, 'of keeping them. For a bit, at least. Now folk don't want veal most farmers shoot the bull calves at birth, or freight them to the continent. Just as cruel, if you ask me, the mothers full of milk and wanting to feed their young.' George looks up at me, carefully. She comes and stands close by, rubs the back of my neck like she's started doing with her favourite Ayrshire, Margery. 'We wouldn't do it how it used to be done. We'd feed them properly, let them suckle for a good few months. What do you think?' she says. 'The girls'll get to mother for a bit. And we'll sell the meat when it's time: rose veal, it's called, when they've been given the chance to grow and roam. Pink it is, not like that pale, white meat when they've not been fed right.'

I nod. But my chest feels tight. Vera, the pregnant, big-bellied, long-lashed Red who likes to lick my boots, is growing bigger and bigger. She'll calve in late spring. I will not think about it. I do not think about it.

When the sun goes down here, the night's black and thick as stout. I sleep fitfully, startling awake over and over, a muffled echo of something bang, bang, banging in my ears.

We're used to hard work. George has looked after herself since she left the farm at sixteen: she's worked in factories and in warehouses and on building sites; she's done deliveries, up and down the M62 in sixteen-hour shifts; she's emptied slot machines and shifted pianos and washing machines and double beds. I've worked in kitchens and bars and pubs, changing barrels, pulling pints, clearing tables, grafting into the small hours for more than a decade now. We're used to working until our bodies ache and our thoughts are blunted.

'You up to this, my love?' George asked me when we first met. We were in the back room of The Swan with Two Necks, her last pub. I'd fetched up looking for casual work, and the job came with the offer of accommodation, which I needed badly. 'This isn't an easy job,' she said. 'You'll get all kinds of bother. And the regulars will try it on. I mean, really try it on.'

'I've worked all over,' I said. 'I've worked bars in Rochdale and Salford and Liverpool. I'm a grafter. I can take care of myself.'

'Is that right?' she said, not unkindly. She was looking at my face, I think: at the darkness around my eye that the concealer couldn't cover, at the flatness of the pulverised bone in one of my cheeks. My hair was shorter than it had been a week before, levelled off by my sister with a pair of kitchen scissors.

'I'll give you a week's trial,' she'd said, and I've been with her ever since.

We're both used to hard work, we are, but by October we're knackered. The weather's turned and our lips are chapped. We ache in new places from the graft – our joints grind and we find new points of tenderness in our shoulder blades, our knees, the knuckle-bones of our necks. My ears ring from the constant wind.

We scrub up all the time, lathering up to our elbows, to keep the milk clean. George's thumbs both split open and my nails start to peel away in soft white layers.

George looks for help with the evening milking. When the men arrive, they park up on the moor and walk down to the house in a style that I cannot read – they are leisurely, they will not be rushed. But they are not relaxed: theirs is not an amiable gait. There are three of them, and the eldest knew George's father. 'Georgina,' he keeps calling her as we walk around the farm, and she clatters about, slamming gates, kicking buckets, trying to murder the sound of the old name.

After they've had a good look around, we sit in the kitchen and George brings them beers. 'You missed a lot, Georgina,' the older one says. He fills her in on local scandals: the horse-meat butchered in the valley and working its way into supermarket lasagnes; the old sisters who used to farm up at Slack whose front door was eaten away by badgers, finally alerting folk to their deaths. He tells her about foot-and-mouth, about the animal carcasses piled in fields around the valley, quick-limed in mass graves while farmers wept. And he tells her about the last fire at Sour Hall. There's real relish in his voice then, as he tells her how her father was put in hospital, how his lungs were ruined by smoke as he tried to get his cows out. 'Lucky he weren't stamped to death,' he says. 'It's the boggart, tha knows.' The two lads jeer and slosh their beer around. 'You can laugh,' he says, 'but Georgina knows. He tried to leave Sour Hall, her father, but that boggart wouldn't have it.'

George looks in my direction now. She winks at me. 'Peter,' she says. 'You've had too much ale.'

''Appen you're right,' he says. 'You ask old Mary. She knows a thing about it.'

'Can I use your lav?' one of the lads asks, and George points him upstairs.

I can hear the cows braying at something outside; several of them at once, a relay of deep calls.

'I'll go up,' I say. 'Have a look out over the fields.'

When I get to the top of the stairs, the lad is standing with the bathroom door open, pissing into the toilet. He turns to look at me, still holding his cock. He doesn't say anything, but he smiles at me, long and slow and wolfish. He shakes his cock, puts it away, wipes his hands on his jeans, and then walks out on to the landing. When he gets close to me, I flinch; and then he laughs and jogs away down the stairs.

Why did I stop? Why did I give him that chance to laugh? I turn into our bedroom and I hit the back of the door with the ball of my fist. I'm stupid. I'm so stupid. I let it happen, I let it happen, I always just let it happen. I hit the door again, bang, bang, banging it until the flesh of my palms starts to throb.

'Ashleigh?' It's George's voice. 'Everything all right up there?'

I move to the window, do what I was meant to: look out on the cows. They're charging across the field, running downhill, away from the milking shed.

'Something's spooked the girls!' I shout. 'You'd best go see to them.'

There'd been no sign of what had frit them, but George and the men had found the cows bunched together at the far end of the field. One of them had hurt her leg in the stampede. 'You can start now,' George had told the two young ones, 'help me get this lot back up for milking.'

'I don't like them,' I tell George later on. It's dark outside now and she's just come back in, carrying the cold inside on her skin. I'm washing up and her cheek is cool, a scrap of dark night sky against my neck.

'They're harmless,' she says. 'They're just lads.'

I tell her about the pissing one. She laughs out loud. Then she sees my face and stops.

'Look, he was probably embarrassed, trying to style it out. You know what lads are like. Don't go soft on me, Ashleigh. If you really don't like them after a few weeks, I'll find someone else.'

She fastens her arms around me. She moves her mouth into my hair, nuzzles across the back of my neck, her lips cold.

'Let's go to bed,' she says.

At the start of November, the first frost sets across the moor: a hard, bright, dazzling white. We need to do something about the horse, Mary, before the fields get too hard. We've tried to stable her with the cows, but she bolts at the door. She grazes as far away from us as she can, only eats the hay that we put out for her when we've backed off a good distance. She bucks when we tether her, bares her teeth and shrieks. But she's limping: her feet have overgrown her shoes.

George calls the farrier. He arrives in a van with a chimney, a furnace built in at the back.

'Normally, I charge twenty-five pound for removal and filing,' he says. 'Which is a fair price. But I've been up here before, a long while ago. I'll need forty quid to go near her.'

We've managed to tether her at the side of the dairy. George and one of the lads brought her up, and now George has a purple crescent of a bruise on her forearm and says she's ready to let the horse go lame and I can talk to the farrier and pay for it myself if I want her seeing to.

Mary's whinnying before we get near her, dancing from side to side.

'Easy, girl,' the farrier says. 'Normally we'd use a slip-knot, so the horse can free hersen if she's distressed. Otherwise they get hurt, trying to escape.' He wears a heavy leather apron, and he fetches from it a long metal file, which he puts on the ground. 'That's not going to work with this one,' he says. 'I'll need to tie her tight.'

He ducks under Mary's head, unties the tether and holds her fast. He double knots the rope, makes it tighter, so that she's right in against the dairy wall. She bucks from side to side.

'Right, I'm earning my money today,' he says.

Mary's head pulls against the rope again and again, vicious nodding like a seizure. The farrier catches one of her back legs in his hand, bends it up and sets to work immediately: he kicks a metal stool into place, rests the hoof on it, begins to prise out the nails from the shoe. Then he's filing away the hard outgrowth of the hoof. The noise is bad, but he works quickly – hoof filings into the air like sawdust.

He's on with the second hoof when I hear it: a sharp, loud bang from inside the dairy. Mary hears it too. She tries to rear up away from the shed but hits her nose against the wall, convulses backwards, kicking the stool away. The farrier jumps back, his tools clattering to the ground. Metal clangs around us, carries on clanging around us. Mary's bucking and braying, her back legs all over the place.

The farrier stands back. We both stand back, just watching the horse. A cold feeling: panic filling my throat.

'Heard the stories about Sour Hall, have you?' he asks.

'Maybe,' I say. 'Do you mean about the boggart?'

He laughs. 'The boggart,' he says. 'That's one word for the old bastard. Though George might have some others. After what they did to her.' He nods towards the dairy.

I don't say anything.

'Not a talker then?' he says. 'Suit yoursen, but that horse i'nt going to get sorted here.'

It takes a while until she's calm enough, but eventually he gets close and sets Mary loose. We follow her up to the top field. He catches her there again, does his work.

'I'll not come back up here,' he says when it's finished. 'I've left her barefoot. She's an old horse. You should set her somewhere with hard ground, and she'll see to hersen until she's done with.'

*

One December afternoon the sky changes colour – it curdles from thin blue to deep grey. The sky is bright and dark at the same time, like the light in a man's eyes the moment before he turns on you. The snow falls and falls and obliterates the road and then the moor and then the horizon. George calls the council, tells them that the road is almost impassable, that our water supply might freeze and then we'll be in real trouble. An hour later we drive out in the Land Rover and see that a snow plough has made it up to the edge of the causeway, has gritted the main road, and then stopped at the neck of our road and deposited a beaten-up sign saying *Road Closed*.

We turn for home: the car judders as we slide back down towards the house. We dig out trenches to the shed so that we can feed the girls. Our hands are raw, our lips are chapped and bleeding. We run the hot water on constant. Will this help? Or will it risk the pipes cracking? We don't know. That night I smother our fingers with Vaseline, and George lies still while I smear it on her lips. The cows are huddled in the shed, their noises muffled in the snow. But I'm sure I can hear it: every so often, a loud, dull banging that makes the animals cry out, and then go entirely silent.

Christmas and New Year come and go. George buys good whisky, gives the lads presents. We work together through the longest, darkest nights of the year.

In January my sister calls. Wishes me a happy new year. She doesn't ask after George.

'I'm pregnant,' she says. And then she says, 'Sorry.'

'Don't be sorry, for fuck's sake,' I say. 'When are you due? Are you okay? Is Paul chuffed?'

She's due in May. She's fine but the size of a house already. Paul is made up. She talks about trying to come to visit; I say something about going back across to see them when the baby comes. When the call is finished I sit on the sofa and make tight fists with my hands, over and over. My skin is dry, and my fingertips rasp in my palm. My nails drag. Rough, rough noise. Bang, bang, bang. A cold current rushes over me and I'm up on my feet, out of the house, running out towards George.

I find her in the yard.

'What's wrong?' she says.

'Nothing,' I say, 'I just . . . I thought I could hear that noise again.'

'In the shed?' she says.

I nod.

'There's nowt in there for you to worry about, Ash,' she says.

'Shouldn't we check?' I say. 'Make sure the girls are okay?'

'I'll check,' says George. 'I don't want you in there all worked up. You'll make them stressed, and it's bad for the milk.'

George is not a person you ask questions of, but that night I force myself to ask how the butter and the cheese are coming along. It's been months now that we've been milking, that she's been fermenting the butter and culturing the cheese; and there's nothing she's happy to sell, nothing she even wants me to taste.

'Are things okay?' I say. We're laid in bed side by side, not touching. 'I mean, out there, in the dairy?'

She's quiet for a while. Then she says, 'It's got to be right before it goes out. You only get one chance. You know how this business is.'

We've been trying outlandish things that George orders from other farm shops: cultured butters made with seaweed and miso and rose petals; raw cheeses high with garlic and nettles; stinking rounds of cheese made by Trappist monks and silent orders of nuns. We're going to be simple, George has decided, but distinctively sour. Our butter will be raw – she skims the cream from the milk, to get rid of any sweetness, then mixes it with a culture and leaves it to ferment. What's left is muddled in a large, steel churn and then she hand-kneads it, salting to taste. The cheese will be raw too. She's working on a signature cheese custard, yellow as Irish butter but gluey and bitter. The hard cheeses she presses and wraps in cloth, storing them on the dairy shelves to ripen.

'I can't get it right,' she says. 'The butter is too pale. It must be because the girls are inside. I should have frozen more milk at the end of the summer. The hard cheese keeps cracking. And the custard keeps spotting with mould.'

'Can I help?' I say. 'I could do more in the dairy?'

'No,' she says quickly. 'No, no need, Ash. I knew it would be a long process. It's just trial and error.'

In spring, things that vanished in the winter start to reappear: harebells, skylarks, the albino stag that the locals say has lived on the moor for an impossibly long time – two decades and more. George tells me she caught a glimpse of him in the pine woods, like a wisp of smoke through the trees. And other things appear, too – things abandoned or lost: a porcelain sink, white and cold, dumped in the middle of the causeway; a desperate fox nosing for food for her new cubs; a lad out in just a T-shirt and jeans, cast up from the night before, walking the perimeter of our fields, off his head. 'Am in Halifax?' he keeps shouting. 'I need to get to Halifax.' George circles him, keeping her distance, then makes him sit in a trailer and drives him down into the valley bottom.

'What is a boggart meant to be?' I ask George one blustery morning. We're out in the field, patching up a wall that's lost a line of stone.

'A boggart?' she says.

I pass her a triangular rock and she jimmies it into place with her big, dextrous hands.

'Well, it depends who you talk to,' she says. 'Old Peter will tell you a boggart lives on a farm and helps when it's happy and hinders when it isn't. Makes mischief. Throws things around, bangs things, sits on your chest in the night. A right little farmyard poltergeist.' She laughs. 'Ashleigh,' she says. 'Don't tell me you're going soft in the head.'

'Just trying to get to know the place,' I say.

'Well,' she says. 'It is folklore round here. The story goes that you can't escape a boggart. Once it's fastened on to you, it'll never leave you. In the old tales of Sour Hall, the farmer sets off to go, tormented by the boggart, but he finds the creature in his butter churn halfway across the moor. He knows then that he can't escape it, so he goes back to the farm and learns to live with it.'

'Is that right?' I say.

When I look up, George is staring at the barn. She's still smiling, but her face is straining against the wind. Georgie has this look sometimes: like she's fighting something you can't see, and she's winning.

In April it rains for two weeks solid. It rains until the grates in the valley bottom fill and the roads begin to surge with water. Then the Calder floods and the valley bottom turns to a wide, brown river. Up on the moor-top, every surface gushes. The fields are spongy, and give way under our feet, starting to turn to bog. It's twilight all day long: the rain stops the light from breaking through. The lads can't get up to us, so I help George with the evening milking again. The cows stay inside all day now; it feels warm and damp and malarial in the shed. We herd them into place, line them up against the back wall, and fasten them up to the clusters. I lean against Vera, shoulder to shoulder. Her belly's big and hard now. She's due next month. She turns her massive head towards me, snuzzling my open hand with her wet, pale mouth as she's milked. She lurches suddenly, knocking me hard. All of the cows clatter, their hooves scrabbling around. Bang, bang. That noise, that noise louder than I've ever heard it. They drag against the clusters. They bray and whinny like horses.

'Whoa, steady girls,' George calls. She walks down the line, checking them over. They're lowing still, big heads down, nosing for danger. 'You okay, Ash?'

'Yeah, I think so,' I say.

'Don't know what gets into them sometimes,' George says.

'Didn't you hear it?' I say. 'The banging?'

'I heard the girls banging about,' George says.

'No,' I say. 'In the dairy.'

'Maybe it's foxes again,' says George. 'I'll check on it.'

'Don't—' I start to say, but George is already through the doorway at the end of the shed.

'It's nothing,' she shouts. I hear her clattering about in there. Then she comes back through, wiping her hands on her overalls. 'It was just that old butter churn,' she says. 'Rolling across the floor. Must've swollen in the damp.'

George doesn't meet my eye. She pats Margery, who's still stamping her front hooves; works her hands against her neck. 'There, girl, there,' she says.

We work our way along the line, uncoupling the clusters, leading the cows back to the pens. One of them half drags me across the shed, sprinting back towards the herd. When I lead Vera back across she turns and blinks at me with whiskery eyes; slowly shakes her head from side to side.

'Ash!' George calls. 'Stop mooning at the girls. I'll finish up. Go and have a nice bath and a big glass of wine. I'll be in in a minute.'

The water here takes a long time to draw from the spring. I strip, and I sit in the first few inches in the bath, waiting for it to fill around me. I try not to look at my body. I close my eyes and sink backwards, until the water fills my ears. Everything is echoey and distant, but close at the same time. The muffled sound of my heart beating, the churn of the blood in my ears. Boof, boof, boof. What is that noise? The banging again? I open my eyes. There are great blooms of orange spreading through the water. Bright streaks of blood. Gritty trails of bright matter. I'm bleeding. I'm bleeding again.

I hear myself scream. I'm screaming so loudly that I've killed the other noise and all there is is this scream, my scream, ringing in my ears and my throat. George is in here now, and she pulls me out of the bath, wraps me in towels. She peers into the bath behind me and then she checks my body over, firm and careful, and she cradles me, just like before, rocking me again, holding me close to her.

Afterwards, she pours us both a whisky. We sit near the fire.

'Ashleigh,' she says. 'It's okay. You don't need to be embarrassed.'

It wasn't blood in the bath: it was iron.

I screamed at the sight of iron.

She tells me now, by the fire, that the moors are studded with old mines. That when it rains like this, the mine shafts flood, and the Sour Hall spring gets inundated with rusty water. With bright, bloody iron, making the water taste of blood. 'I should have warned you,' she says. 'Didn't think to. I'd almost forgotten about it myself.'

She's careful with me all evening, fixes me something to eat and more drinks. When we go to bed, she holds me close. And when the light's off, she says: 'Maybe you should talk to someone, Ash. You know, if you're still thinking about it.'

'I don't need to talk to anyone,' I say. 'I'm not still thinking about it.'

'All right,' she says.

Once George has gone quiet, I don't think about it. I don't think about it really hard. There's a weight on my chest, or in my chest – as though I've swallowed water and my lungs are heavy with it; as though something is pressing hard and heavy against my heart. I remember a girl who used to work with us in the pub, a young girl, with dark hair and blue eyes and big, creamy cheeks, who used to complain about her boyfriend: how gentle he was, how he didn't know how to take control, how it was pointless asking him to be rough – if you had to ask for it, it never felt real, did it? I never answered her.

Is it my heartbeat? Is that all it is? This bang, banging. I put my hand across my mouth, bite down on the flesh of my palm. Bang, bang, bang.

It's May. The light has come back into the sky and the air is green and the cows are outside again. George says that the cheese is almost ready, that we're nearly ready to start making some money. She's cheerful. She tells me that it's Vera's time: she's been pacing; the weight of the calf is low in her belly; her udders are engorged and the soft ligaments under her tail have loosened, making a new spill of vulval flesh. We take her up to the shed, put her in a side pen, and she lows and thrashes her tail around as though agitated by flies. When she has a contraction her body is something else: her tail shoots up in the air, her back arches like a cat's. She's silent and rigid then.

'Is she okay?' I ask George.

Her body is back to normal, cow-like again, but she's moving from side to side, and she's turned steadfastly away from us.

'Yeah,' says George, 'she's fine. They don't always like company in birth.'

The labour is not quick. When Vera finally drops to her knees and down on to her side, and the calf starts to show, it is like an obscenely large, glossy egg, pulsing at the centre of her swollen vulva. It moves out, and then back in again, out and back in again. Finally, the calf starts to slide out. At least I think it's a calf, in this bluish, opaque sac. I can't tell which part has come first, until the whole thing slithers out, and then I make out the front legs stretched in front, followed by the head and body. There is a small amount of bright blood left behind under Vera's tail, but quickly something contracts, and the blood disappears back inside of her. There's a vivid smell of fresh cut grass and blood and rancid milk. She's up on her feet, Vera, almost immediately. She sniffs at her calf. It's still: entirely still inside its caul.

'It should be moving,' George says. She climbs in the pen and pulls at the white sac, which breaks easily. The calf moves its head ever so slightly and Vera begins to lick him, vigorously, all over. The calf's nostrils flare and then it barks, a hacking, old-man cough.

George moves off, back out of the pen. 'The placenta was covering its mouth, I think,' she says. 'Look at that. Our very first calf, clearing its lungs.'

The calf lies there for a while longer, coughing, eyes only half open. Vera turns away from it briefly to eat the afterbirth, then comes back to her calf and licks its face roughly. She licks and licks with her big pale tongue until the calf is pushing back, struggling to stand up. Its back legs straighten first, and then it's on its front knees for a while, face grinding into the hay, until it finally judders up – thin legs splayed, body an unstable trapezoid. It's shaking and it jumps uncontrollably when it tries to move, but it's up and it's darting under Vera, stabbing its snout towards milk.

'Well,' says George, 'that is one of the quickest calves I've seen to feed. What a little beauty. And a bull calf. Look.'

I do look. I watch the calf feeding until my chest is tight, and then I turn away.

That night, the wind is high. There's been a gale warning. The slates lift on the roof of the house, and I think of hair being pulled up at the root. It's dark and George is already asleep when I feel the weight on my chest again. A heaviness that is also a tightness; my breathing constricted. I don't think of it. I will not think of it. It was hardly alive at all, what use is there in thinking of it? Of the darkness; of the muffled sounds it might have heard? I think instead of a pub I used to work at in Liverpool that had a flat roof over the bar area, and a staff-room that looked out on the flat roof. I'd sit there in my breaks, reading the news, watching things on my phone, looking out at the sky and the plastic bags and crisp packets and parking tickets that got blown up on that roof and caught in the guttering. There were seagulls that nested over the pub, and made a great racket all through the summer, creaking like great, old, unoiled gates; yawping at the dawn like an airborne colony of seals. One summer a chick appeared on the flat roof. A large, grey seagull chick. Lifeless. Established dead by our team of bar staff who took up a rotating vigil in our breaks. No one knew what had happened to it, how it had come to be there: whether it had fallen from the nest, whether it had been caught up by plastic or poisoned by one of the objects that we saw the birds carry to their chicks – milk-carton tops and ring pulls and the slices of lime discarded from customers' drinks. When the mother bird discovered the chick, her cries were pitiful. At first she stamped around the roof, cawing: enraged, belligerent. She did this for several days. And then she sat down quietly, which was worse. She did not leave until the bar manager got out on to the roof through a hatch, bagged the chick up and disposed of it in the large wheelie bin.

Bang. That weight on my chest, pressing down on me. Bang, bang. Something's banging out there again, banging in the wind. What a night for Vera and her calf, their first night out in the dark together. Our first veal calf. Is this really what kindness is? To let her lick the blood from her young, to let her smell and feed him, to let her believe in his life for weeks, for months, and then to take him to slaughter? Better, perhaps, never to have seen your young live. Better the old-fashioned way, the bullet in the calf's head. Bang. Bang. The cows are braying. The wind lifts the slates again, and then they clatter back into place. I should go and check on the shed. We must have left something unsecured.

George has been working so hard: she needs her rest. And she'll only say I'm imagining things. I leave her sleeping. Downstairs, I pull on my boots, grab her long coat. Out on the moor-top, the wind is wild and warm. I can smell earth and straw and the bodies of the animals. There's a torch in George's pocket, which I use to light my way. Detritus swirls across the yard – hay and small clumps of mud strobing the concrete. When I reach the shed, there's no sign of anything left undone. The door is fastened properly. I open it, step inside, close it carefully behind me. Some of the cows are lying down; some of them are standing together, heads jostling, big eyes reflecting oil green in the torch's beam. Vera is standing diagonally in her pen. She's blocked the calf into the back corner and she's swaying from side to side. I reach my hand out towards her, but she doesn't respond. Bang. Bang. Her hooves skitter, the whole herd skitters. They're all up on their feet now. Low mooing. Vera brays, head low, stamping her front foot.

They can hear it. They can definitely hear it. The bang was from the back of the shed. The bang was from the dairy.

The door handle is cold to the touch. The air, as I step through into the dark space, is cool on my cheeks. A cold current rushes me, makes my skin prickle. I flick the light switch and the space is bright white. The smell in here is different now; sharp and yeasty. Curds of milk and rennet and something right bitter. The vats must be full of cheese. Fermenting. Aging. There are large muslin cloths on the side, crusted with milk skim. On the floor, in a corner of the room, is the old butter churn. On its side. Knocked over in the wind, perhaps, though it looks so heavy, so sturdy. Bang, bang. Something banging in there, or in my chest? I take a step towards it. Bang, bang. What would it be like to spend your life trapped inside something, only knowing the dark? This is what I used to think about, over and over, after it had happened. Bang, bang. There's something in the butter churn. There's something in that butter churn. I had a baby once, or the start of one. It did not live. Or, it lived inside me and then it died inside me. It spent its whole life in the dark. It bled out of me the week I met George; it was kicked out of life, he kicked it out of me, then he set my hair alight. Bang. Bang. There's something in the butter churn. When George rang the doctors, they asked me to bring it in. Can you bring the matter *in*? they asked. The matter, whatever is the matter? George scraped what she could from the bath-tub, put it in the only thing we had to hand – an old margarine tub. A margarine tub, for pity's sake. Bang, bang, bang. My hands are on the butter churn. The wood cool and tacky to the touch. My chest is tight, so tight. But I'm going to do it. I'm going to see what that banging is. I stoop and look into the dark barrel. Nothing. There's nothing in here. Just a blank, empty space, the wood inside black and waxy too. I stand up. That cold current in here: the east wind must have blown the butter-churn over and about. I *am* soft in the head. The banging I can hear now, that thudding in the background, is the hooves of the cows next door. Is my own heart. Is the blood in my own ears. I right the barrel, shift it back against the wall, check that it's on even ground. I put both hands on the barrel edge, breathe out. Ready myself to face the wind again. And that is when I see it: I glance back down into the darkness of the barrel and see it there: its unmistakably foetal shape; its clot of a face; its small, curled, hairy body. That is when my body floods with the cold, and I cannot scream, because my throat is filled with something cool and sour and dense, and I turn and I run, I run through the stalls, back out into the darkness. I run and I run, and I drop the torch on the concrete, and the wind is a roar around me, bang, bang, banging in the amniotic black.

*

I leave a note for George. I have a small bag always ready, still: I know how to perform a flit. I set off when the pale, dawn light seeps up from the horizon. The wind has died away, leaving behind a dead quiet. There is no bird-song; sheep cower silently on the ground; a whitish mist rises over the pine woods on the other side of the valley. I walk and I walk, and all I can hear is my breathing and my feet against the road. It takes me an hour to reach the bottom of the valley, the edge of the town. I will catch a train. I will catch a train back to Manchester and disappear into some new work; I always do. George doesn't need me – I needed her, but she's never needed me.

I stand on the platform with my headphones in. I stand on the platform trying not to think. I press my fingernails into the flesh of my palms one by one, over and over. A train is coming, a train is coming, a train is coming along the tracks. The noise fills my ears like blood churning; like butter churning. Bang. Bang, bang. I can hardly breathe, my lungs so heavy, my chest so tight. Bang, bang. Why is it still here? Why can I still hear it, even here? I turn away from the train, I turn to try to escape the noise again and that's when I see her. George. Standing at the gate to the platform, her face blanched, her hands loose by her side and empty.

We sit in the greasy spoon in the station. She orders coffee, but neither of us drink it. I'm silent for a while and she doesn't ask any questions. But then I tell her everything: I tell her about the banging and the butter churn and the boggart. I tell her that I've always known how to get on with things: how to work and work, how to ward off the bad things. But I do not know how to get on with this – with Vera licking her calf into life, and George taking care of me, and the bang, bang, banging that makes everything come rushing back in: all of the sourest things; that final kicking I got and the bright, bloody scraps of life that Georgie and me collected up together.

George stays quiet for a long time. Then she says: 'This is what

I know, Ash: If you try to run away, it stays with you. You can't escape it like that. Come back with me. If you still want to ... be with me, then come back to Sour Hall and we'll see to this together.'

The next summer the sky over the farm is a haze of brightness; the hills are drenched with gold. The night-times are a brief, greyish blur. George is making sour, delicious things, and she's selling them, selling them well – her fermented butters and custards and casein and hard, rancid cheeses. Vera's calf has grown to a yearling, a mad creature who charges the matriarchs. He'll soon go out to stud.

I go out there often now. On the short summer nights when I cannot sleep, when I feel my chest start to tighten, when I hear the bang, bang, banging, I go out there to the shed, and walk through the warm, animal space of the stalls. I go into the cold dairy and I sit next to the old butter churn. I feed it with memories of violence, and I coo to it, and sometimes, when the banging has finally died down, I put my lips to the cool, dark, tacky wood, and I tell it that I saw it. Yes, I saw you, and George saw you too. We've both seen you, and we know what it's like to live in darkness and in fear. You were there with me at your very beginning. And you'll be there with me until the end. You bloody, fragile clot. You bright little scrap of life.

ROSHEEN

Irenosen Okijie

Based on
The Dauntless Girl
NORFOLK

The heads suspended in the old barn's ceiling glimmered seductively. All four bobbed, hovering like a fractured constellation before gathering again. Their bloodshot eyes flickered. Their expressions were pinched and strained. Their mouths moved frantically, expelling short breaths in between garbled language that was not local to Norfolk. Or at least, not that Rosheen could tell. She herself a stranger in the land before she had dreamt of the wide flat skies and horizons, the sprawling dappled green landscape, windmills dotted along the Broads' periphery spinning like moored gods. Her fingers were numb and cold clutching the bucket handle. The sound of it swaying by her muddied legs was a creaking alarm that the crows chased in frenzies around the yard.

Rosheen edged forward slowly. With each step, the weight in the bucket rocked from side to side. Grains for the chickens spilled from her pockets in yellow rivers. The tension thickened. The barrels on the side were silent witnesses. There were red stains on her clothing. A line of sweat on her top lip. The heads lifted their tongues. With each step she took, the memories in her limbs were cushioned by the sleep state, her soil-smeared face a shadow moving in the cavernous space. The air in the barn seemed to have shifted just recently, as though before Rosheen even entered the heads had been foraging through their loneliness. The creepers on the walls were dusted with moonshine. The heads had no bodies.

Stumbling momentarily, she knocked the bucket against her leg. Its contents sloshed, dangerously close to spilling over. The heads began to shriek. Still in her stupor, she dipped her hands in the bucket. Fingers covered in blood, she raised her arms up and began to spin. Rapturous tears ran down her cheeks. The barn door clattered shut. The creepers on the walls multiplied. The contents of the barrels sank through an opening into the bottom of a pale-blue thrashing sea. Stray body parts appeared on the bales of hay like drunken hallucinations before dwindling to nothing. The heads roared, circling Rosheen as though she were a defective sun.

She had come to England from Ireland's County Kerry – from a town called Killarney, which rested on the shores of Lough Leana – the daughter of a Trinidadian father, Horace, and an Irish mother, Maureen. Maureen had told her such glowing stories of the father she never knew that Rosheen had begun to wonder if Horace, a good-looking fighter pilot who had fought for Britain in the Second World War and passed through Killarney with the same restless disposition she had inherited, was in fact a saint, the fourth Wise Man or an optical illusion Maureen had conjured one lonely night after drinking too much stout. Such was the loyalty she afforded this man who seemed to have vanished from the face of the earth once he left Ireland, but he had been real all right. She knew that every time she looked in the mirror. He had passed on his dark looks. People could barely tell Rosheen was mixed from the molasses hue of her skin, the spiral curls of hair she kept short for efficiency, a slightly wide nose that sat proudly on her face. She had flashing large, dark eyes and dimples which became more prominent when she broke into laughter. In the beginning, the judgemental residents of Killarney had often asserted, 'Good God, the shame of Maureen having that black baby. Her pa would be weeping in his grave, I'll tell you. Why doesn't she get rid of it?' Or a variation along those lines, as though Maureen could leave Rosheen in the arms of the Mary statue that stood majestically outside St Mary's Cathedral, who in turn would make her vanish to the heavens. Maureen was ostracised for the most part, except on Sundays when she stubbornly refused to be banished from

God's house. She sat in the pews in her finest garb, gently rocking Rosheen, ignoring the sly, knowing looks the residents exchanged.

When Rosheen got older she sat up some nights in bed thinking about Horace. She wondered whether he saw creatures moving in the dark sometimes the way she did, whether he too could hear the rumbling of weather changing by pressing his ear to the ground or saw light forming between bracken scattered along the town's pathways. Yet Rosheen, in her mix of barely contained eccentricity and pragmatism, did not romanticise him. She had questions. The last Maureen had heard was that after the war Horace had returned to Norfolk, England, where the airfields had beckoned like distant relatives.

When Rosheen turned twelve she began sleepwalking through the crumbling limestone house in which she and Maureen had coexisted fairly harmoniously for the most part. She had been a wilful, precocious child who loved her mother, although it was not unusual for her to misbehave. She would throw Maureen's pearls and brooches into the fire, watching curiously as the flames licked them to melted bits. She would invite local children to play, then block the front door so they couldn't leave, or walk around in the mud in Maureen's polished black leather shoes with stumpy heels which she saved for church. There were visits to services where Rosheen would sneak off to scoop the holy water into a bottle, then pour the contents inside the jacket pockets of residents as though the Lord himself had instructed her to do so.

The night Rosheen began her sleep wanderings things shifted as though in orchestral synchronicity. The bracken that littered the ground outside their home crackled softly. The stones formed makeshift paths covered in a fine mist. The moon was a silvery bruise in the sky, waiting patiently for Rosheen to limp silently towards it in an act of devotion. The clock hands in the sparsely decorated hallway faltered and Rosheen sat up in bed, dazed, her expression blank, her hair messy, her white nightdress soaked to the skin. She swept the rumpled, flowery bedspread aside. Standing awkwardly, her left hand twitched. She walked out of her room barefoot, the corner of her right eye bloodshot, and crossed the stairs, down into the hallway then out through the front door. She headed into the gusty night, the earth cool against her naked feet. By now the wind winding through the holes in the garden wall was hissing even louder. The copper taps there were spitting at angles. She walked towards them in her stupor, curled her body over them in an awkward embrace, as if the water would propel her into different directions. She slid down to the ground, curling her limbs like a snake introducing itself to a new surface.

She crossed several acres of land, her nightdress a ghost against skin. She appeared in flashes, a strange entity in a trance state. The surrounding houses in her peripheral vision were shrouded by dense darkness imbued with a certain melancholy. After a while, scratches appeared on the bottom of her legs from brushing against twigs. She scaled a wall leading to a structure which leaned to the side as though bracing against unforeseen interruptions, its thatched roof thinning at the edges. Her throat was dry. Short streaks of dirt covered her cheeks. Bits of soil were lodged in her fingernails. Still she moved, a fever dream let loose on the land. The soft din of dawn was yet to arrive. She was barely aware of the scratches. Other injuries edged towards her in search of skin to occupy. Subconsciously, Rosheen called things to her body in this state: an accordion, its black keys like teeth in the air, the march of swallows before a migration, the glimmer of reflections from shattered mirrors, weather in paperweights made real – things you could trace and hold tenderly before the morning swallowed them whole.

When she finally returned home, appearing in her mother's bedroom gripping a rake from the thatched house and wearing that vacant expression on her face, Maureen was awakened from sleep. Screaming, she thought a stranger had entered their home, but it was Rosheen, who in that moment, aged twelve, bore an ominous adult presence that Maureen recognised with a slow, unsettled wonder.

At twenty, Rosheen decided it was time to leave Killarney. Despite its wild, rambling beauty, she ached for more: new experiences that would take her outside of the familiar. The horizon had other things for her to discover that the town could not contain. She did not know its form yet but its malleable shapes bloomed within her bit by bit. She knew it would reveal itself one day. She had been told of new opportunities by the candelabra-maker Conn whose cousin Aidan worked at a farm in Norfolk, England. Aidan had told Conn, who in turn told Rosheen while she stopped by the shop, that there were several farms looking for workers out there. Conn warned, 'They're not always the friendliest bunch, so mind yourself, but if you do go you might want to try your luck on that front. I suppose sooner or later a young lady such as yourself would want things you can't find in Killarney. But be very careful, you know . . . with the night wanderings. I've seen you a few times on my way back from old Darragh's place.'

'I'm not in control when it happens,' she said, feeling somewhat exposed. A knot of tension formed in her right shoulder. 'I didn't know people had noticed.'

'You and Maureen are a favourite topic – the nosy folk will always talk. As long as you're all right?' His concerned expression contorted his rugged face a little. She had seen him in passing many times over the years. He never seemed to be in a rush about anything – as if he could bend time to his will rather than the other way round. She had quietly admired that. He handed her a slip of paper. 'That's the farm Aidan works at. If you find yourself in any trouble, you can contact him.' He shook her hand gently then, in a formal way that seemed incongruous, as if to get a hold of himself. He pursed his lips. The intricately decorated shop suddenly

became too small to contain what was unsaid. Their handshake
was suspended between them. She felt the tremor in his fingers as
though his hands would turn to wax in hers.

She left a note for Maureen on top of the fireplace at home.
Because she had a flair for the dramatic, Rosheen sealed it with her
blood. Inside the white envelope there was a shamrock for good
luck and the promise that she would return to visit. She caught the
ferry to England with some gypsies who told raucous, colourful
tales in between songs and enthusiastic drinking. Their bodies
jostled like new pennies. The smell of alcohol lingered in their
cabin. The women's skirts billowed as if they harboured secrets. A
baby screamed for the nipple. A tambourine clattered to the floor.
A gaunt, emerald-eyed woman began to cry at one point, claiming she was mourning the loss of her shadow for the second time.
Rosheen absorbed it all with a wry smile until the noise became
warbling in her ears.

On arrival in England the sum of thirty Irish pounds was
all she had to her name, rolled inside a small, black cloth purse
stuffed at the bottom of a bag of few belongings. It was bitingly
cold on the quaint Holt streets in Norfolk when she finally got
there after taking three trains. The cold was harsh in a way she
had not been prepared for. The pretty but unfamiliar winding
roads were picturesque. The flow of cars was at a steady pace. The
town centre, filled with carefully decorated shops, was warmly lit.
Ridges of ice on dark imposing lampposts melted like separating
continents. Pangs of doubt growing inside her were exacerbated
by the suspicious, discreet looks people threw her way. She wondered if Maureen was missing her already. Had she cried over
the letter or her stealing away before she had been persuaded to
do otherwise? Would she find a special place for the shamrock
to wither away as a timekeeper till her return? The thought of
finding her father in Norfolk, perhaps longing for something he
did not know he had left behind, sent a warm feeling spreading

through her. She walked for a while, listening to cars moving past her. Thoughts circled in her head like a merry-go-round. She was turned away for work for one reason or the other from a few places: the woman at the dressmaker's shop said they did not have the time nor inclination to train someone new; the baker's was a small operation of four people – unless one of the workers got very sick they were not hiring for the time being. 'You might want to tempt Lady Luck into action by trying Crookborne Farm,' suggested the kindly woman who ran the confectionery shop. Rosheen took directions from her in relief.

It was early evening when she got to the farm. Her limbs ached, her head was throbbing and tiredness was evident in her face. She was so thirsty she felt she could consume the contents of a stream. She opened the crooked wooden gate, entered. She walked a little way to the chestnut-coloured door of a thatched house. A strange feeling of familiarity filled her body. She knocked. A large, rough-looking man answered. He had beady brown eyes, a swarthy pallor and a sunken quality to his face. His thin lips pulled tightly at a pipe lodged in the right corner of his mouth.

'I'm looking for work,' she said calmly, despite wanting to collapse into a heap. 'I'll take whatever you have going. I learn quickly. I'll keep out of your way when I need to,' she countered, reading his expression of disinterest before he swiftly declined. He must have liked her gumption. The cold air blew from their mouths like a quiet currency.

The farm itself was ten acres of land nestled between the Broads, a scattering of lakes and intersecting waterways. There were steep surrounding valleys dappled with light. Windmills spun in the distance like taciturn guardians. Fuller, the owner and overseer, put her to work the next day. He said he had a few workers pass through over the years but it had been difficult to hold on to good ones. Farming life was not easy. He bore an odd, removed quality about him that would have alarmed some, a coldness in his eyes.

Rather than feeling threatened by it, Rosheen took it as an indication that it was perhaps a form of defence. Lonely people often shielded themselves as a way of protection. She cleaned the kitchen and sorted the pantry. She heard the billy-goats stuttering back and forth as though caught in an invisible lined web. Later, she watched Fuller gather the sheep for shearing, tersely calming them when they became restless. The goats broke out from their holding, rushing into the field of pumpkins as though they hid wonders inside. Fuller made cheese from goats' milk as well as other produce. She assisted him one afternoon, stirring large copper pots of milk in the roomy kitchen until her arm hurt. On one errand, she passed an old barn at the further end of the farm that appeared to be out of use. Its wooden doors were eroded. There were worms at the bottom slithering up. She peered at the slimy gathering, resisting the urge to place her finger there. A slightly fatter worm was ahead of the others as though leading a charge. 'What's that old barn for?' she asked Fuller in the sheep pen on her return, her sleeves rolled up. 'It seems a shame not to make use of it.'

Fuller took the pipe out of his mouth, his eyes narrowing. 'That barn's not open to anyone. You're to keep away from there. Accidents have happened. Mind your own.' He turned his body away, back to the task at hand, sorting a batch of ewes ready for the chop. A humming began in her head. She watched the sheep. Their cries were a sly distraction, a clarion ringing in the frazzled atmosphere. She noticed that all the animals had tiny red specks in the corner of one eye.

Three months passed during the winter season – days of bitter cold, uncertainty and a growing restlessness that felt inevitable. In that time Fuller worked her to the bone. Some mornings she rose at sunup and did not collapse into bed in the tiny, freezing attic that sufficed as her living quarters until long after sundown; her limbs burning, a chasm deepening in her chest. She had pilfered a few books from the house library – if the mahogany shelf of books that stood between the airy kitchen and the upstairs part of the house could be called one. She borrowed Charles Dickens's *Great Expectations*, *Nicholas Nickleby* and Jane Austen's *Sense and Sensibility*. If she was not too exhausted of a night, she would pore over the books, aware of the lamplight flickering and shrinking, absorbing it as a comfort. She enjoyed them. They provided a form of escapism from a hard life but she wondered about the tales of people who looked like her. Why were their stories not considered of value too? She knew her father Horace had seen some of the world as a pilot in the war. Maureen had told her about The Tuskegee Airmen. She had told her Norfolk was the strongest clue she had to Horace's whereabouts – that was why Rosheen had come. She promised herself one day she would find him. She would rise above the station people imposed on her and write his adventures. She began to think of him even more: how he walked, if he talked with an accent, whether he was bow-legged like she was. She wondered if he had the same tendency to daydream or if he harboured the piercing loneliness that never went away. She started to see aspects of him on the farm: his green infantry uniform floating through the pantry, his sleeves brushing against perishable goods, his gold cuffs glinting on the long, wooden kitchen table between cold cuts of ham, broth and cabbages blushing purple in the daylight. His injuries bloomed on the windows before moving in search of other surfaces around the farmhouse. Horace was trying to tell her something from afar but she did not know what it was, and there were crescent-shaped smudges on the books' pages that were not from her fingers.

The demand for the farm's cheese grew in the county yet Fuller paid her sporadically, sometimes only half of what she was due. When she confronted him, he growled, 'You're a mouthy madam. If you don't like having a roof over your head and food in your belly, you can go elsewhere. See if you'll be trusted in someone else's business. You're ungrateful.' He spat in the dust and jammed the pipe back into the right corner of his mouth as if to punctuate his comments. That evening her night wanderings started again. She saw parts of a dream gleaming inside the pumpkins. The next morning she awoke to find herself in the pumpkin field, their insides gouged out, her fingers slick with pumpkin juice. The memory of how she had got there had dissipated. Fuller was screaming at her, winding his belt strap, striding towards her. His face was fit to burst, his mouth spewing profanities. Through groggy eyes, she spotted the swing of the belt above her like a flash, then raining on her body, bolts of lightning against the bone. She raised her arms in defence, kicking at his shins. He grunted in surprise as she landed one in his groin. 'Aargh, you bitch!' The belt slackened in Fuller's hand. He fell to his knees, clinging to it as an anchor. The audience of gutted pumpkins lay scattered like stranded disciples. Above, a flock of grey marsh harriers streaked through the sky. The wheelbarrows spilled soil from a lost dawn. It was a bright, beautiful morning. The slow hum of the town rising from sleep could be heard in the distance. Now that she was fully alert the anger inside Rosheen grew. Imagine being awakened by an attempted throttling. She could not believe the audacity of the man. Why, even the boys in Killarney had known better than to take her on. They called her the bonny, bow-legged, black wonder.

She knew for certain that she was not the first worker Fuller had attacked in such a manner. The next day he pretended the incident had not happened, which surprised her. She had sat up in the night thinking, staring at the gauzy moon for answers, bracing herself for another confrontation or to be let go. She needed time to find other work. She did not have the luxury of just leaving, to go where and to whom? There was Conn's cousin Aidan south of Norfolk, but other than her fairly loose connection to Conn there was no real guarantee he could help her. He no doubt had his own problems to contend with. As the days went by she watched her reflections in the farm windows with terse lips. They were slender, melancholy versions of herself that faded like a fine mist. Is this the England you sought, Rosheen? She cursed the day she flung herself into a hard, lonely life, a perpetual sense of isolation. Two meals a day, if that. The occasional visit into town brought respite. She would stand outside the sweet shop eyeing the artful window display achingly until she conceded, buying handfuls of small balls of cocoa, stretchy wine-red strips and sour sugary droplets which melted on her tongue. There was other relief from Fuller himself now and again, on evenings when he took off drinking or with his raven haired, hard-eyed fancy woman. She was a hollow-looking character who rarely deigned to visit the farm because she considered it beneath her. On the one occasion Rosheen had met her, offering a small platter of the finely cut cheeses she took pride in making, the woman had raised her nose haughtily, fingers hovering uncertainly before begrudgingly selecting a slice as though she had been presented with a plate of horse manure, barely glancing at her. Her red hat was comically balanced at a precarious angle. The bulbous skirt of her cherry and black rock and roll dress swished about her as if parting the red sea. *Jesus! Mary Fecking Magdalene*, Rosheen thought, *I should have pissed on those slices before giving them to her*. She promised herself that the next time she would. They were cruel people who deserved each other. On those evenings when she knew Fuller had gone to visit her, Rosheen slipped away into the town's taverns, dancing with abandon while the gypsies played, filling the rooms with merriment and song.

One evening she spotted Horace's clothes flapping on the roof of the old barn, bending a wind to their will. They beckoned her. A tingling feeling trickled down her back, spreading all over her body like wildfire.

A few more weeks passed. Spring arrived. Fuller began to drink heavily and he did not care to disguise it. There were dark empty ale bottles unceremoniously dropped outside his room door, left in the pantry or on the windowsills. She even discovered one in the sheep pen. The sheep cried around it. There were red specks gathering again in the corners of their eyes as though the gods had marked them as a flawed batch. She fed the sheep: tenderness before a slaughtering, much like Fuller and his fancy woman. She suspected that things had soured between them because he was even meaner when he drank. She knew he still harboured a grudge when he docked her wages again, claiming that demand for their produce had slowed due to competition from some of the bigger farms in the region. The truth was, people had noticed his heavy drinking in town and some as a result were reluctant to give him their business. He nursed his resentment against her the way a person would a bruise: assessing its gravity, running a finger over its circumference, pressing it to sharpen the pain. Some days he left her making the various cheeses while he disappeared, the rancid stench of his breath still in her nostrils.

She wrote to Maureen and Conn. She could not bring herself to reveal the true nature of her circumstances. Her pride would not let her do so. Instead, she painted an idyllic picture of life on the farm, fabricating several characters she brought to life with relish. She knew the truth would only make Maureen worry to the point of exhaustion. As for Conn, she pictured his sardonic smiles, his curious calm gaze, the way he said her name slowly, as if to savour it, as if it left a particular taste in his mouth. Her heart fluttered at the memory. She wrote to Conn again, informing him that she saw them wandering through the secret parts of Killarney together. She watched him in the sleep state too, barefoot and running towards her as she stood by the thatched house she had once visited. She saw his hands stroking the widening girth of her stomach in time, his soft breath on the stretchmarks blooming there in gratitude for what was to come. In another letter, she told him that she had seen them lying on that rooftop together. A few days later, she called him on the telephone, and the steady reassuring rumble of his voice made her feel like a thousand intoxicated butterflies.

It was a blustery evening when she headed to the back of the property to stretch her legs. Surrounded by woods, and some yards from the main farmhouse, it was slightly removed from everything else. There was a well there. As far as she knew it had no water in it, but a nagging familiarity bloomed inside her every time she passed it, a little like the first night she had knocked on the farm's front door. The well was a big stone mouth springing from the ground, daring the sky to fall into it. She walked to it, looking down into the darkness below. She stood there for a while, so engrossed in thoughts of home she barely registered quick footsteps coming from behind until she felt hot breath on the back of her neck, until it was too late. She was shoved in. She felt the hands on her back, a sudden pressure, the sensation of falling. A scream curled in her throat. Only the mouths of creatures in the woods making shrill noises and the undulating Norfolk Broads acknowledged her fall conspiratorially.

She landed awkwardly, arms splayed out to cushion the impact, legs bowed like a crab. The pain was so intense at first she thought she would break in half. The smell of rotten flesh was so pungent she retched, heaving then placing a hand over her lips. Her stomach convulsed. Her thoughts were scrambled. A buzzing in her brain began as though a procession of hornets were shedding their wings in the matter. The terror of the fall gripped her again. The shock crippled her body for a few minutes. Her knuckles were scraped. Her clothes were soaked in sweat. The water had gone. After the shock faded and the reality of her situation hit her, she felt around the well floor gingerly. There were four bodies which had decomposed to the point of oozing in parts. The smell was inescapable. In her gut she knew they were former workers at the farm Fuller had got rid of when they no longer served a purpose. The true nature of what had originally seemed an act of kindness – offering room and work – revealed itself in that moment. Holding her breath, she felt the bodies again.

Their heads were gone. A tremor wracked her limbs, a spasm in the dark followed by a crushing feeling of inevitability. She looked up at the well's opening appealingly, hoping to catch a glimpse of the night sky. Exhaling, she touched the walls searchingly, looking for ridges or gaps on either side she could slip her fingers into and climb to the top. Over the next few hours she failed repeatedly. She lost her footing multiple times, a nail tore off, her fingers got sweaty. On several attempts she would get a quarter of the way up only to lose her grip and fall. She scraped her elbows, banged her knees. She felt beaten and alone. Each time she fell the bodies awaited her. They were seeping, speaking what had been done to them. They waited, signalling the end of a stunted, macabre ceremony. Was this what fate had in store for her all along? To die alone at the bottom of a well with rotten bodies she did not know. Tired and frustrated, she shrank back against the wall, curling into a foetal position. Outside, the trees shook. She howled, her cry ricocheting beyond the well's walls.

Eventually, she sat up again. It was difficult not to heave. Once or twice when she sensed tears coming she pushed them down into the crook in her heart. Besides, what good would crying do? The crook trembled, rippling through the sky and its blanket of unnamed stars. She shivered. Her clothes felt heavy and seemed like inadequate protection, her various cuts and scratches stung. Her pulse throbbed. She heard the sound, faint and then increasingly close: the rhythm of soldiers marching, the beat persistent, the thud of their feet hitting the ground. The air crackled, as though the regiment had changed formation again. Horace's uniform appeared through the crevice of air, shrouded in a feverish yellow light. It flickered gently then became more defined. Its sleeves were frayed from scouring the secret parts of the farm. Its gold buttons winked. Its green hue faded slightly at the breast. It folded as though collapsing against a stray wind then swelled. The sound of soldiers marching faded. The carcasses around her seemed to lean in, an accidental act of camaraderie. Her breath caught in her throat. A man appeared in the uniform. A man who had skin like hers but darker. Handsome. His nose was broad, his face almost perfectly symmetrical. 'Rosheen.' His deep voice was like cold water over her skin. Was this a phantom? An apparition she had conjured in a desperate state? It was Horace. She was sure of it. He repeated her name again. She uncurled her body, moving towards him, her limbs stiff. His lips pursed. He grimaced, showing her his hands. They were bloody, mangled, a contrast to the rest of him which looked in perfect condition. His hands were storytellers in the night. She realised then that Horace had died on the farm. He must have come there after the war, taking whatever work he could find. A sob caught in her throat. She trembled. The sense of loss was immediate, overwhelming. Her body caved again.

She left Horace flickering between the carcasses. After several more failed attempts, she reached the top of the well climbing scissor-legged, carefully placing her fingers in crevices again, plotting a route by feeling her way through. She concentrated deeply till she no longer feared it. On reaching the top, she hurled herself over, landing on the cold grass with a cry.

When she arose she was in the sleep state, her eyes blank, vacantly staring ahead. Her limbs propelled her forwards of their own accord, moving towards the farmhouse, towards Fuller who was deep in the throes of a treacherous slumber.

In the old barn, Rosheen the defective sun watched the heads of former workers resume their shimmering in the ceiling. Horace's head was amongst them. Their bodies still sang in the well. They bobbed in the thatched ceiling approvingly. She turned to the bucket she carried, its every sway and movement a sweet lullaby. The weight in the bucket needed to be released. She bent down reaching towards it. It was Fuller's head inside. His lips were blue, his eyes frozen in shock. She lifted his head out, began to spin around the room in a dance. Now her eyes had a vengeful gleam in them. Shaking, she opened her mouth, released a breath that was a soft pronouncement. Fuller's head left her fingers, ceremoniously taking its place amidst the others, howling in abandon.

BETWEEN SEA AND SKY

Kirsty Logan

Based on
The Great Silkie of Sule Skerry
ORKNEY

SKYE

Oh my darling wee fishie, I won't let go of you
I cannae hear you speak but I know you love me too
Oh my darling wee fishie, I'll hold you close to me
I cannae see your eyes, but your love is clear to see
Oh my darling wee fishie, I'll never put you down –

Aye, well, Mammy will have to put you down now, won't I?
Keeched your nappy, so you have, and it's squirted all up your back.
I knew I'd taped the bloody thing on too tight. If I didn't know
better I'd say you'd eaten a bad curry. Good thing Mammy bought
the double pack of wet wipes, eh? Right then, wee fishie. Clothes
off, nappy off, up on the table, legs in the air. Jesus Christ, how
can such a titchy thing be so full of such disgusting—
    Wait, no no no. Mammy shouldn't do that, should she, fishie?
Mammy heard that if she shows disgust when you've messed your
nappy or sicked up on Mammy's shoulder, then you'll hear and
understand even if you don't know the words yet – you'll know the
sounds and the look on Mammy's face. You'll know that Mammy
is disgusted by what you did, even though you can't help it, can
you? And then you'll grow up to have weird complexes and feel
shame about the natural functions of your wee body. But there's
no need for shame, my beautiful fishie. We all do the same things
in secret, you know. I don't know why they have to be so secret,
but that's the way folk do it.
    I'll not have you growing up to feel shame about the things

you do. Folk around here try hard enough to make your Mammy feel shame about the things she does, you'll see that soon enough. As if I didn't feel enough like an outsider already, coming all the way up here to do the job I do! No one likes to give up their secrets; the people in this village least of all. They'd rather I just put those bones—

Ah yes, I see you, wee fishie, that was an excellent yawn; right to the tonsils, it was. You just close those big eyes, now. I'll just try to get these bloody awkward poppers shut.

They'd rather I just put those bones right back in the ground and covered them up and forget all about it. Bodies can reveal all kinds of things that we want to hide – isn't that right, wee fishie? Except you, of course. You've got no secrets to hide, have you? Your Mammy knows you best of all, no surprises. And even the smelly surprises you make for me aren't exactly unexpected, are they? No secrets here. No shame.

Hush now, wee one. That's you nice and clean and ready for a sleep. You go off to your dreams now.

You know, I'll never let you know how much worse you made it for me, living here. Since the day it was clear you were on the way, I've never been given the right change in the supermarket or had an invite to the shinty match on Saturday or been left alone with anyone's husband. Aye, there's still the odd man will let his eyes linger on me, even now with you in my arms. But they're all afraid now that they'll be named the daddy. As if paternity tests weren't a thing! But you're more special than all that daytime talk-show stuff. And so am I. No man from the village for me! Your daddy came to me on the tide, and he left again the same way. It's not every woman can be with a man from the sea, and it's not every wee fishie can be fathered by one. I don't have to prove anything to anyone. Let them talk. I feel like they built that new mobile tower just so everyone could gossip about us all the clearer.

But I'm big and strong enough for both of us. You're still wee enough that I can pick you up like this and hide you in my arms. I'll keep you safe from those evil eyes. You'd think times had changed. And I suppose for some things they have. But not for a woman who comes to the village and digs up the dead and stoats around town in a red dress and ends up with a babby with no daddy, hmm?

Right then. No more waffling. We've got work to get to. Well, I've got to work. You'll just sleep through it as usual, no doubt. Some help you are. Worst assistant ever. Still, at least you're cute.

> *Oh my darling wee fishie, no evil eyes for you*
> *You don't need a daddy, I've love enough for two . . .*

MUIR

I was very small back then, even smaller than a regular baby. I was dark-eyed and dark-haired, with a baleful stare and a petted little mouth. Well, so I assume – I have all of those things now in an adult's face, so I must have had them back then in my baby's face. We often say that small stuff doesn't matter, but it seems to me that many of the things we most desire and fuss over are small. Diamond rings. Newborn babies. A single true word.

There were other things about me that were different too, and it's not just that I was small, or even that I remember all this, when it's more usual to forget. But we'll get to that.

Small as I was, I had two eyes and two ears – big ones, always open to the world. So I knew all about it when my mother took me to a café one morning before work. She carried me around in a sling then, a length of seal-grey fabric binding me to her front. It kept her hands free for her work and meant I could hear her heartbeat. I imagine she did that because she thought it was soothing. I imagine it was too, though her heartbeat is one thing I don't remember.

The café was busy that morning. Summer was in its final throes;

not that it gets much of a pulse in the north of Scotland anyway. More of a blink-and-you'll-miss-your-annual-vitamin-D situation. But the day was fine and bright, the stiff wind coming off the sea only making you shiver a little. It was a Sunday, and it didn't go down well that my mother was going to work that day. The village had changed, left its old ways behind – but also, it hadn't. It was still considered bad form to hang your washing out on a Sunday, and going to work was even worse form. Unless you're the priest, I suppose.

Still, my mother knew her work was important, and she'd already lost so much time on the dig from having me. Most people would say that six weeks is not a long time to take off after childbirth, and perhaps most people would also have waited until Monday to get back to work. But my mother was not most people. So she strapped me to her chest and took me to work with her, that day and every day from then on. Until ... well, I'll get to that.

She had her black coffee and her slice of iced gingerbread, and after I'd had a fidget and a bit of a wail, banging my fists against her heart, she figured I wanted something to eat too. Out from the sling I came and latched right on. It might have seemed that I was in my own world then, but I heard and saw everything that happened next.

'Excuse me,' said some squinty-mouthed lemon-sucker of a woman. 'Excuse me, but would you mind doing that some-where else?'

My mother lifted her head and pointedly looked around the café, as if to say, *like where?* The coffee machine chose that moment to cough to life, and even if my mother had said anything, she'd have had to shout to be heard over the hissing suck of milk steam-ing. Instead, she just smiled vaguely, as if the conversation was over, and turned her attention back to me.

'I'd really prefer you didn't do that,' went on the lemon-sucker. 'I don't mind, personally, but it's William. He's easily distracted.'

My mother looked over at the woman's table, where a boy of about seven sat with his father, who was staring at his phone with an intensity usually reserved for hostage negotiations. It was clear he'd already decided not to engage in this particular negotiation. My mother turned back to the woman.

'Wouldn't you say,' my mother said slowly, her smile sickly sweet, 'that this might be a good chance to teach your son that it's not polite to stare at people?'

'Oh no,' said the lemon-sucker. 'Not wee Billy. I mean William, my husband. You can do what you like at home, but there's no need to parade – *that* – around in front of men.' At this she leaned in, like they were in a girl's club, sharing common ground. 'You know what they're like.'

At that, my mother couldn't help herself: she let out a laugh. She pushed her shoulders back and stared right at the now-reddening face of William, who was staring at his phone as if the fate of the world depended on it. Luckily, before my mother could start a war over my suckling head, someone else waded in.

'Och, leave her to it,' the other woman said, 'the baby's got to eat. It's either he gets fed now or he'll scream the place down, and what would you prefer?'

'Well,' said the lemon-sucker, not ready to give up yet, but she lowered her voice, which was suspicious as she didn't mind people overhearing before. She thought she had the higher ground then, but that had grown shakier. 'Well, she could go to the ladies' room.'

'How about a deal,' the other woman said. 'If you away and eat your sandwich in the toilet, then this lassie will let her baby have his lunch in the next cubicle. That sound fair?' This last was to my mother, who grinned and nodded. Well, what could the lemon-sucker say to that? Off she popped, back to the table with her lecherous husband and her glaikit son. I don't know which of the three of them got the worse deal in having to hang around with the other two.

'Thanks,' said my mother to the other woman. 'You're Heather, aren't you? You work on the wind turbines. You must have a good head for heights, climbing around up there.'

'Och, it's fine. There's harnesses and that.'

'Still,' said my mother. 'Don't think I could do it. I'm far too much of a scaredy-cat.'

Heather laughed in a friendly way. 'Says Skye Gillies, the ghoul of Glenecher, the woman who plays with bones all day!'

My mother didn't laugh. 'Is that what they say about me round here? That I'm a ghoul?'

'People say all sorts. Doesn't mean anyone listens. But you know yourself that it's a difficult topic. You're raking up old graves. Literally.'

'Those bones have always been there; just because no one knew about them, doesn't mean they didn't exist. I think it's important to find out what happened to them. Everyone deserves to know where they come from.'

'That's what I'm saying,' said Heather. 'People here – their roots grow deep. There's more going on than whisky and gossip and old wives' tales about selkies and fairy folk.'

'My mother was born here! She lived here until she was twelve. Doesn't that count for anything? I've been here over a year. Will I always feel like an outsider?'

'A year?' said Heather. 'That's the city girl in you talking. You'll need to be here for three generations before they'll stop thinking of you as a blow-in.'

My mother sighed. 'I knew none of them liked me. They gossip about me, they give me the wrong change, they comment on everything I do, even when I'm just feeding the wee one.'

'What's his name?' asked Heather.

'Muir.'

'Sea warrior, eh? Makes sense. A baby surrounded by the sea needs to be able to hold his own with it.'

'Wish I could hold my own with the folk around here,' said my mother, and if I didn't love her so much I'd have said she was being a bit of a sulky bint. You'd have thought she was sixteen, not thirty-six.

Now it was Heather's turn to sigh. 'Listen, Skye. The village isn't a hive mind. One sour biddy has a dig because her creepy husband's got a roving eye – so what? She doesn't speak for the whole village. No one does. We've all got our own thoughts, each one different.'

'Doesn't feel that way,' said my mother.

'Speaking of the wee one. You know that's why they're talking.'

'What do you mean?'

'Ach, Skye. You know well enough. You've not said who his daddy is, so none of them know who his daddy *isn't*. They each think it could be their own husband.'

'Do they really think I've shagged every man in this whole village?'

'Not every man. But if you'll not say who it is, then it doesn't have to be all of them. It only needs to be one.'

'Can't each man just say for himself that I didn't – it sounds so ridiculous to say *seduce him*. Like we're in some nineteen sixties' erotic thriller about what the postman got up to.'

'Oh, this goes further than that, way back to Eve in the garden,' said Heather. 'But you're smarter than that. You know they've all denied saying more than two words to you, and even that only in public. The only person in this room that you need to tell about the boy's father is the boy himself.'

'I wish they'd all just mind their own business,' said my mother, and at that she pulled me off her nipple and tucked me back into the sling, though to be honest I wasn't really finished. She always did have to do everything on her own schedule, everyone else be damned.

'Look, Skye, we don't really know each other,' said Heather, getting up to leave. 'So I hope you don't mind some advice. I mean it as a friend. Sometimes the thing we think we're the most sure about actually turns out to be our biggest mistake.'

SKYE

Oh my darling wee fishie, you stay there in your dreams
I'll make the world to suit you, I'll bring you all you need
Oh my darling wee fishie, you sleep there on your own
Your mama is too busy list'ning to these old bones –

Oh Sweet Jesus, that last one was bad. No more making up songs today, Mammy promises. Talk about forcing a rhyme until it creaks! I never was much of a writer, I'll tell you that right now. Luckily there are lots of stories round here that I can tell you, so I don't have to make anything up. Mermaids and changelings and selkies, mysterious creatures that can transform from seal to human and right back again. Folk will tell you that they're good stories, but they're not true stories. So let's stick to the truth, me and you.

Give me some ancient bones, and your mammy can tell a good truth. I know how to make them speak. They can call me the ghoul of Glenecher all they like, but I know this work is important. And why is it ghoulish, anyway? Eh, wee fishie, do you think your mammy is a ghoul? What I'm doing, it's just finding out the truth hidden in the story. We're all bones inside. We're all skeletons, just walking around and flapping our jawbones. Bones and a bit of meat and some skin to hold it all together.

It's funny to think of it that way, isn't it? I made all of your body with my body. Bones and meat and skin growing inside more bones and meat and skin. Humans are more than that, I suppose, but I couldn't really say how. It's not for me to say though, eh, little fishie? All I have to do is listen to these bones until they tell me their story. Until I can figure out their truth.

The folk round here just don't like to be told the truth of things. That's why none of them like me. That's why all of them gossip about me. That Heather from the wind turbines can say there's no hive mind, that everyone thinks different things, but it doesn't seem that way when—

Ah, hang on a minute – keep that leg straight, wee fishie. I need to adjust you. Lift you up, fix that strap, and— there we go. Right then. I've got everything laid out, so we can get started. And there was me hoping you'd sleep through it all today! Those big dark eyes, taking it all in. I swear sometimes you're looking so hard you forget to blink. All right then, you can be Mammy's assistant. Don't take it personally – it's not that I don't trust your note-taking, but I'm going to use this recorder just as a back-up, okay? Okay. I'm a little out of practice, so bear with me.

Skye Gillies, resuming initial uncovering of human remains found on the outskirts of Glenecher. Remains were uncovered by – as TV-drama-cliché as this unfortunately sounds – a dog, who tugged part of a distal femur free and brought it to its owner on a walk. As far as I know, this is the first osteoarchaeological find in this area. Location is not one usually conducive to preserving remains, but the soil here is less acidic than is typical in Scotland. It's difficult to conclude too much at this early stage, but already it is clear that these are deviant burials. Rather than the typical Christian style of burial – all in the same direction, bodies lying on their backs, hands by the side or crossed over the stomach or chest – this body appears to be lying on its side in the foetal position. Lack of a brow ridge, small mastoid process and broad sciatic notch all suggest that she is female. Top crest of the pelvis was still fusing and third molar was erupting, suggesting she was aged between eighteen and twenty-five when she died. I hope to be able to pinpoint this more exactly by sending the artefacts to the relevant experts, but my personal analysis of a few small coins buried with the body suggests that she was buried between eighty and a hundred years ago. There also appear to be infant remains, though it is unclear at this stage whether the child was in utero or if it was added to the grave at a later date. The infant remains seem ... irregular. I can't comment further until I've lifted and examined them.

Okay – wait – let me check my list. The first part of an assessment report should comprise ... bone assemblage, okay ... quantity and provenance of skeletal ... general condition of remains ... got it.

You still awake, wee fishie? We've got work to do here. I'm nearly ready to dive back in, but before we can get a proper look at these bones, we'll need to uncover them. I've got my pickaxe, my pointing trowel, my lolly sticks, brushes, bags, pens, callipers, camera. Are you ticking these off? We can't mess anything up, or the folk around here will throw a party. Throw darts at photos of my face, I don't doubt. But I'll not let anyone shame me away from the truth. These bones aren't just bones. They're people – or at least, they were.

Okay, fishie. I've finished excavating this layer, so you hold on tight while I— Oh, my back! Did you hear your mammy's knees cracking when she got up then? I swear you must have a cannonball in your belly to be this heavy.

Now we have to sweep up the dirt from this layer to get rid of all my footprints to make it look nice for the photo. Yes, I know how silly it is to sweep some dirt away from some other dirt for the sake of a photo, particularly as we're going to destroy this layer after we've made it pretty. Sad, isn't it, how many beautiful things we have to destroy to find out truths. But I've worked pretty damn hard with this brush and these lolly sticks to uncover as much of the remains as I can, and I'm going to get this right. Anyway, people do all sorts of strange things for the sake of appearances, don't they? Even if it all gets destroyed in the end.

MUIR

I wish I could get as technical with the details as my mother did. Truth is important, and I don't want to gloss over specifics. But let's be real. I was a baby, not even two months old when she started back on the dig. The days did blur a little for me then. I was less interested in some stranger's long-buried bones and more interested in figuring out how to use my own bones. How to flex my fingers and kick my legs. None of us remembers the world-changing joy of finding out that we can clasp our hands around an object and make it move, which I find a shame. There's no harm in seeing wonder in the world.

But I had many, many, many hours on that dig, and even small eyes can see a lot. My mother did that dig right. She was good at her job. And while I was being entranced by the brand-new things I found my hands could do, her hands were busy too.

After that first pair of bodies was unearthed, she kept digging. Underneath them she found another pair. Osteoarchaeologists don't like to jump to conclusions that aren't backed up by clear facts, but it didn't seem much of a leap to say that the pairs were mother and child. Based on her best guesses at dating grave goods found with the bones, the first pair had been buried about a hundred years ago; the second pair about a hundred before that. And I think you know where this is going next. Under that pair was another, buried three hundred years ago. A mother and a child, buried together once every hundred years. And each child was too small to have been born alive, particularly back then when an even slightly premature baby was a dead baby. Perhaps if they'd been born now there would have been a chance. But there's no point now in playing with what-ifs.

I'm glad I was there with my mother, slowly growing in my sling as she uncovered wonders. Perhaps not everyone would think of a series of centuries-old corpses as a wonder, but my mother did, and so I did too. She was always interested in the mysteries of things. She thought that things shouldn't be kept buried. She thought that truths needed to breathe, needed to be set free. Except her own truth, of course. The truth of how she got me.

It was slow work, that dig. It takes a whole day just to correctly lift one skeleton from the ground, and that's after it's been fully excavated. Once it's fully exposed and documented everything is lifted, then sealed in zip-lock bags: one for each hand, one for each arm, one for the left ribs, one for the right ribs, one for the spine. And so it goes, until the whole skeleton is safely stored. Then the final layer of soil is carefully cleaned away, and that's what takes the time; especially with foetal bones in the mix, as they're so small. Easily moved and easily missed. It wouldn't be hard to mistake a tiny, stained bone for a chip of stone if you didn't know what you were looking for; though my mother, of course, did know.

Every step has to be documented, narrated, photographed. I was there with her every day for four months. There was a lot of time for her to talk to me.

I'm not trying to pretend that I can tell you all of it, but I remember a lot. The fact that she did almost all of the dig alone stretched it out even further. Some digs are trendy and much-fought-over. Dozens of interns and students, PhDs, professors, historians, curators, journalists: everyone scrabbling for a bit of dusty glory.

But a century-old woman and her dead baby wasn't big news, even when the further layers were revealed. Even when the baby bones began to look a little ... unusual. Fingers and toes and neck too long. Legs and arms and spine too short. And teeth, full grown teeth in a baby's skull. Sharp ones.

I listened as my mother tried to convince herself that everything was normal. The greenish tint on the bones could have been copper staining. If bodies are buried wearing copper jewellery, the metal can leave green patches; she'd seen it plenty of times on previous digs. But when she pulled the child bones out of the ground and looked at them properly, it was harder to cling to the belief in normality. I don't know if she realised it, but when she saw those elongated hand and feet bones, those compressed spines and sharp teeth, she held me tighter.

The thing is, I heard more than my mother told me. I heard what she said on the phone; or rather what she didn't say. As more layers were uncovered, as more pairs of bodies were revealed, she began to clam up. More bones; fewer words. No, she said on the phone, nothing of larger interest; she'd do her work and document it well, write a paper perhaps, but nothing of interest to any others. If she found grave goods or unusual pathologies, she'd send details to the relevant experts for their analysis; but other than that, she had it all under control, the whole predictable lot of it. I don't know why she was so secretive about it all. Perhaps she wanted to shock everyone with a surprise paper, turn that into a series of lectures, a book even. Perhaps she liked to do things alone. Perhaps she just liked being in control.

When my mother said that she had it all under control, she was referring to the dig – but she meant me, too. I was just a regular baby, and this was just a regular dig.

But none of it was regular, and she didn't have it under control.

SKYE

Oh my darling wee fishie, it's time to go to bed
The fire's warm, the bed is soft, no worries in your head –

And a bloody good thing we've got that fire, wee fishie! I feel like I'll never be dry again. You know, I once worked on a dig in Egypt, and one day the tiniest bit of rain fell, and the whole dig was called off for the day. Can you imagine if we did that in Scotland? We'd never get anything done. Your mammy's got a theory that the rain in Scotland is why we *do* get so much done. All those famous writers and musicians and inventors – well, what else do folk do when the weather is bad? They stay inside and make things. Yes, wee fishie, I see you looking at me. And I know that doesn't make sense, as it's not like the pyramids showed a lack of productivity, did they? Only six months old and already you're pointing out when your mammy talks bumf.

But I see how your mammy's voice is making you nod off, so I'll keep going. Speaking of weather, and of making things, it wasn't the best day when I made you. Well, it ended up being a great day, but weather-wise – no. A house by the sea like this one is a beauty when the sun's out, but when storms come in it can be right scary. I don't mind telling you that night was a scary one. Rain lashing, wind squalling, the sea reaching its black fingers up to my windows like I'd made it angry. Not unlike tonight, come to think of it.

But I wasn't scared, even though I should have been. All I felt was a strange pull towards the sea. I've always been drawn to it, but that night it felt irresistible. I knew that to venture into it would be death. But it was so wild and so loud, and the wilder and louder it got, the stronger the sea pulled at me. I kept thinking – it will be quiet down there beneath the waves. All I'll hear will be my own beating heart. And just when I couldn't resist any more and I reached for the door to go outside and walk into the sea, there was a knock. I opened it, and—

Did you hear that, wee fishie? It sounded like knocking.

Don't be scared. I've got it under control.

I'll just go and open—

Sorley! Christ, you scared the hell out of me. Standing there on my doorstep in that big grey cape. I'd forgotten how tall you are. And those eyes! Do you even know how terrifying you can look when you want to?

Well, come inside then, the wind's fair fierce. It's been a while, hasn't it? Back from the sea already? No, no, just stand there on the mat, just inside the door. I'm guessing you want to see the wee one. I named him Muir. He's just gone to sleep, but you can have a look.

Six months exactly since he was born, and here you are, just like that. I didn't realise you had calendars down there. Or do you go by the moon? Or . . . tides, I don't know.

Sorley, aren't you going to say anything? No— wait! Don't go clumping about the house like that, you'll wake Muir. And you're getting my rugs all soaking. Ah, now you've done it – he'll not get back to sleep for ages now. Okay, that's fine, you can hold him for a bit, but— wait! What are you doing? You can't take him outside, it's pissing down! You've no idea how to look after a baby, honestly. He's not even got a hat on.

I said wait! You can't just stride in here and grab the baby out of his cot like that. Don't take him outside! Stop it, Sorley, you'll scare him. You're scaring me, for Christ's sake. What are you doing? Stop it! Where are you taking him? Would you just bloody well *say* something?

No! Sorley, no! Stop! Give him back! You can't take him outside! Where are you— You can't take him into the sea! He'll drown, Sorley, he'll drown! Please give him back to me! Don't hurt him, please!

MUIR

Just like that, Sorley swept into the house, picked me up, and strode down the beach and into the water. It was all over in seconds.

The sea was cold, but I didn't feel it. The moment my feet touched the water I began to change.

The bones of my fingers and toes lengthened.

My legs and arms shortened.

My neck stretched; my spine shortened.

My teeth sharpened.

I ballooned with fat.

My eyes blinked black against the salt water.

All of that, too, was over in seconds.

In the length of a breath, I had become something entirely different. Or rather; I was exactly who I had always been, but now on the outside as well as the inside.

Beside me swam not a man in a grey coat, but a huge grey seal. I stretched out my flippers, gave a huge pulse with my tail; and I was swimming beside him. He led me away from the shore, deeper into the water.

My mother was right about the quiet of the sea. The storm raged above me, but all I knew down here was the sway of the waves and the sound of my own heartbeat. I'd spent six months flailing around with my clumsy limbs and grasping hands, failing to balance, failing to pick things up, failing to do even one thing for myself. But now, as a seal, I felt strong and sleek and free. It was the best feeling I'd ever known.

Even at that moment of bubbling joy, I didn't entirely forget myself. I knew I should reassure my mother that I hadn't drowned. That I should pop up above the water, give her a cheery wave with my flipper, bark out how much I loved her and that I'd be back with her soon. I loved her, and I didn't want her to think that anything bad had happened to me. I wanted to convey to her even a tiny part of my joy.

And although I remember much about that time, I know some of it must have slipped away. I wish I could remember waving goodbye to my mother. But I don't remember it. Perhaps that's because it didn't happen.

SKYE

Skye Gillies, Sunday the ninth of September. Conclusion of findings of human remains found on the outskirts of Glenecher. All layers have now been excavated and all human remains have been removed, examined, tested and photographed. Total number of bodies found: eight, including foetal remains. Bodies consist of four females aged between eighteen and twenty-five, and four sets of foetal remains, apparently dead in utero at between twenty-eight and thirty weeks. Bodies were buried one on top of the other, and there appears to have been minimal co-mingling of remains. Based on approximate dating of grave goods, each body appears to be about a hundred years apart, which is to say each woman died around a century before the one above her. As for the foetal remains, there are some major inconsistencies in the bones, including—

Ah, wee fishie, I miss you. Remember when you used to come with me on those early digs? Tiny you in your little grey sling, those big black eyes taking it all in. I hope it's okay that I still talk to you. It's only six months now until I get you back. I've only just handed you over to Sorley, but I'm already counting the days. The hours, even. All I can do is keep busy. It's not just work, wee fishie, don't worry. I'm not a total recluse. I used to go swimming a lot, but – I don't know, it just doesn't appeal to me much these days. I don't even like to look at the water; I keep the blinds closed most of the time so I can't see out. But I have my monthly film night with Heather, and we meet for coffee sometimes too. She's the closest thing I have to a friend here, but I still feel like there's still a distance between us. A lot of things unsaid.

My work here is just about finished. Soon I'll be able to lay these bones down, their mysteries solved, their truths no longer secret. Just a few more things to conclude, and then I'll be able to go back . . .

Well. I was going to say *go back home*. When I had you, I felt like I could make my home anywhere, because you were my home. But how can I leave here now, when you might not be able to find me?

In conclusion, I have taken these findings as far as I am able. The next stage is to pass the remains, photographs and my thoughts on to other experts to examine. In this way, we can all work together to find out how these remains came to be, who buried them, and what we can learn from them. It is my hope that the existence of these remains, which I will tentatively call hybrids, can be used to further investigate—

Oh, what's the point? I can never publish any of this. It's just more grey literature, a useless excavation. Six years of my life, the best work I've ever done – work that could change the world! – and it's just going to sit on a shelf somewhere, rotting away. Such a waste. Such a stupid, stupid waste. I should be touring conferences and universities, starting debates, opening eyes. But I don't see how I can get a single lecture out of this, even if I fudge some details and tone down my conclusions.

What can I tell them? That I found remains that prove that one woman every hundred years conceived a selkie child here, but none of them ever made it to term? And that I know that although the bones seem like an impossibility – a hoax, a mistake – I know they're not? And I know this because I'm the first woman who had a selkie baby and lived to tell the tale?

Either they wouldn't believe me and I'd be laughed out of a job, or they *would* believe me and you'd be taken away and locked up in a lab and tested for the rest of your life.

I can't tell the true story of my work. I can't tell the true story of my child. So what story is there for me?

Oh my darling wee fishie, I won't let go of you
I cannae hear you speak but I know you love me too
Oh my darling wee fishie, I'll hold you close to me . . .

MUIR

At first, I suppose my mother thought I was never coming back – that I'd gone into the sea, and that was the end of me – but six months later Sorley brought me back to land. And six months after that, he came for me again.

We went on like that for a while: summers up on land with my mother; winters down in the sea with Sorley. I don't know that my mother liked it, but she didn't have much of a choice. I was half a child of the sea, and I couldn't live all my life on the land. If I did, perhaps I'd end up as tiny bones in the ground, like the babies she dug up.

I didn't mind the split of my years at first; I actually quite liked it. Or at least, I never knew otherwise. It was easier being a seal in the winter than it was being a human. As a seal I was as roly-poly and fat-rounded as a . . . well, as a seal. You've seen them. You know yourself. I was pretty much a furry grey sphere with flippers. You've seen seals on land; it's not really a good look. We flop around like bags of unset jelly. We're huge slugs with feet. Inelegant. Unsuited. Cute, but in a pathetic sort of way.

But in the sea, I was a different story. I was powerful there. I was sleek and sinuous, like I was water myself. Like I was liquid pouring out, like I was black oil pooling. I was quick, too; snatching fish faster than you could blink, my teeth sharp and white as ice.

It was nice, also, to get away from that small chunk of land. Scotland has plenty of empty space, but walk for long enough and you'll always butt up against a shore-line. You just can't go that far without feeling hemmed in. But under the water, there was space to spare. Sometimes I'd just let myself spin in a drift, head down and floating, flippers a slow-dance. In winter, particularly when storms are raging, if you ever get a choice between human and seal I highly recommend that you choose seal.

A few times in the winter we swam close to shore, and I saw how the people suffered with the cold as they walked by. That makes it sound too leisurely; they practically sprinted, some of them, galumphing along as fast as they could in their rain boots and heavy coats. Or the wind and the rain would be going, or sleet maybe, and they'd have to lean their bodies right in to fight against the wind. Sometimes they were lucky, and the wind would be going the same way, hustling them along, dragging its fingers through their hair and trying to flip up their skirts. Those poor people were no good at winter! Their hands chapped and bleeding, their visible skin either white and bloodless or red-raw. How Sorley laughed to see them. He didn't think much of people. He said the only good thing a person had ever done was give me to him.

I never really figured out who he was. He told me every day that he was my father, and I did eventually call him it, just to please him. But I didn't believe it.

I don't know where I came from. The only thing my mother would tell me is that I was hers, and hers alone. If I asked her out-right whether Sorley was my father, she wouldn't answer. Surely an absence of *yes* means *no*? She was the only parent I had, the only one I would ever need. She had given everything to me, and what more could a boy want than everything?

Being with Sorley was fine. I liked being in the water. I liked playing with the other pups. I liked catching and eating fish. But as the years went by, a feeling grew in me. A feeling like something was missing. Some nagging lack in me; a narrow, deep hole where my heart should have been.

I missed my mother.

I wanted to be with her all the time.

I didn't understand why she couldn't live here with us.

She was my only parent, and I could live under the water fine – so she must be able to as well. She'd taught me enough about bodies and their functions that I could understand that. But if she could live here, I didn't understand why she chose not to. I'd tried to ask her, but she'd always manage to talk me round, to the point that I forgot what I was asking in the first place.

I knew what I had to do. There was no use in trying to convince my mother to come with me. She was a great talker, and if it was possible to build a bridge of sentences to get us out of this, she'd have done it before now, and we'd be together all the time. But here we were, apart and incomplete. It was clear to me that words could never be enough to get to the truth of things. The time for words had passed; I needed actions.

One day, right in the middle of winter, I swam to shore to see my mother.

SKYE

Well, wee fishie, here we are, all settled in for the night. I've got my spag bol and bottle of wine for dinner, my fire all lit, and my DVD box-set ready to go. Another evening in by myself, talking to you as if you're here. I feel like I might have officially crossed the line into Small Town Weirdo now. As if the folk round here didn't think I was odd enough already!

Here's an example for you. The other day I had my film club with Heather – she always likes to sit around in the pub afterwards, picking over the film, talking about what worked and didn't work in the script: the lighting, the acting, the editing. How she knows to separate out all those things, I don't know. Something's either good or not good, as far as I'm concerned. So Heather, she didn't like this film at all.

'The script was rough as hell,' she says. 'The dialogue from the main guy! *I'm broken, a hundred shades of broken, and I don't know if I can be fixed.* It doesn't even make sense! Honestly, that actor deserves an award just for saying it with a straight face.'

'I don't know,' I say. 'I thought it was romantic, the way he came back for her.'

'You *would* say that,' says Heather, but she smiles when she says it, and before I can reply she carries on. 'The problem was that I just didn't believe it. They bring in all this fantastical stuff, dragons and

bogles and mermaids, and then they give this half-arsed explana-
tion. We all know those creatures don't exist, right?'

'Right,' I say back, though I don't need to tell you, wee fishie,
that I wasn't at all sure she was right.

'Well,' says Heather, 'then they shouldn't even try to explain it.
In the film, these things just exist. Would you have questioned it
if they just existed?'

'No,' I say, and I couldn't help a wee laugh to myself at that.

'Either explain it properly so it makes sense, or don't explain it
at all,' says Heather, and then she goes and gets us another bottle
of wine to share, and that was the end of that.

Oh, my wee fishie. I know what you're thinking. I could have
told her about you then. She's opened a door to me like that before,
and it makes me wonder just how much she knows. But it's not
as simple as that. She might think she wants the truth, but she
wouldn't know what to do with it. It doesn't fit with her perception
of the world. None of the folk here would understand you the way
I do. I reckon I should have just given them a lie like they wanted.
All that stuff about your father – if I'd been a bit smarter I'd have
said it was just a man from down south, that I'd gone back to the
city one weekend and had a drunken night with a stranger. Or
maybe I could have really shut them up by saying you were an IVF
baby, that I'd done it all myself, no father at all – or not one who
needed to be a part of things, anyway. I could have said anything.
Perhaps I should have, just to stop them all staring at you.

But I didn't want to lie. Does that sound silly? I know that
saying nothing isn't the same as saying the truth. But I thought
that if I said something I knew wasn't true, they'd be able to tell.
They'd know the way a lie scrapes your throat when you tell it, the
sour taste of it on your tongue. I thought that I could get away
with just saying nothing, and that eventually they'd all go away
and forget about me. Six years on, and I suppose the village has
changed – but also, it hasn't. Now they all think that your daddy

really is a man from down south, and that we have some kind of shared custody, six months each. They've already started asking me how that's going to work when you start school, and I have no idea how I'm going to explain that one away!

I know it's not true, wee fishie. I didn't mean to lie to anyone. I just said nothing and let them assume what they wanted. I always thought I was smarter than them. Smarter than everyone, including your daddy. Seems like maybe that didn't work out so well, now that I'm here alone with my dead-end career and my mouth full of lies, and you're—

Was that a knock at the door? Hard to tell when the wind and rain are wild like this. Another stormy night, another knock at the door – but at least this time I know it's not a hulking great seal-man come to steal my baby, eh? All right then, let's go and see who—

Muir! My wee darling! What are you doing here? No, never mind, I don't even care why. I'm just so happy to see you. Come in, let me shut the door. Come by the fire.

Are you hungry? I've already made dinner, but you can have it. Why aren't you saying anything? Is this a new game?

Muir, what are— My, you're so strong now. You don't have to pull so hard. I'll come with you. Are you okay? Is there something wrong with Sorley?

Just wait a minute, let me get my boots and my coat on, it's wild out—

Muir! Don't pull me so hard. Okay, fine, I won't put my coat on if it's that important. I'm following, okay? Now can you please tell me what's wrong? Tell the truth, now.

MUIR

I didn't say a word to my mother. I led her out of the house and towards the beach. What with the wind and the rain and my insistent hand on her wrist, I'm not sure she knew what was happening.

I led her down the beach and into the raging sea. When the first wave swallowed her feet, I felt her try to pull away from me. But the wind was blowing in my ears and I couldn't hear what she was saying. I was glad of that; there was no good in talking.

We were in the water now, so I'd started to change. As a six-year-old boy I wasn't particularly strong. But as a seal I was muscular and broad, powerful. Before my arms could change I wrapped them around my mother and pulled her over in the shallows. The sea was wild. A wave swallowed us, pulling us deeper.

My mother was not sleek in the water. She was not sinuous. She didn't drift or sway. I kept hold of her, swimming hard. She fought against me. She was strong, but under the water I was stronger.

I knew this was the right thing to do. I was my mother's son; she had made my body with her body, so everything in me must have been in her too. Under the water we could be together. I wouldn't have to live this split life, half my year with her and half my life apart from her.

My mother's mouth moved, like she was trying to say something to me, but I couldn't make sense of it. The only sounds that carry under the water are long and low like whale-song; human speech is no good at all. A high-pitched scream can be heard if you're close enough, but my mother didn't scream. Of course she didn't; why would she? I was her son, and she loved me most of all. She was always happy when she was with me.

I kept tight hold of her and kept going. Further out to sea, deeper under the water. The chaos of the storm was long gone. It was just us now.

But she didn't seem to be changing. As soon as I hit the water, I'd begun to transform: fingers and neck longer, limbs and spine shorter; teeth sharper; body rounder. But I could feel that her body was the same as it was on land. She'd closed her eyes against the salt water. Her mouth flapped open in the currents. Her muscles felt loose, her body heavy.

I didn't understand. It didn't make sense. Wasn't she like me? Hadn't she told me that she made all of my body with her body; bones and meat and skin growing inside more bones and meat and skin? She was going to change. She had to. I just had to keep swimming; to take her deeper under the water, down where it was calm and quiet. Any minute now, she'd change.

Oh my darling wee fishie, I won't let go of you
I cannae hear you speak but I know you love me too
Oh my darling wee fishie, I'll hold you close to me
I cannae see your eyes, but your love is clear to see
Oh my darling wee fishie, I won't let go of you
I won't let go of you
I won't let go of you . . .

THE PANTHER'S TALE

Mahsuda Snaith

Based on
Chillington House
STAFFORD

H ere is where the story begins.

A panther is prowling in her cage. The cage is on a ship, sailing from the topaz waters of the Malabar Coast through the bustling trading ports of Portugal before reaching its final destination on the greyer shores of the British Isles. Tanned, weather-worn sailors have loaded the ships with crates full of monkeys and king cobras, cages of parakeets and peacocks, along with peppercorn, cloves, cinnamon and mace. The ships are overloaded, yet not quite as overloaded as the ones from Africa, filled with the trembling bodies of slaves.

Although the lizards and monkeys intrigue them, it the beast in the largest cage that holds the sailors' attention. Her eyes are the colour of the finest jade. Her midnight black fur is worthy of any royal robe. Her pale whiskers, thick as wire, fan out like sparks from gunfire when agitated. And the crew make sure she is agitated frequently. They poke her with sticks through the bars of her cage, laugh raucously. The panther backs into the corner of her prison, her growling guttural, like the shuddering noise of cartwheels riding over rocks.

Because of their boredom, their foolishness, their drunkenness, the crew find longer sticks with which to rile the panther. She flashes her teeth revealing four fangs as smooth as ivory tusks and a large pink tongue that ripples like the deadly sea they sail across. Her ears flatten back in the same manner as a farm cat, fooling the men into thinking she is as tame as these creatures. A young man, inexperienced with the seas and life, cannot reach the creature with his stumpy stick so pushes his arm through the bars and juts at her with it. The panther leaps, swiping her claws as he falls back in terror, clutching his arm, his face drained of all colour. There is a little blood, a graze at most, though his cuff has been torn to shreds. The young man's eyes fill with tears.

The men are silent, then they hoot in a chorus of laughter that rings around the deck like sirens. They jostle the boy side to side with their feet as he wipes the wetness from his face. They move their attention back to their duties.

They do not goad the panther again.

She stretches her front legs forward and lies down on the bed of straw lining her cage. Her pale eyes watch the men intently, ears pricked up as she listens. Though she is unable to understand their speech, she hears one utterance over and over again.

Giffard.

The panther licks her paws and waits.

He asks for her to be carried into the west chamber. When he arrives, a line of servants are staring at the cage with fear swimming in their expressions.

'This has gone too far,' says the cook. 'A beast like this is the devil's work.'

John Giffard coughs.

The servants hush their tones, step back and bow their heads. He is a tall man, with an umber beard that is as well-groomed as the fine clothes he wears. On his shoulder perches an infant Barbary ape. It is agitated, running along his shoulder blades and chattering into his ear.

It has been a long time since John Giffard has visited his home at Chillington Hall. His work in the king's court as Gentleman Usher as well as being Justice of the Peace means that he is here less than he'd like. But he has returned today specifically to receive these new guests: a whole new selection of exotic animals to add to his menagerie. His wife Jane, whose family has brought him the wealth that allows him these luxuries, is lying ashen-skinned in her sick-bed upstairs. The animals bring a light relief to Giffard's otherwise gloomy days, and it is this one creature in particular that has delivered the same anticipation he felt when receiving his first crossbow as a child.

He bends down, taking the ape from his shoulder. He can feel its small heart pounding against his palms as he examines the largeness of the cat in her cage, the sheen of her handsome coat, the savagery in her pale green eyes.

He smiles.

'I could never have imagined anything so beautiful,' he says.

The panther lifts her head and roars. The noise ricochets off the wooden panels that line the chamber. The cook yelps, picks up her skirt and runs back to the kitchen like a frightened mouse.

Giffard laughs.

'Where will we keep it, Father?'

He looks at his son Thomas, a young man who is still green as the hills. He feels the eyes of the servants turn to him with eagerness. The monkey releases a howl.

'We will place her in the forest,' he says.

Then he returns the ape to his shoulder and leaves.

She lies flat in her cage as the men transport her to Brewood Forest. It is late, the sky pale pink, as they pass a lake that shimmers like crystal cut glass. They enter a clearing and place her down, looking at the panther with curiosity. She looks back equally as curious; she has never seen skin so pale and freckled. Before they get any closer she flashes her teeth, then watches as they scurry away.

The sapphire night cloaks the forest. A moon, full and round, shines down upon her cage as the panther surveys her new environment. She is surrounded by ash, walnut and sweet chestnut trees. She smells the scent of the trunks and feels settled by it. She hears the occasional sound of nocturnal animals; the call of a tawny owl, the yapping of fox cubs, but compared to the constant chatter of the jungle this place is peaceful, private. The panther stands up on all fours and walks to the middle of her cage.

It is time.

She breathes in deeply, filling her lungs, then performs a cat stretch – paws extended, hind legs lifted in the air. Her body begins to morph. Tail shrinks into tailbone. Padded paws flatten into palms. Claws reshape into crescent-shaped nails as hooded lips rise into a curved smile. Her black robe of fur sheds to reveal dark skin that shines like polished rosewood. Chest swells into breasts as bottom becomes round behind. She remains prone, shaking her head as hair cascades from her scalp into long flowing locks that reach the floor of the cage. She is completely naked except for one item: a ruby tikka headpiece that dangles over her forehead. The chain, made from rose gold, falls down the middle of her hair parting. The stone, as large as a minted coin and crimson red in colour, is surrounded by freshwater pearls.

When the panther has transformed fully into her human form, she rests for a few moments; sorcery can be tiring work. Then, when she is ready, she slips her hand through the bars of her prison, reaching up to the rope hanging from a hook. On the end of the rope is a key.

At least for tonight, she will be free.

The child has been ill for a week. Her mother, Agnes Brown, tends to her with cold towels and herbs collected from the roadside: cowslip, heartsease, yarrow and white dead-nettle. She makes rubs and broths, strings the plants to ceiling beams but still Beth's breath is strained, her body tossing with fever.

The doctor has visited. He blood-let the girl which only seemed to make her worse. Then he told Agnes there was nothing left to do but pray.

So Agnes prays: morning, noon and night. She kneels by Beth's bedside, hands clasped so tight together the moon shapes of her knuckles turn her skin pure white. Her husband, the miller of

Chillington Estate, tells her to stop her muttering. She can tell he has given up on the girl and thinks there is no hope for her. In the same way, Agnes has given up on him.

It is early morning and, before the miller rises, Agnes heads south from the village with a wicker basket hanging from her arm. She leaves the sound of the watermill behind her, walks down the dirt path lined with ferns until she reaches the forest. She hopes to collect the herbs she needs to restock her pantry: meadowsweet, feverfew and black elder. As she tries to identify each plant, pulling the flowers close, studying the shape of each glossy leaf, she sees a flash of something dark running through the trees.

She wonders if one of Lord Giffard's creatures has escaped from his collection. The year before, an animal with black and white quills came ambling through the village. It was short and squat, with a humped back that made it look like a moving mound of earth. Whenever someone tried to approach it, the quills would rise into an angry cloud as the creature clattered its teeth. The blacksmith's apprentice was sent to get the gamekeeper who lured the beast away from the village with a trail of gourds and carrots. Later, he told them how fortunate they had been that the porcupine, as it was called, had not attacked.

Agnes has no time to be frightened of whatever beast has been set loose in the forest; all her thoughts are with Beth. She thinks of her musical laugh and fiery eyes and cannot imagine the world without them. She searches the ground for meadowsweet and feverfew but to no avail. She checks for elder trees but only comes across sweet chestnut, ash and walnut. She decides to pick anything, everything, in the hope that one of the plants will break her child's fever.

Agnes approaches the lake. The waters are clear and, through breaks in the forest canopy, sunlight streams down and dances across the surface. She thinks of Beth, how she would find such joy in this sight, then realises someone is watching her.

On the other side of the lake is a woman. Her skin is as dark as just turned earth, her hair ink black, cascading down her naked flesh like the flowing locks that covered Eve in Eden. On her forehead, a ruby is balanced in the middle as if held by some force of witchcraft. The stone is like nothing Agnes has ever seen, bright in colour and cut with crisp lines, but it is the woman's eyes she is most drawn to. Sage green. Unflinching.

The sight of those eyes, the glistening skin and the smooth round hips, sends a tingling feeling across Agnes's body. A feeling she has not felt for many years.

She takes her basket and runs.

When she stumbles into her house the miller is passed out by the hearth with a bottle of ale clutched in his hand. He has been drinking more frequently lately.

Agnes kneels by Beth's bed and observes her daughter's eyes flicker in a foggy sleep as her mouth continues to whine. She puts her basket down and it is only then that she sees the herbs she had filled it with have disappeared. In their place are other unusual plants. Thin, shiny red fruit with a waxy skin, the knobbly stem of a green plant with heart-shaped leaves, and a root, sliced in two, with pure orange flesh inside.

As the miller sleeps, Agnes boils the herbs to make a broth. She does this partly out of habit; she has become such an expert in making herbal brews. But she also does this from a new-found belief that the woman by the lakeside has given her these gifts for a reason. That she somehow knows about Beth's illness and is trying to save her. That she is the answer to Agnes's prayers.

As she stirs the concoction, the fumes make her choke, though are not entirely unpleasant. She waits for it to cool and feeds it to her child in a wooden bowl.

Then she kneels down and prays.

The panther is fed by the gamekeeper. A rabbit carcass here, a hog's head there, deposited through a hatch at the top of the cage.

Occasionally he delivers her loaves of bread, turnips and whole cabbages; he has had no training in what to feed a panther.

She is starting to feel a stab of loneliness in the forest, a home-sickness that makes her stomach ache. She hopes the gamekeeper will stop and talk to her, but he is a gruff man and always leaves without a word.

The panther thinks about the woman with her basket of herbs. She had always wanted to be a healer herself, though her father said this was no kind of occupation for a woman of her station. Nonetheless, before she was cursed, she would walk through the jungles foraging for spices and mysterious fruits. She was aware of the creatures that lived behind the vegetation, could hear them cry and shriek, but was never afraid. Padma (for that had been her name) had always felt far more akin to the animals than man.

One day, Padma returned from the jungle to find a golden chariot drawn by four horses sitting outside her father's house. It belonged to the prince, an unpopular man who was far more concerned about flaunting his riches than the poverty of his kingdom. But the king was aging and was wise enough to know that his son would not succeed him without the good will of his citizens. Padma was the eldest daughter in a noble family whose father was well respected by the locals. Their marriage would be a gift to the people.

She had never liked the prince. Everyone said he was a hand-some man yet when he spoke the ugliness seeped out like poison from a wound. He was spoilt, insensitive, controlling. On the day that he came to her home and after she had been promised to him, he had presented her with a ruby tikka and instructed her to put it on. Padma had said she would wait until the wedding, imagining how the villagers would talk, seeing her parade around with such extravagance hanging from her head. He had hooked the tikka on her hair himself, draping the ruby over her third eye and telling her she must wear it at all times to prove her loyalty. Her younger sisters thought this so romantic. Like so many before them, they were spellbound by the prince's wealth and status. What they did not know was that on that very night Padma had started to remove the tikka from her head and suddenly had become short of breath. The goddess Kali appeared before her: eyes veined red, tongue stretched long against ebony skin with a skirt of human arms around her waist and a garland of human heads hung from her neck. In one hand she held a machete, in another the severed head of a moustachioed demon, in the third a dish to collect the blood dripping from his neck, leaving her fourth hand free.

'You must never remove the ruby,' Kali warned Padma. 'For it is your heart, and without it you will die.'

Kali explained how the prince had ordered this to be so, paying a holy man handsomely to bind his new wife into such loyalty.

'Then I shall run away,' Padma said.

'No, dear child, for the prince has put a spell upon the palace gates. You will be cursed if you exit them.'

And so Padma realised that she was not only bound into a loveless marriage but sentenced to a life of imprisonment. She fell to the floor and wept like she had never done before. The goddess Kali, who looked so fierce, had much compassion for she was the divine protector and the destroyer of all evil. She stroked Padma's cheek with her one free hand, feeling great sorrow.

The panther is so distracted by the story of her past that she almost misses the scent of the healer as it drifts along the breeze. It is sweet, like passion flower. She transforms into Padma, slips her hand through the bars of the cage and takes hold of the key.

When she walks to the edge of the lake the healer does not hold the same surprise in her eyes as she had the day before. In fact, there is something close to affection. She begins to speak but the princess cannot decipher any of her words. They babble and wash straight over her.

The healer steps towards her and places her wicker basket on the ground. In it are garments: a long white petticoat and blouse, a woollen skirt and bodice, and a pair of tanned-leather shoes. Padma smiles. She is quite content in her nakedness yet still she is touched by the sentiment. She reaches down to the basket but when she begins to pull out the garments they are transformed into a single, long, yellow cloth of silk. Upon the border is a magnificent golden pattern that shimmers in the moonlight. Padma wraps the sari around her body the way her mother taught her to, pleating the front, throwing the end piece over her breasts and shoulder. She touches the ruby tikka as it hangs over her forehead, which means she is really touching her heart.

The healer seems troubled by this magic. She grabs her basket and hurriedly leaves. But the princess has already given her thanks, filling her basket with a sari that is equally as splendid as the one she wears but peacock blue in colour.

That night the panther sleeps with a belly full of kindness.

The next morning Beth's fever has passed. She is weak, but feeding on solid food and is no longer soaking the sheets with sweat. After a few days she is able to sit up and begins to chatter as freely as a bird.

The miller, displeased with the scent that Agnes has filled the home with, remains cynical.

'But she is better,' Agnes tells him. 'Surely that is a blessing.'

'For now,' he says.

When he leaves for the mill, Agnes begins her day of household chores and tending to Beth, all the while thinking of the woman with sage eyes and wonderful skin. She imagines what it would be like to touch her: whether she is as smooth and supple as she looks. She begins to dream about holding her in her arms. Staring into her exquisite eyes. Kissing her shapely, full lips. As the days pass and Beth begins to stand and then walk, Agnes starts to wonder whether the lake-side woman is even real – whether, in her frantic need to cure her child, she has fabricated this mystical creature because that was what she needed. The thought latches on to her like fleas on a dog. Even when she scratches, she cannot free herself of it.

Agnes takes Beth to the forest.

The child is still weak, so Agnes carries her part of the way, but she also seems excited; she has spent so long inside. Agnes decides the woodland air will rejuvenate the child, even if what they are searching for proves impossible to find.

Agnes and Beth sit on a mound by the lake. Beth asks if she can plait Agnes's hair the way she used to, before she got ill. Agnes removes her cloth bonnet, loosens her locks and lets spirals of auburn hair tumble down her back. As Beth runs small fingers through the strands, Agnes searches the forest for the round-hipped figure with dark, polished skin. Then Beth stops combing.

'Cat,' she says.

Agnes turns to look at Beth. Her face is pale and blinking. Agnes laughs.

'It must have wandered from the big house,' she says. 'Animals come from there all the time. Once, in the village—'

A shadow falls over them. The woman with the green eyes is standing beside them dressed in her yellow wrap. Even with the darkness of her features and the pure black of her hair she looks as if she is glowing. Agnes smiles. The lake-side woman is real.

She looks down at Agnes and Beth with soft eyes and an easy smile, then bends forward to stroke Beth along the cheek. She begins to speak. Her words are rhythmic, like the sound of water rushing over rocks.

'Her name is Padma,' Beth says. 'She tells me she is a princess.'

Agnes is shocked, but only briefly. She believed the plants in her basket had the power to save her child, but now she realises that, by consuming them, they have given Beth powers of her own. The princess sits down with crossed legs and continues speaking as the child interprets her words.

The princess had been young when she had been married to a heartless prince. She had been told by a fierce and gracious goddess that she had been bound by magic to stay in his palace. Yet, after one year of marriage the princess had tried to escape. The goddess caught her at the gate telling her that if she went any further, she would be forever cursed. The princess told the goddess about all her husband's cruelties: keeping her at court while he travelled across the land, philandering with many different women and men as he left her to deal with the ruling of his court, leaving her in poverty while he spent the kingdom's riches.

The goddess's eyes filled with rage.

'The women of your world are treated like vermin yet the men continue to behave without admonishment. I will allow you to escape the gates of this palace, but it cannot be in your current form. I will turn you into a beast of the jungle. Some will call this a curse, but the real curse shall befall the prince. He will soon realise the true power I have bestowed upon you.'

And so the goddess, fulfilling her duty to give moksha to her children, turned the princess into a panther.

Beth, who has translated so fluently and without rest, begins to blink slowly and releases a yawn. The princess strokes her cheek once more. She looks deep into Agnes's eyes. Agnes feels a stirring in her heart and loins. It is both exhilarating and frightening.

She picks up Beth and leaves.

The miller sits by the hearth with a stoneware bottle in his grasp. He brings the spout to his lips at regular intervals as he stares at the glowing embers. Occasionally, he moves his gaze to Beth curled up against Agnes's body as they share the same bed. Agnes had brought the bed closer to the hearth when the child first caught the fever. She said it was to keep Beth warm but he knows it is also so she can check on her regularly. The miller's parents always told him that, if milk is left to sit in the heat, it spoils. It was the same with children.

Agnes was giving the girl too much sun.

He takes another swig from his bottle remembering how today, when he had returned from the mill, he had found the house empty. The pungent aroma that had come from Agnes's recent concoctions lingered in the air. The smell was unlike any that came from the broths she had made before. Neither woody nor floral, this smell was stinging and overpowering. A potion, the locals would no doubt say. Their talk had never bothered him before this day.

The miller goes to the pantry. It is dark, the shelves barely perceptible, so he lights a candle, almost burning himself in his inebriated state. He surveys Agnes's store, picking up bundles of herbs before sniffing them, then rummages through her potted balms and jars of tinctures, creating chaos in her neatly organised collection.

The rumours had followed Agnes her entire life. Her mother had been the wise woman of the village, curing minor ailments with her own pantry of herbal medicine. The villagers respected her greatly in those days; she never asked for money and did not boast of her gifts. But folk healers were always under scrutiny, especially when they were women. There were some who refused to ask for her advice, who steered clear of her home as if it were a plague house, who muttered words such as 'witch'. It didn't surprise him that they accused Agnes of the same: she had been trained in the lessons of healing by her mother the same way he had been trained in milling by his father. But he always knew his Agnes was a good, Christian woman. There was no place in her heart for black magic.

Yet that broth, that smell, the secret journeys to the forest of which she thinks he is ignorant: these do not feel like the workings of a woman who has nothing to hide.

The miller punches the stone wall of the pantry. His knuckles bleed. He is about to abandon his search when his foot hits upon something hard and solid. He lowers the candle which illuminates a chest, of walnut wood with wrought-iron fixtures, given to them as a wedding gift. He places the candle down, lifts the lid and is hit by the fiery smell he has been searching for. Inside the chest is a cloth as blue as cornflowers with a gold print along the borders. On top of the cloth is a bowl filled with a strange orange root, a pimply green stalk and red fruit. He picks up the fruit – small, bent, shiny-skinned – and bites into its flesh. Instantly, his mouth burns as if it has been filled with the embers he has just been sitting by. He spits out the fruit, wipes his tongue against his cuff, coughs and splutters until returning back to the hearth to down the remainder of his bottle.

This, he thinks, is the devil's work.

He does not go to the mill that day. Instead he waits by the house until he sees Agnes and Beth depart. He follows them: out from the village, out past the stream that turns his watermill, out on to the path lined by ferns and into the forest.

He hears Beth singing – an old tune her grandmother taught her. She seems to have recovered so well, too well, considering how sick she had been. He hides behind trees and brambles until eventually they reach a lake. He hears a new voice join theirs. Joyful. Loving.

The miller bends low behind a buckthorn bush. He has always suspected his wife of seeing other men. Her fire-coloured hair attracted them, had attracted him. But when he lifts his head, he sees no man but the figure of woman with skin as dark as the bark that surrounds her. She is standing tall, regal, wrapped in a buttercup-yellow garment. The same type of garment, the miller notes, that he had found in the walnut chest. Her hair is raven, reaching long past her buttocks, her eyes goblin green. She embraces Agnes and Beth and when she lets go, the miller sees them both look at her with transfixed eyes.

He was wrong in doubting his wife. It is this woman who is the witch.

Agnes sits behind the woman on the side of the lake, a comb in her hand as she pulls it gently through the witch's locks. The witch is speaking, though her words are too fast and strange for the miller to understand.

'It was only after the third night of living in the forest that she saw her husband again,' Beth says.

She is looking directly at the witch as she speaks and he realises that, somehow, she is translating her words.

'He had come to search for her with an army of men,' she continues.

Agnes is plaiting the witch's hair. The miller can see she is finding pleasure in the intimacy of this act. He clenches his fist around the leaves of the buckthorn, squeezing the black berries until the juice bursts out.

'She waited for him to be alone,' Beth says.

The witch leans towards Beth, curls her fingers in the air as if they are claws and speaks with a sudden ferocity. Beth gasps. Agnes stops plaiting.

'What is it?' Agnes says.

Beth looks at her mother with her mouth agape.

'She pounced upon him and ate him,' she says.

Agnes holds her hand to her chest, then bursts into laughter. The witch and Beth join in. The sound is musical.

The heat rises in the miller's veins as he tears the branch with the berries from its bush. When he creeps out of the forest, he does not return to the village but heads west, to Chillington Hall.

Thomas Giffard examines the miller. His clothes are splattered with stains, morsels of food stuck in his beard, but it is the smell that marks him out. Sour and sharp, the reek of sweat and intoxication.

After the miller came banging on the door demanding to talk to the master, John Giffard asked his son to deal with the man. He was too distracted by his wife's illness, the upkeep of his menagerie and demands from the king to deal with trivial, estate matters. When Thomas arrived in the library, he could tell the miller was not pleased. But it did not take him long to begin recounting his tale, wiping his hands up and down his tunic in agitation as he spoke. He had seen a woman, skin as dark as night, who was living by the lake in the forest. She was a witch, he was sure of it, who had already put a spell over his wife and child and was sure to spread her black magic to the village and perhaps even the hall.

'She is of the devil,' the miller says. 'Something must be done.'

Thomas thanks the miller for his account, then nods to the page to show him out. The miller's cheeks flush mulberry red.

'Will you do anything is what I'm asking?' he says.

Thomas knows his father would say a drunkard should never be taken seriously, especially one who accuses others of witchcraft when his own wife has been accused of the same before. But he also knows he will one day inherit this estate; he does not want to make any enemies. Not yet.

'I will look into the matter personally,' Thomas says. 'You have my word.'

At dusk, Thomas Giffard walks into the forest. He hears the hoot of a tawny owl, the breaking of twigs which he assumes is from deer. He sees a dark figure dash through the thickets. For a moment he believes it is human; the hair is long and dark, and he thinks he sees the flash of bare buttocks. He runs ahead, heart in throat.

Then he hears a growl.

It is only when he gets to the clearing that he sees the panther in her cage. She is standing on all fours, eyes fixed upon him as though he is prey. Thomas walks slowly towards her. He has been exposed to fierce beasts from his father's menagerie since he was a boy and knows that they can smell fear. He tests the cage door – it is locked. He looks down at the creature and her pale green eyes. There is something dazzling about them, bewitching. He wonders if the miller would be so foolish as to mistake a panther for a woman.

Yet still, before he leaves, Thomas takes the key hanging from the cage. He loops it around his wrist and returns to the hall.

Better safe than sorry.

The child is hot with fever.

Agnes rummages through her chest in the pantry but finds the princess's herbs have vanished, though the wrap remains. She knows this is the miller's work. He is drinking even more now, barely visiting the mill at all. When she speaks, he is agitated by her every word. Agnes hopes he will not begin to get rough, as he did when the crop was poor last year. It began with small actions: objects tossed across the room, the slamming of doors, then he started grabbing at her wrist, pulling at her hair. Soon there were slaps, punches in places where no one would see the bruises. He had only stopped when she had taken a knife to his groin and threatened to cut his balls off.

After the miller has passed out by the hearth, Agnes drapes Beth's dozing body over her chest, wrapping her arms around her neck and legs around her waist, and walks to Brewood Forest. It is sunset when she reaches the lake, an orange sky making the water seem like it is ablaze. She sits and waits, but the princess is nowhere to be seen. Beth begins to wheeze and cough.

Desperation rises in Agnes's body. She gets to her feet, leaving Beth curled up on the mound, and creeps further into the forest. It is getting dark now, the light dimming to a navy blue. The trees surround her like giants from the folktales her mother recited: dark, looming, with crooked arms. Agnes hears the shuffling of animal feet, the rustle of wind in the trees. She can feel the forest breathing, smell its spirit in the deep woody aromas.

She reaches a clearing and sees the outline of a cage. It is the same height as her, with bars that could be mistaken for saplings if they were not so straight. A large padlock is hooked through the front door and, inside, there is something lying flat, covered in what looks like a black cloak. Agnes sees the slow rise and fall of this cloak and realises that it is the fur of a living animal. This is one of Giffard's beasts. She waits and listens to its breathing. It is slow and rumbling; the sound of deep sleep. She creeps closer, circling the cage so she nears the creature's head. It has small ears, round jowls and flaring nostrils. She bends down.

The beast opens its eyes. They are bright, fierce, sage green in colour. Agnes falls back in horror, recognising but not believing. The beast rises to its feet. She scrambles to her knees and prepares to run.

'Wait.'

Beth stands behind her, hand leant on a tree as her body gasps. She nods to the beast who has walked to the cage door. It is reaching through the bars, pawing at the padlock.

'The key is in the big house,' Beth says. 'Giffard's son took it.'

Agnes looks back at the beast. She had thought it was a tale, but now she realises the lake-side woman had meant it when she said she had pounced upon her husband and devoured him. She is not just a woman: she is a panther princess.

Agnes runs over to Beth, picks her up, and heads back to the village.

Beth does not speak again. Her temperature rises and she finds it difficult to keep fluids down. She returns to her sick-bed, shivering and sweating, while Agnes searches the pantry for something in her own stock. The shelves have been upturned and jars have been smashed on the floor. When she returns to Beth's bedside, she detects scarlet blisters dotted across her neck.

Agnes looks at her husband as he sleeps by the hearth. She is stoking a burning hatred towards him. It blazes from her gut, rising to a smoky hiss in her eyes. It is not just the drinking that angers her, nor even that he has disposed of the herbs that could well have saved their child, but the fact he does not even look at Beth any more. It is as if he believes her dead already.

Agnes kisses her daughter on the forehead, swings on a shawl and makes her way to the hall. When she arrives, she enters via the kitchen door. This was the way they took her when she was sent to see the mistress, guiding her up the servant stairs with a basket of tinctures and balms clutched to her side. The master had been by her bedside, bags under his half-shut eyes, and only glanced at her momentarily. He had already sent for the finest doctors. Requesting the village healer meant he was at his wits' end.

She only needed to look at the mistress to know there was nothing she could do, yet still she made a rub which soothed the coughing, took down the swelling and helped her sleep through the night. The master had been grateful for this, had insisted on payment even when Agnes refused. Of course a rich man like Giffard, with his fine estate and collection of exotic animals, could not understand that some things could not be bought.

This time, Agnes remains on the ground floor of the house. She searches the cupboards, makes her way into the hall entrance with huge dressers and fine portraits on the wall. She rifles through the drawers but they are empty. Agnes decides she is running a fool's errand: the key could be anywhere, if in the house at all. She turns to leave before hearing a sharp squawk from a room nearby, quickly followed by a laughing noise, too high and unashamed to be human. She sneaks down the corridor. The low glow of lamplight radiates from the main hall. She stands by the open door and listens for voices. Instead, she hears deep breathing and snuffling noises.

Agnes steps into the hall and reels back. It is filled with cages, crates and glass tanks, each one housing fantastic creatures – some which she has seen in pictures, others which are the stuff of dreams and nightmares. She sees large cats covered in spots; frog-like creatures with long tails; small apes, one of which is not even in a cage but sitting on a beam with a chain around its neck. The popinjay she heard squawking is on a hanging bar; its feathers are turquoise with a mustard chest that is as striking as the cloth of the princess's wrap.

The eyes of creatures not yet asleep turn to look at her. They flash green in the low light. Agnes turns to escape the hall then notices a row of keys hung along the wall. Above them are miniature portraits of each strange beast. Every tail, claw and plume has been intricately detailed in ink before being washed over with fine strokes of watercolour paint, except for one key, large with a laced head, that is hanging separately on a rope. This key has no picture. Agnes doesn't know why she believes this is the key to the panther's cage. She has no time for wondering. She grabs it and slips out of the house.

When she gets to the forest clearing, Agnes treads slowly to the panther's cage. The panther is awake, tail swishing side to side like a cobra swaying to a snake charmer's tune. She places the key on the floor in front of the cage, then looks at the bright eyes staring out from the dark.

The princess had saved her child, now it is Agnes's turn to save her.

The miller is waiting for her in the doorway when she returns. His huge bulk seems to touch all sides of the frame. His expression is rumbling with thunder, eyes flickering with bolts of lightning. She has seen this look before, though not for months. He asks her where she has been.

'To gather herbs,' she says.

He walks into the house and she follows, checking to see Beth is still in her bed. The miller picks up Agnes's wicker basket from the side of the hearth and tosses it across the room. It hits the wall and spins back across the floor until it stops before her feet, the handle cracked in two.

'Where have you been?' he says.

She finds her fingers are trembling. She lowers her head, keeps her eyes averted.

'I can't remember,' she says.

Agnes feels the back of the miller's hand strike her cheek. She falls to the floor, breath suddenly rapid, the room spinning. She hears his voice again.

'*Where have you been?*'

She sees Beth sat up in bed, eyes round with horror. The miller shoves Agnes's body with his foot. If she stays down much longer, she knows he will kick. As she rises, Agnes wraps her fingers around the handle of a cast iron pot. She twists her body and swings it hard, hitting the miller in the jaw. He staggers back, eyes blinking, not with pain but surprise. She swings the pot again, this time aiming for the crown of his head. His body crumples and collapses.

Agnes keeps the pot handle clenched in her hand. Her husband's body lies like the half-filled sacks lying across the dusty floor of his mill. Her breath is hard and heavy so she bends down, cranes her ear over his mouth, so as to listen for his. It is weak, but still audible.

Beth climbs out of her bed and holds on to her mother. Agnes tells her to dress, then spreads out the blue wrap the princess gave her across the floor. She fills it with food, clothes and herbs before strapping it to her back. She grabs Beth, letting her curl her body around hers. Before she leaves, she looks down at the heaped body that is her husband.

'It is not where I have been that matters,' she says. 'It is where I am going.'

*

After the healer releases her from her cage, the panther princess begins to feel weak. The strange foods, cold climate and many transformations from beast to woman have taken their toll. To conserve energy, she remains in panther form outside of her cage. She knows the panic that would ensue if she is seen, that soon the gamekeeper will become aware of her disappearance and alert the main house, but until then she will roam free.

She prowls the forest, drinks from the lake, walks to the dirt path outside its perimeters. The ferns by the path are tall and thick, yet she is not brave enough to use them as cover. She returns to the lake instead, waiting patiently as the hunger to see the healer and her child gnaws away at her stomach. Their company had given her such consolation, more than she has ever felt from a human being.

It is not long before the panther smells the sweet scent of the healer in the breeze. She runs to the edge of the forest and sees she is walking along the path with the girl in her arms and the peacock-blue sari attached to her back.

The panther princess lowers her shoulders, creeps through the ferns with one paw gently treading in front of the other. She does not want to be seen until she is close enough to change into her human form. Then she will stand before the healer and take her into her embrace with a passion greater than a thousand roars.

The healer sees her. Instead of running away in fear, she releases a warm smile of recognition. The panther princess stands tall, ears pricked up. But before she begins to transform the healer screams out, eyes transfixed on something beyond the panther's shoulder.

The panther princess turns her head in time to see John Giffard and his son – the same man who took the key from her cage. The father is holding a crossbow, arrow pulled back as he narrows his eyes in her direction. His boy cries out a warning she cannot understand.

The panther princess feels the sharp hit of the bolt in the side of her skull. She stumbles as her vision flickers, seeing the flash of green ferns, the brilliant blue of the sky before the pale image of the healer's face hovers over her. She hears Giffard shouting to his boy whose feet resonate through the earth as he runs back to the house. She knows she has little time and paws at her forehead.

'Take it,' she says as the ruby tikka comes loose.

The girl is sat next to her mother and translates her words. The healer looks unsure. The panther princess paws at her head in such a violent manner that her claws make gashes in her own flesh. The healer unfastens the tikka and tucks it into the pocket of her apron as if it is a secret.

The panther princess smiles, looking down at her paw to find it has become a hand. She is Padma once more. She looks up at the kindness of the healer's face as tears stream down her cheeks. She has never had someone love her so. She looks at the child, who coughs weakly, and conjures her last fragment of energy to restore her back to full health. Then, behind the figures of the healer and her child, Padma sees the goddess Kali. Her face is still ferocious, yet now Padma can see the serenity that lies within. She is the destroyer of all evil, the protector of her children. She will guide Padma into the next life.

The world turns dark. The panther princess is no more.

Long after his wife has passed, after he has been Standard-bearer for Henry VIII and granted a crest with a panther head placed above the shield, John Giffard has nightmares about that day in Brewood Forest.

He saw it all. The panther stealthily moving through the ferns, ready to attack the figures walking along the path. He heard the miller's wife cry out in terror as she clung on to her child. He was out of breath when he reached the path, standing strong, ready to shoot.

'Take breath, pull hard!' Thomas had cried.

Little was he to know this would become their family motto.

Little would he know that this day would be glorified by all that knew of it. The day John Giffard had slain a panther.

But, of course, those people would never know the entire story. How, after he had shot the beast, John Giffard had seen the miller's wife running over to its side with tears running down her cheeks. He thought her mad, that surely the panther would strike her down with her last breath, but instead the beast had rolled softly towards her. Then he saw her body curl up, the black fur shortening until it smoothed into dark skin, a river of raven hair flowing out from the scalp to cover the body of an Indian woman.

He ran up to this woman, watched as she passed a red jewel to the miller's wife, then took her last breath as the sky clouded over.

'This cannot be,' he had said.

It was the miller's wife who found the sack on a cart left by the path. She helped him put the body in, before whispering a final prayer for the woman inside. She told him she would not breathe a word about what had happened if, in exchange, he told no one in which direction she ran with her child.

He kept his promise, did not tell a soul. Not after he watched her flee and the house staff and his son came running to his side, dread shuddering through their faces. Not later, when the miller was found stumbling around the village with a wound to his head.

He told them the panther's body was contained in the sack, that it must not be opened as the creature had been frothing at the mouth, riddled with some toxic disease. They buried her immediately, on the spot where she had been killed, making sure the hole was deep and wide.

As John Giffard watched the sack being lowered into the earth, as soil was thrown on top and his secret was buried, he felt a great sadness. The panther had been his favourite animal from his collection. Such a magnificent creature, it could never be replaced. He would, he decided, erect a cross to mark the spot where she had passed. Then everyone would know what a fine creature he had possessed.

But nobody would know about the nightmares.

And so, as our story ends, let the tale of the panther princess be a warning to you that not all things are as they seem. That, and to treat the female of your species well, for if they are provoked, they will one day surely pounce.

THE TALE OF KATHLEEN

Eimear McBride

COUNTY GALWAY

Long ago, a long time now, a hundred years before the ocean took back the island, before the south-easterly hounded the last locals from its shore, there lived a fine young woman who, inevitably, was in love. Innis-Sark was the island. Kathleen was her name. The ocean was the Atlantic and Ireland was the mainland. This great love of hers was a fisherman, as plenty around had been before. That the love indeed was a great one I have nobody's word for but, for the sake of pathos, I'll profess it to be true.

It was a hard life but a good life and you may take as read all the usual obeisances which, at the mention of rural life, must be made. Particularly the old kind before sanitation ruined everything, along with electricity, the A-bomb and the discovery of penicillin. Not that I'm suggesting it wasn't lovely. I'm very sure it was and, as an act of good faith, I'll even offer up the tropes: the landscape was rugged but beautiful etc., exposed to and hewn by the elements; the people were hardy but honest and could rely upon their neighbours; everyone was close to nature – although everyone went to mass and felt there was no contradiction in a belief in fairies while golloping down the body of Christ. Indeed, the old ways and the new ways were companionably arranged in order to discourage dissent from either strand or the asking of logical questions. We are all together so we all must be the same and hell's mouth will open at the moment of deviation – you already know it, that 'life is a team sport' sort of thing. But this is not our story. Our story's about the doings and undoings of Kathleen.

*

Briefly then, what is expected but doesn't really count – or in any way propel this chronicle forward – what did she look like? Well, whether her hair was as black as ebony, or not, we cannot possibly know. Neither if her lips were the blown red of a summer rose. Nor if her skin was of the milkiest white. Nor if she sported a shapely calf. Not even – to diverge briefly – if the music of her laughter filled every heart with gladness. Island life being what it was though, well-developed muscles may be supposed. A healthy weather-beaten complexion. A great capacity of the lungs. Given how few photos survive of then we are, generally, at liberty to envisage her as we fancy. Such is the way for all lives back when light's primary purpose was demarcation. Hours and days. Seasons, then years. In fact, Kathleen's whole life may have been spanned before light ever succeeded in getting itself trapped. She never knew of its existence behind a lens, repurposed for the human past's reflection from ever further away. Perhaps if she'd been born into that world, later on, this story would never have been at all? This is only idle speculation though. Besides, as already has been said, the specifics of her appearance have no bearing on what happened and do not account for the curious quirks of her fate towards which I now tentatively creep. Indeed, had her hair been blonde or her skin ruddy with tint or her eyes blue and bloodshot or her lips a little anaemic, what took place would have taken place just the same. So, while it matters little how she herself looked in that time, her whereabouts in it amounted to something. She lived before the last century's exodus of Innis-Sark, yes, in the century before but also before photographs – or the widespread taking of them. Definitely before science had put paid to the seriousness with which mystical phenomena were greeted. But also – and this is significant – after the church had started to get its claws in. So, let's say at the start – which appears to be again where we are – Kathleen's story takes place long, long ago.

*

Lightly then, to edge us in, I'll assume you think Kathleen's whereabouts require a mention. Although I am aware that I am to-ing and fro-ing, fear not, I'll get us there in the end. By the way, to say 'Our Kathleen' keeps popping into my head but I worry this relates to a baser instinct. It would be a fraudulent display of intimacy on my part and feigning intimacy with women with whom I have none is a bit of a rubbish thing to do. For instance, do you need me to imply she was a distant relative of mine to have your interest piqued? And should that pique then be used to encourage an emotional investment in her? And for you to be emotionally invested in the well-being of an unknown woman, must she be someone you like? You know, she might not have been but, sure, I also might not be and you might be absolutely horrific. Let's face it, we can never know. So, I'll take the chance you're wise enough to suspect that the obligation to create likeable female protagonists is only pandering to a certain kind of audience and we're all trying to do better than that. You've been given the benefit of the doubt so try not to waste it, all right?

Anyway.

Where Kathleen – not 'our' but her own – lived . . .

Off the coast of Galway. I always like to say now 'Next stop New York' – which I only draw attention to in case anyone's read my books. Innis-Sark was prone to wallopings by the Atlantic and getting cut off from the mainland for weeks or more. These details aren't central to our business but do no harm to know. Only the isolation is significant for, as we are aware, many wonders and horrors may befall us when we are very far. Returning to local news though: stone cottages dotted the terrain, dry-stone walls, trees growing swept back by the wind. There was the aforementioned fishing, also farming. Turf-cutting. Butter getting churned. Milking cows and fetching lobster pots and dragging the currachs in. A TV documentary I watched suggests the islanders were great ones for smoking a pipe. A male habit, I assume. Of course, I've seen old photographs of grannies in shawls smoking them too but their whereabouts in place and time, for the life of me, I don't know. Anyway, the tobacco for this, along with the post and nearly everything else was usually brought from the neighbouring island of Inis Boffin. Three miles' row away, the documentary says. Steam rising from the rowers' necks. The hardiest being the steamiest, they said, and all the usual marking of real men. But whatever about all that, music too was a thing and dances, whenever they managed to ship musicians in. More often over to Inis Boffin. Rowing in the early hours back, in the dark and dangers attendant upon it. For what word is a currach inside the story of the sea? In truth, it barely punctuates the Atlantic which rises always as it wants and takes what it will away.

On that note now, all initial exposition is done. You know where we are and in whose company. The last little fact before we go on is simply that it was after one such dance that Kathleen's lover – or does discretion demand 'beloved young man'? – was lost at sea. Drowned. Alas, alas to be him in the cold as the current dragged him down, and out, and far. Further than hands could clasp or prayers could reach. A young man's young body in the penetrable deep and then gone forevermore. There were sad days after for all concerned and although its like was not unknown, none were the better for that. Poor Kathleen was left in a body collapsed by the loss of her great love – and yes, I agree with myself about making it her 'great' love, it really does add something to the pathos. With no one to console her then, she grew haunted, pale and thin. I use this description simply because it's the way to write about sympathetic grieving women. I'm pretty sure just as many grieving women get red and shiny and fat, but I did say 'sympathetic', didn't I? As everyone knows, you don't get to eat a hearty meal and have sympathy too. So, the misfortunate, thin Kathleen got wan and found only increased savagery in the arrival of each successive morn. No ease either or drowse by the afternoon and, after a day's long work, no restful exhaustion. Just the pillory of grief bearing down on her neck and the smirking laughter of all that she had once thought might be. There isn't often a connection made between humiliation and grief so I accept this connection may be particular to me but I do think there's something there.

One evening though, as she walked back home – sun skulking off to below the watery horizon – she was confronted with . . . how best to say? – an unanticipated sight. There, between the jaws of the lane leading home, neither in nor on the wall but somehow floating in front, a beautiful stranger in a beautiful dress – obviously certain clichés are playing into this but let's let that pass for now. It was most likely a woman, she guessed, and an apparition – to be clear. Not the Virgin Mary, as you might think, given Kathleen had taken to walking around with her rosary beads 'just in case'. 'In case of what?' you might well ask. 'Apparitions' I would say, as I'm obliged to hazard an answer, because grief can be funny that way: encouraging you to imagine if you'd only prayed what wonderous alternatives to your present reality you might instead now face. Or that, since your heathen lesson has probably been learned, it's now time to get to work on some serious warding off. And who might not come a-visiting to ensure these fears found home? Aren't all immortals generally mad for disrupting the human present with needling reminders of failures past or what should have been better done? But I only suggest Kathleen's thoughts may have been these and accept, equally, they may not. She did tend to go her own way in her mind but, still, she was a product of her times and it takes an unusually adventurous kind to get on the outside of that. Plus, we must take the rosary beads into account for they imply a particular bent. However, after all that, it not being a visitation from the Blessed Virgin makes the matter moot. In fact, as rapidly became apparent, there was nothing Catholic at work there at all. It was the floating first gave it away. Nice shoes it had and an unchristian amount of leg protruding from the rich-looking stuff of its skirt. It also smiled most merrily and, beatific as she undoubtedly was, it's pretty hard to imagine the Virgin Mary smiling like that. Anyway, all this gave Kathleen a land but, to her credit, she stood her ground and let the emergence in.

Weird it spoke inside her head, drying cascades of tears before they'd even descended the outskirts of Kathleen's eyes. As the ensuing conversation occurred within her, it's hard to accurately relay but the general gist of what Kathleen heard was 'Be not afraid' – except that sounds too overtly religious, for which I've only my own upbringing to thank. I don't feel like thanking it though so I'll have a go at something else. Right ... Then ... The voice said, the weird voice said:

> 'Kathleen, sorrowful Kathleen, there's no need to
>   be afraid,
> Kathleen, poor sorrowful Kathleen, there's no
>   reason to grieve
> for I bear tidings to make your sore heart glad.
> We in these last days have been moved by your sadness
> and are come here to your aid.'

Now, I don't really know if what she said was in verse but in the interests of expressing her 'otherness' this is the method I've alighted upon. Humans of the modern(ish) variety rarely have truck with speech as poetry, especially when they've a great bit of bursting news to tell. The other folk though, the ones from under the hill – well, they keep a different measure of time in their skull and can easily speak how they like. So, I will persevere with this but know that I know it's only a trick and may not be at all representative of the exchange which actually occurred.

Anyway.

Poor Kathleen was startled half sideways, as you'd imagine, by the unexpectedness of all this – for who plans a quiet weep on their way back home but ends up gawping through a fairy woman (?). No one over the age of ten expects this, or even less these days I think it's safe to bet. Let's say over seven or eight.

Anyway.

Poor Kathleen having no idea what to make of all of this – for she, despite growing up in the double faith, had never before been exposed to a supernormal experience – said something along the lines of: 'What are you going on about?'

'Your weeping,' said the fairy, 'and the sufferings of your heart are burdens from which you may unburden yourself, should you choose our game instead.'

'What?' cried Kathleen, now confused.

'The crying,' said the fairy – for she was quick enough to realise that verse may not be the best way to invincibly convince – or, you know, I got sick of devising it. 'I know why you're doing it,' the fairy added. 'And why would you not? But I'm here to inform you it's a wasted effort.'

Now this was not something Kathleen was willing to hear, heartbroken as she was, she would not forbear to have her suffering brushed off in this way. 'My love is lost!' she cried. 'And my heart is broke for my beloved who lies cold on the floor of the ocean and will never be seen again.'

'Ah-ha!' said the fairy, grasping her chance before the threatened teary deluge could recommence, 'that is where you're quite wrong!'

'Am I indeed?' said Kathleen, affronted but also stopped dead because, at that very moment, the fairy clapped her fine hands and a twisted ring of blackthorn appeared. Lifelike enough it looked too, shedding the odd white blossom and giving off the right perfume.

'Oh yes,' said the fairy, glad to have Kathleen's full attention snared. 'Far from lining the ocean floor, your pretty young lad is where you, if you choose, may yet go. For he caught our eye when the waves grew high and imparted into his pretty mouth and body the salty gift of themselves. Oh, we watched undecided while he spluttered and coughed – no human can be beautiful while emitting brine of course. But when, in his mortal anguish, he called your name, we found ourselves experiencing a flicker of concern – which is an awful lot for us to bestow on mortal calamity. As you may imagine, we've seen an abundance of ye drown and never managed more than mild irritation at the almighty kerfuffle being made. As he went down through the water though, his love glowed and we liked the colour of it. So, we reached out and saved him – a rare exception to our normal wont (we leave pretensions to mercy for the Catholics, same as their inventive punishments). By the time he surfaced he was already half dead but we still dragged him over the entrance to the other land and, if we say so ourselves with a touch of pride, he spat up a good load of ocean and now appears to be fine. Pining though, somewhat annoyingly and ungratefully, for you.'

'Oh!' cried Kathleen, clutching her chest as the fairy stopped for what appeared to be a breath. 'Show me him, show me him. I'll do anything you ask.'

'No need for dramatics,' the fairy replied. 'I realise our reputation is of being demanding but, you know, there are two sides to every tale. All you need do is look into this ring and there you will see everything for which your heart has ached.'

With no hesitation, or even the thought of a prophylactic Hail Mary, Kathleen gazed right into the very centre of it. And oh, there was love. Tall and thin or short and fat or short and thin or the other way about – do we really need to go over this? We all know I can't really say – beautiful to Kathleen though, most importantly. All her cried-dry body drank it in and knew nothing would ever be good again without him, in whatever shape or form.

'What can I do,' she begged, 'to keep looking at this? Anything you want I will give. I will perform any task. I will repudiate Christ, if you ask.'

'Now, now,' said the fairy, edified but modestly so. 'There's no need for the surrendering of mortal souls. I know it's a matter over which you and your ilk get confused. These last centuries especially there seem to have developed rumours that we're in league with the devil and all that crack. But, in actual fact, we don't know who this devil is or why he would ever want that which can't even be proved to exist (you see, we have read our Kant and approve enough to throw him a quote, although we know not to expect that kind of reading from you). No, from you we want nothing more than the cessation of this infernal woe and to see a smile spread on his face – of which we have, of late, become inordinately fond. To this end, we have concocted a delivery system of you, if you agree, to him.'

'Oh how?' asked Kathleen, all a flutter now and as eager to oblige as to abandon her sorrows.

'This larger ring,' said the fairy – producing it from thin air (because she could and enjoyed the effect) – 'will facilitate travel between our world and this! All you need do is pluck a leaf, burn it and deeply inhale its smoke. On the instant of doing this, you'll be borne to under the hill where our world and your great love await. And it's a fine world, Kathleen, where you may shed every care. Therefore, take this and later, I will see you there, if you dare!'

Once the blackthorn dropped into Kathleen's hand, away with the fairy, as quick as she'd arrived. Kathleen just stood there wonderstruck, trying to believe she had just been picked clean of her former woes. Then from the cottage below the rooster crowed – thrice, or is that trying too hard? – and she waked back to herself again. The ring was there though, in her hands and real enough to prick to blood her fingers and thumbs. But with the dark coming down, swooping now, she picked up her feet and headed on home.

*

There her mother waited and smiled to see her daughter smile, ladling more food on the plate from which Kathleen now wolfed down a helping and a half, then two. She raced through the evening as though she couldn't wait. Throwing turf on the fire before being asked. Scrubbing off the dishes. Taking a broom to the kitchen floor. Only on her mother's sharp insistence eventually sitting down to stretch her poor tired feet across the hearth. She stared off into the embers a bit before playing dog tired and slipping off to bed. Her mother was delighted by the lightness in the face that bent down to kiss her own. 'At last some lift in the weather?' she asked, smoothing the hair from Kathleen's face.

'A little, a little' was all Kathleen said, thinking only of what worlds awaited once she could get herself alone.

'Blessed be to God,' sighed her mother, meaning every word, leaving Kathleen to briefly think *'If you but knew the half of it.'*

Filled though with thrill of what the night would bring, she did not pause to draw blood from her mother's sensibilities, confining herself to the spare remark that, 'Yes, indeed, God is good.'

'There'll be others,' said her mother, not yet permitting her to leave and keen to nail down the advantage which this light respite allowed. For before the drowning, it should be said, Kathleen and her mother had tended to disagreements aplenty – about the boy and going to mass and not taking in vain the name of the Lord Jesus Christ, which Kathleen was in the habit of now and then. Tonight though, seeing the smile again, her mother was confident enough of the good graces of heaven to hold her tongue and let her daughter go.

Up then Kathleen to the rafters under the roof and the quietude of her little room. In the storm of it all she could barely wait for the settle of the hinge before proceeding to her secret and laying the twisted blackthorn out. The matches buried in her apron pocket were hastily withdrawn. *Was there an incantation?* she wondered, but recollected none beyond the burning and the breathing in.

However, instructions are not always easy to precisely recall, especially ones given after a shock. For although Kathleen could not have known about FBI agents in television programmes capable of remembering numbers twelve digits long, after hearing them only once, *we* know about them and so must make allowances for untrained memories. Not that there was a mistake. What she remembered was essentially correct. I just thought I'd mention, for my own credibility's sake, that she'd wondered about it, that's all.

Anyway.

Listening out for footsteps from downstairs, she pulled off an already drying bud and felt foolishly romantic in a manner she had not for some time. With trembling hands then she struck and lit the signifying match. On touching to the tinder leaf, she felt vaguely surprised by how thick was the smoke which emanated from it, but remembering the fairy's words she shut her eyes and breathed in, then even deeper so that there could be no chance of getting anything wrong. She was not altogether clear about what happened next. A whispering in her ear, then a sensation of swiftness converging inside some unknown spot in her brain. Whatever it was, on opening her eyes again, she found herself in a place she had never been or even known could truly be.

She was away. She had arrived at far. How could she be inside the hill? How did she know that was where? But why ask when the fairy had already told her? And where else did she think she may have meant? None of this, however, helped to mitigate the bizarre. How was it she could be this far? See herself as a body and the hill as a place, but find herself inside it while still seeing without as though layers of rock could not obstruct the view? How could she press the cavern walls yet smell the ocean out there? Feel no chill but still know the wind ripped through her hair? Or watch her feet take her forward while sensing no ground beneath? The essence of this conundrum being: how could she be of the body and not, all at the self-same time?

But suddenly the question grew tired and everywhere was light. A thousand candles dripped from vaults above right into the void and black below. Angels sang, except she knew not to call them by that name. Inside her head in secret though, she whispered, 'Angels sang,' as if perhaps readying a tale she would one day relish to impart. But she never would impart it, for angels they were not. All this lies ahead though and can't be known yet – well, not by the one who isn't making this up: you. Instead I'll say there were entertainments on view which, for Kathleen, were beyond her ken. But bewilder as they would attempt, she fought to hold her ground or what space within the teeming she was apparently allowed.

So, she held and held until a voice she knew said, 'It's called the fairy sight.' A voice reborn from beneath the waves, the one she'd thought was lost, and forevermore. 'That's a long time,' the voice reproached, as if it could hear inside her which, it turned out of course, it could. 'You, you, you. I've missed you,' it said, both outside and in the depths of her head.

'But where am I?' Kathleen felt compelled to ask.

'Don't act the goat!' the voice fied. 'You know fine well where you are.' This then was the end of coying herself out of her own understanding and the real start of the dance instead.

'He is alive, so be alive,' her heart commanded. 'You are alive, so live,' it said, and Kathleen, being who she was, took this sage advice into it.

So away they went together into the night. Vault to void and to either side with the flight of birds and the fast passing of light from hand to gripping hand. From cups to lips, the sweetest sound. The air all music. No feet drumming alarm. Just drumming whirl and whisking around on and on and on. Herewith past has never been and the bold future waits in its own suspension. Here their time has no dominion and the heart may do all it wills. No more toil against unforgiving ground. No gloom tolling of bells. No nets cutting hands where the salt must sneak and sting. There is no sea in here and no lost out there. No more bellowing Atlantic in winter uproar. The ocean here's a great cat lapping on the shore. And where stones are ground to sand are sown such waters as to make small children laugh. Here for the human only delight and faces raised to the abandon of it. Here there are no armies, only dancers of the night. Hurly-burly does not exist – although we have also liked the lies of your poets – and where elsewhere pleasure is the foreshadow of death, this place breeds multiplicities of it. Here, no cosh or rote or thumb with which to be hit or bound to or pressed under. Unheard are such words as never or none. No one knows us and we devour everything.

This is the world that approached Kathleen. It gradually stole in through her skin, then made right across the threshold of herself. Where lips sip lips and life is sloughed off, this is the place in which she found her body. And all the voices clamoured in her ears for her to come but come of her own free will. 'Tempt, tempt!' they said. 'And grieve no more, nor ever be grieved again.' They offered her food and they offered her wine. Intimations were made of eternal life and these did not fall on fallow ground.

To find myself released, Kathleen thought, *of this infestation of suffering, to never know harm, nevermore know fear, to strip off the work of the island that has ever been. To be forever young. To always be in love!* She was young, so of course these were the things she would think. Too young to love the marks life had left on her yet or appreciate how useful they might be. Already she was thinking how this could be always but, for now, it was too late, or too soon. For even this night had its ending song. The dancers' dance slowly winding down. The harp thrums stilling. The still of the drum. The creep away of wonders in the face of the sun, coming more and brighter and real.

'The day must part us now, Kathleen,' said the lover to his

beloved. Woe betiding both of them as the insistent day came roaring in, parting their tight hands.

'But again tomorrow night!' she cried. 'I will see you then!'

'And I will wait,' the lover sighed. 'I will wait here always just for you.'

So, the day killed the night. Kathleen woke in her own bed. Footsore but heart salved and her future near determined, as far as she could see. From this day on she would bear no cross, just do what she must and wait for the dark and the woman she would be inside it.

There was some time of this then. Weeks, perhaps. It's hard for me to be precise as there were no calendars to be synced or any of that kind of thing. What's important to know is that these events recurred. Nightly, I'm inclined to think, for youth, by its nature, is disinclined to restraint and is in fact prone to mostly more of the same – if the same happens to be what it likes. So, Kathleen was going great guns, all her miseries swept clean and all the 'my life is over' stuff quickly forgotten. She adopted a faux sobriety, in order to keep face. This was aided by her body suddenly thinning to its thinnest: skin dwindling, grey and ever closer to the bone. 'Probably all the dancing,' she thought.

'Loss's fitting manifestation,' was the judgement of the island and, 'nothing more than should rightly be.' It was in the revival of her spirits, however, they sensed something amiss and much revived she was, so the whisperers whispered: 'Have you seen her?' 'I've seen her.' 'What did you think?' 'She's awful happy in her loss.' 'My own thoughts exactly.' 'Did she love that poor boy at all?' 'They say she half lost her reason when he drowned but it's not yet his month's mind and she . . .' 'What?' 'Well now, I've no wish to gossip but . . . I'd say she's gone a rose in her grief.' Now, whether or not there were many roses on Innis-Sark I couldn't say but I

think we all recognise the point being made. And it wasn't far off
the truth, this noted twinkle in her eye. All the more noticeable for
not being the usual, and preferred, deadened irises of the women
left behind. They'd call this hussy-like, were her family not so well
known. As it was, there were swallowed tuttings at this bold face
she showed his mother. Like a wilful abnegation. Like a kick in
the teeth. Where was her stricken visage? And when had she left
off with the rosary beads? Kathleen, never utterly oblivious, nevertheless let barking dogs bark and turned her living eye in, waiting
for the night, her lover and the music in her head.

Neither was her mother's joy at this rejuvenation short-lived, and
who among us here would raise an objection to that? What cal-
lous eejit would stay nostalgic for their child's recent brush with
despair? Militants and monsters? Those who genuinely don't care?
Those invested in a studied ambivalence towards impending disas-
ter? Kathleen's mother, being none of these – although apparently
of the 'content-with-what-little-freedom-she's-been-allotted' variety (of which we could argue the politics until kingdom come but
it would still not be immediately relevant) – thought exactly that:
that her daughter was now better off than she had been before. So,
she was happy enough – Kathleen's mother – for a good long while
and mostly preoccupied by shovelling a good meal into her cheer-
ier, if still decreasing, child. However, as can often be – oftener
in those times but in ours yet occasionally – her mind flew to the
Lord Jesus Christ and the holy Roman Catholic church. I won't
hop forward to get into all the muck of what would eventually
surface about the doings of those in the religious life. For our
purposes it's sufficient to say, back then, the church communi-
cated very inflexible positions about the routes to going straight to
hell. Islanders had little choice but to believe, there being few in a
position to object philosophically (see the previous, and not unfair,
assumption about Kant). But perhaps it was simply expedient too,

given that the gap between your average islander and perdition might frequently be just the height of an unlucky wave.

Kathleen's mother – though unlikely to have had recourse to these specific thoughts – circled the cause of Kathleen's smile in quiet, thinking but not consciously thinking of the possibilities she feared. She'd probably have only admitted to wondering how this reverse could have, so expeditiously, been brought about? Being older, and of the island, she'd borne griefs of her own and could remember none quite as quickly gone. There was also Kathleen's mismatch to be pondered: wreaths of smiles atop her lessening flesh. God-fearing as she was, she knew plenty tales of the fairies and their wicked rotes of tricks. Stories of malevolence, and changelings, and spite – none, however, of the dead rising so she never considered that. Bargains she feared though, and their inevitable price for meddling where Christians should not. Being Catholic of the old guard, she's unlikely to have possessed much in the way of direct biblical knowledge but would have known the gist of: 'What shall it profit a man to gain the whole world but lose his own soul?' This is a bit too 'King James' a version but you will take the point.

Kathleen, in her happiness at the prospective choice of all eternity joined in the dance, would probably have argued the toss, but her mother, in neither happiness nor alteration of any sort, was incapable of viewing irreligiousness with anything but dismay. Not that she ever broached the subject or even admitted to the forefront of her mind. She could simply not help looking out from the accumulations of her antecedents' eyes. And the previous generations did not like what they could see: the unsavoury gleam of 'other solutions' in their Kathleen, further evidenced by an increase in her vituperative shouts of 'Jesus Christ!' when anything annoying occurred. So, first Kathleen's mother was happy and then she was not.

*

Less happy again come the Sunday Kathleen wouldn't countenance getting out of bed, wouldn't hear a word of the row to Inis Boffin for the taking of mass. 'Get up!' her mother called. 'The men are readying the currachs and we've to leave before the weather turns.'

'Let it turn,' groaned Kathleen, nursing a foot blooming blisters from her revelries in the night.

'God forgive you!' cried her mother. 'Can you not do this for the good Lord Jesus Christ?'

'And what has he done for me?' Kathleen answered, rubbing life back into lips gone numb with night wine.

'Will you not at least come to pray for the souls of the lost? Must they languish in purgatory because you will not raise yourself up from your lazy degree?'

'Lies! All of it!' laughed Kathleen, feeling quite unbuckled now from religion and its generally thankless approach.

'I'll be speaking to the priest,' her mother warned.

'Speak all you like!' said the brazen Kathleen – and how else could you describe a dissenting young woman? With that, out her mother went in rage, half praying for her daughter and half cursing, her maternal heart though becoming one with the waters and the forbidding of their cold.

That night, with the whole family at the rosary on their knees, and barely having given out the Sorrowful mysteries, Kathleen's mother spied her daughter's face. Bowed in the light but full of nothing but contempt and impatience for the prayers, or the inflicting of them (as would become a far commoner occurrence in just over a century). Two times more, she saw this, maybe three – certainly both during the Joyful and then Glorious mysteries. Very evidently Kathleen was away in herself and far from deep thoughts on the creed. At the finish, her mother made much ado of the sign of the cross and horror ran through her on Kathleen declining to at all. 'Kathleen!' she said. 'Bless yourself.'

'I did,' Kathleen replied.

'Bless yourself so I can see it,' she persisted. Kathleen would not. 'For your mother,' said her mother. 'To give my heart ease.' Kathleen though, in her adamance, prevailed and the cross remained unblessed. 'Kathleen!' she beseeched. 'You're putting the heart crossways in me.' Impervious however, Kathleen left the room.

I won't say she was hard-hearted, that wouldn't be what it was – not that I disapprove of hard-heartedness in women, not at all. She'd just lost the sound of her mother's God. Its hollowness had ceased echoing within and, truth be told, Kathleen felt nothing for any forms of God now. How purposeless it seemed, all that confessing, against the scintillation of the new. Cruel too, she thought, to insist the so briefly dwelt-in body not live greatly while it could and make very much of what might bring it joy. 'I will never fathom' she concluded, 'this love of lack, but at least I am now become my own body of Christ, enough for everyone and sometimes more.' And this little spasm of blasphemy did her good. It buoyed inside as she fetched out her blackthorn twist. Even its pricks just intimating the approach of delight and what was the spill of blood to all that? Her body now in her bedroom but her head halfway there, with nothing but the stretching out before her of hours where no proscriptions need be seen or heard. So filled was she with anticipation her ears did not pick out the step. Or the creak of the door from her mother's pressure. She did not sense she was seen or worry she would be. Her haste and freedom just plucked the leaf and burned it quick to ash. Then, breathing its smoke in, she fell from her body into the hill.

Vault and void and the candles lit and the hands which clutched hers with their icy fingers. Convulsed in her dance, she had no way to know of the mother's lament at work back in her home.

This she had lost or become lost to. No earthly sounds reached so there was nothing she knew of her mother's cry of 'Send for the priest!' Rather, in the glad frisk of the night, she turned herself to the face of her love. None to forbid and no one to forestall the giving of mouths as gifts to strange bodies, and bodies she already knew. Further they sought and took of her now and she, in her glee, gave away. Until the voice marked God split right through her head. Ripping her now from the arms of the loved. Suddenly all music was the Holy Ghost invoked and Kathleen dragged back into her room.

Now were frantic crossings above her. Blessings she knew. She burned against and as the sweetness withdrew before the dank scent of home, before her mother's human breath and her own future as old, she sat up in her bed and screamed, 'The dead are coming! The dead are here for me!' Terror, they recounted, in the years after this. Terror was what they all heard in the cottages and fields, across the island and into the sea. Fish drowned themselves up on the shore-line in fear. Birds clung to their nests. Rabbits to the earth. Eggs soured in their shells and butter in its churns. There were, it was said, three calves stillborn before Kathleen finally fainted away.

In prayerful watch then her mother sat, afraid in her marrow of her daughter's state; more afraid the priest would not arrive soon enough and invoking all the angels and saints. There was laughter in the hill and at the window at this – if she'd heard it and she didn't. Perhaps too much time had passed for her ears still to hear those sounds of wanton youth? Instead her reverend thoughts mulled on religion and the priest. With unfounded certainty, she believed he would put this pagan misfortune right and everything back as before. It is, perhaps, too easy to judge and with the gift of hindsight suggest that if she'd known her daughter, she would surely have known this solution would be the very death of her.

But, as the fate of mothers has so often been, she had succumbed to the persuasion to put her faith in almost any old place but herself. And in this, she was in no danger of being disabused by the priest.

Through the door he came, cause encased, kissing the chasuble slung round his neck, patting the mother's shoulder, asking after the girl, insisting on candles and meting out holy water with all the interminable gusto of his kind. 'Father, Son and Holy Ghost' along with the liberal dissemination of the aforementioned liquid on and all around prone Kathleen.

'Father, can you save her?' wailed her mother.

'With the help of God' he said, betraying no doubt about his medicinal effects. And who would doubt, if they believed the tenets of a faith which said that, on this earth, they were literally God's representatives? Kathleen, in her new-found atheism, however, was unimpressed – although it still appeared to have some kind of placebo effect. So, despite being out for the count, her face creased into a laugh, even as the blackthorn ring fell to disarray in her hand. Then, dipping his thumb in his chrism, the priest smeared her forehead and mouth, all with the sign of the cross. We cannot say what happened within her but what was visible from without didn't appear to be all that pleased. A frown like a tear ran right across her face, as if resisting the wrench expected by the man who knew everything. Nevertheless, he persisted, and was later roundly celebrated as a hero for it. Kathleen, however, merely opened her eyes.

'She's come home to me!' cried her mother.

'Satan is vanquished!' boomed the priest.

'Oh fools,' said Kathleen. 'You have taken from me all you ever will.' With that, she lay back, white as the sheet and soft in her breathing until it stopped. Dead. And that was that.

There then ensued calamity all around. But her body kept still in its death and whether the rest of her had gone off where it wanted cannot be with true confidence said. The world from under the hill gave no hint. And if tales of her spirit seen dancing there surfaced, it should be remembered such stories are common enough. They are almost to be expected and should be looked sceptically upon – depending, of course, on how much of the rest of this story you believed anyway.

But to tie it all up, as this is the end, I'll mention the various outcomes of the other participants. The gossips gained plenty. A few unlucky animals died. Initially at least, the priest got a fright. As you might imagine he soon recovered himself, given his sort's cultivated repugnance for the doings of females, the non-compliant ones especially. That Kathleen's mother found comfort in her faith may be readily supposed by those with a stake in such things. I have some sympathy. Not much. A century or so later hers was the type who kept making ham salads for the parish priest despite revelations about where he'd been shoving bits of himself. As for me? I leave the island and I leave the past, or as much as I can. Meaning: now there's only you. So, I hope you put your best foot forward as you heard all this and, if you didn't, you might want to have a think about that.

THE SISTERS

Liv Little

Based on
The Brothers
LONDON

The hospice was eerily pleasant. As soon as Grace and her girl-friend, Chlo, arrived at the main doors, there was a plump, freckled and rather affable-looking woman eagerly waiting to greet them. Grace hadn't wanted Chlo to come with her. They were mid-argument when Maya had called with the news that Mum's condition had worsened and that she was being transferred to live out her days at St Catherine's Hospice, situated in a muted, lifeless part of South London.

'It's the last chance you have to make it right with Mum,' Maya had said. Chlo had always been reliable in an overzealous sort of way; she thrived when presented with an opportunity to play the hero, and so she had gallantly offered to hop in the car and cart Grace over to the hospice. This despite the fact that seconds before they had been at each other's throats. Without her, Grace probably would have remained still and in a state of numbness for several hours after Maya had relayed the news. She didn't know if they had days or weeks or hours, but she hadn't seen her mum in almost three years.

Grace couldn't keep her focus in one place; her eyes darted around the room nervously as she absorbed every detail of the hospice's reception area. The first thing that she noticed was the bile-like colour scheme that coated the walls and furniture. Grace had always despised beige on account of it being an unremarkable colour. She also noticed accents of yellow, dotted clumsily through-out the lobby, which reminded her of the faded gingham school uniform she used to wear. Grace was drawn to bright things, and today she was wearing boxy red flares with an oversized printed tee and a chunky pair of red Dr Martens. Her eyes eventually settled on the chaotic splurges of paint that decorated the pinned-up messages from children thanking the nurses for looking after their parents. Grace could imagine these parents, in their last moments, applauding their children's artistic skills even though these abstract images resembled the Willem de Kooning paintings she had studied in school; they could quite literally be interpreted as depicting anything, depending on the angle at which you were holding them.

She was trying to take it all in, in particular the fact that this was where the living knowingly came to die. Grace couldn't avoid thinking about how the hospice walls must have been home to countless regrets, unsaid I love yous, and relationships left unmended, visits from grandchildren who in a few years would not remember that their grandparents had ever lived. Was it better to know how and when you were going to die or be surprised? She wasn't sure. The thought of spirits wandering the corridors, the ones who remained in limbo still to be transported to another realm and those who had come to welcome their loved ones to the other side, was compelling. The last time that Grace and her mum had been in the same space was for Maya's birthday party, three years ago. Grace had become expert in dodging interactions with her mum. However, on this occasion, because it was their twenty-first birthday, her sister Maya had convinced her to make an appearance.

Eight years prior to this moment in the hospice, Grace's mum had kicked her out of the family home, turned her back on her as though the only thing that they shared was their proximity on this planet. Her mum had always had the ability to emotionally disconnect when it came to what she termed 'ungodly' acts – an uncomfortable reality that Grace mostly blamed on the lasting effects of intergenerational trauma at the hands of the British

Empire – yet she still couldn't quite forgive her. Sickness, however, *had* forced Grace into a state of partial forgiveness. Grace
had barely been afforded a moment to decide whether she wanted
to make amends in the time it took for Chlo to speed her over to
the hospice.

'Can I help you with something, love?' the freckle-faced woman
asked Grace, in a tone so artificial and polite that Grace mistook
her friendliness for condescension.

'I'm …'

'We're looking for her mum. Her name is Sandra. I think her
sister said she's on the fourth floor,' Chlo interjected, as Grace
opened her mouth and a flat and undecipherable whisper came out.

The woman paused to think for a moment, scrunched up her
face and finally exhaled and said, 'Oh yes, I know who you're talking about. I thought you looked like the other girl, though she was
dressed smarter than you. If you go through the doors just there
and walk up four sets of stairs, you'll find her. I think your sister
is still up there too.'

She pointed to a narrow staircase and explained that someone
would be back in the morning to fix the lift, which had given in
about an hour before. The staircase was filled with faded photographs of patients: women, men, children, the elderly, smiling
with an innocence that suggested these had been taken before
they'd ended up here. Grace and Chlo made their way up the
steps, and Grace's mind continued to wander as she pondered who
these people were, who they had left behind, what their temper-
aments had been and what diagnosis they had been given. She
settled on the idea that it was both morbid and beautiful to have
pictures that memorialised the dead plastered up and down the
stairwell; Grace was a firm believer in the afterlife and respecting
those who had come before her. Perhaps it was a grim but necessary reminder that our time on this planet is only temporary
and that although our lives may seem remarkable to us, we are

nothing but a part of a greater ecosystem. Her train of thought was interrupted by Chlo.

'It's just so sad, isn't it? So many lives lost – it kind of gives me the creeps.'

As they approached the fourth floor, Chlo squeezed Grace's hand firmly. The two remained silent as Grace walked through the doors and towards the ward. Grace had always been referred to as the fearless twin, the child who would climb up to the most unstable-looking branch of a tree without injury. That was her role. The first night that Grace and Chlo met, Grace had told Chlo that she was going to make her her girlfriend. Chlo had shrugged off the assertion and dismissed her as being another overzealous lesbian with a little too much self-confidence and yet, here they both were. For a girl with a dark, berry-like complexion, the colour was draining from Grace's face with every step. She moved in the shadows amidst a sea of unsettled spirits.

As they approached the desk and were redirected down the hall, Chlo whispered, 'Baby, I think I should go. It might give your mum too much of a shock to see us both together, so I'm going to leave, okay? I'll be waiting for you in the room down the hall.'

Grace thought it odd that Chlo assumed her mother would even know who she was, but she nodded and replied, 'I'll be fine.'

Chlo turned and watched Grace disappear into a sea of white, plastic hospice curtains.

Grace's mother had been a constant source of tension between her and Chlo. To Grace, Chlo's family was your stereotypical nuclear family, an advert for multicultural Britain, and it had embraced Chlo's decision to date Grace with open arms. Grace thought that this was because Chlo's relatives viewed it as a passing phase, but either way, her partner would never be able to understand what it was like to have a family that wasn't so open. Her naivety meant that she'd often come out with lines like, 'You should tell her. I'm sure after all these years she'd rather have you in her life than not at all,' or 'I just feel like if I were able to meet your mother, I'd be able to understand you more. We've been dating for a while now. Maybe it's time.'

'Go! Get out. I don't know what child of mine you think is going to be living under my roof and talking such foolishness. You must have lost your mind. No, uh-uh, not my child,' proclaimed Sandra as she shook her head back and forth, locks bouncing accordingly. 'You need to put this nonsense out of yuh head. You must have watched too much American television. I knew I should've sent you back a yard when you were a yout. You always did have a hard head.' She kissed her teeth. 'From day one I knew it would never be easy, even before mi did give birth, yuh had yuh own ideas about how to come out.' It was a rare moment when Sandra referred to Grace and Maya as a single entity. 'They don't know how to raise them pickney over here.' The more angry Grace's mother got, the more bits of her patois surfaced. She'd taken to speaking in the most British of accents and it was only when she was at boiling point or amongst Grace's aunties that she'd let slip.

'Them likkle friends of yours must have corrupted yuh mind – their parents let them run riot. Uh-uh, not my child. Not my child. This isn't natural.' The only voice was Sandra's uttering 'not my child' and lecturing Grace about how western values were to blame for this foolishness.

Grace didn't say anything. She just stood there, her poker face firm, something that would come in handy for her later in life. Her sister tried to interfere, almost chirping as she begged for her mum to let her stay. The two had been inseparable since they were old enough to move and a simple but heavy blink was enough for one to relay that they could feel the other. They fought for each other, in ways that they wouldn't fight for themselves. Maya's nose and eyes were streaming as she begged and pleaded with their mum to let Grace stay in between increasingly panicked sobs, but Sandra was having none of it.

'Are you going to carry on this foolishness?' she asked Grace as she actively refused to acknowledge her other daughter's plea. 'Because if you are, you better find somewhere else to call home. Cha. What will people think?' She paused. 'No, no. Not my daughter. Not today. I can't even look at you. Get out.'

Her voice, which was usually rich, like melting honey, had grown coarse. Sandra remained still, cleaning a single spot on the window, back turned to her children.

'Blasphemy,' she murmured. Her face remained hard. It remained hard while she heard her daughter pack her things, walk through the hallway and close the door gently behind her. It remained hard for the duration of the evening as her other daughter continued to beg for her sister to be welcomed back in. It remained hard as her thoughts loudened and continued to carry her into another realm until later that evening when Maya had gone to sleep. Sandra sobbed all night, and once she had finished crying, she vowed never to sob over Grace again.

Maya stood at the entrance to the ward opposite her sister as she offered her one slow blink. Her sister mirrored this, a single tear streaming down her face. Maya led her down the ward, where they walked past five gaunt-looking women on either side of them, all between the ages of forty and sixty. Grace observed the fact that the white patients had one or two guests at most, whereas the two black women had families gathered around them who struggled to fit around the narrow hospice bed. They had come bearing food and gifts; hospice meals remained untouched in the corner of the room.

The journey from one end of the ward to the other felt eternal – Grace felt as though she was getting a glimpse into moments to which she should not be granted access. At the end of the ward was a skinny, unremarkable black woman. She must have been in her late forties. Grace thought that it must be her mum, but, at a glance, she couldn't tell. As she drew closer, she recognised the person who sat before her. This figure was thin and without hair, but she could just about make out her mother's sharp, signature cheekbones, which were now even more pronounced. She wasn't sure how to address her; it had been years since she had uttered any version of 'Mother'.

A few seconds had lapsed. 'Hi, Mum,' she spurted unnaturally.

The woman looked at her, still, eyes fixed for several seconds. Grace's mother was taking in every last detail of her child's face. While Grace bore a striking resemblance to Maya, who Sandra had seen nearly every day for the last eight years, the details in the faces of her two daughters were distinct. Grace's eyes had always been slightly softer than her sister's. Without speaking, she ushered her to take her hand and approach the top of the bed where she could see her clearly.

Meanwhile, Maya left the room and headed to the waiting room where Chlo was sitting anxiously.

'Hey, stranger,' Maya said, softly.

'Hey.' Chlo got up and embraced Maya for slightly too long, in an uncomfortable display of sympathy.

The pair sat in silence for a while until Maya said, 'You sounded tense when I called earlier – everything okay?'

Maya's interest in Chlo's life was unexpected. Usually she would avoid prying into the lives of other people and so the two typically shared mundane conversations.

'Well, you know how your sister can be at times.' Chlo laughed nervously as she shrugged off the intrusive question. 'It's nothing. You know what it can be like living with a partner. It's not always that easy but it's worth it overall.'

Maya nodded. She had spent all of her life living under her mum's roof, which meant abiding by her mum's rules. She'd spent a lifetime shrinking away from who she was and her mum's illness had brought twenty-four years of suppressing how she felt to a head.

'How did you know you were into women?' she asked Chlo, without looking her directly in the eye.

Maya couldn't believe what she was seeing. Joanna and Grace were kissing behind the bike shed in clear view. Her best friend and her sister. She was livid but made the conscious decision not to say anything. The girls were a trio and had become inseparable, so much so that teachers had nicknamed them the triplets, a label that the twins' mother hadn't been best pleased with. Between them, the girls had formed an unbreakable bond over a shared love of the supernatural and in particular Harry Potter, on which their mum had tried to implement a ban time and time again on account of it promoting devil worship. Grace, Maya and Joanna had had their own private reading group-cum-witches' circle where they would attempt to cast spells on other children in their school from their hiding spot near the hopscotch in the juniors' playground. They were now fourteen and these witches' circles had become few and far between.

Joanna had been Maya's friend first, a detail of which she was particularly proud. She had found her, not Grace. They had been in the same class and sat next to each other on their first day of year seven. Their relationship had been cemented when they had both dressed up as Hermione for World Book Day. The white girls in their class had sniggered at their outfits and proudly asserted that 'Hermione wasn't black'.

Joanna had stood up and said, 'Hermione was supposed to be black, actually. In the books, they talk about her having frizzy hair. You would have known that if you'd read them and not just seen the films. Losers.'

From this point on, Maya had been in awe.

*

Maya had always thought that if anyone were to kiss Joanna it would surely be her. It was, after all, Joanna and Maya who could recite all the lines from *Harry Potter and the Goblet of Fire*, which they had unanimously agreed to be the best of the films. Grace did enjoy Harry Potter, but not as much as the two of them. She had moved on to carving out a spiritual philosophy based on piecing together inspirational quotes, phrases and mantras for daily living that she had picked up in religious studies and cemented on Tumblr. Joanna wasn't the first girl that Grace had kissed behind the bike shed. From the age of twelve, Grace had made it known to her sister (who was already aware) that women were far superior to men. Grace had kept a picture of Ciara circa *Goodies* stuck in her planner while the other girls in their school had opted for Chris Brown before everyone discovered he was trash.

When the girls reconvened for lunch, Joanna and Grace were sitting a fraction closer than they would ordinarily. Maya was trying to play it cool, avoiding eye contact with the both of them and only answering questions with 'mmhmm', while Joanna and Grace discussed the pros and cons of William Paley's watch analogy. Maya tried not to scoff at their overwhelming need to impress each other. She had seen Grace put on the charm offensive time and time again but now it made her feel nauseous.

'How was it with your mum?' Chlo asked awkwardly.

She had been waiting for Grace to say something during the journey back, but she had been completely silent. Now that they'd walked through the front door and made it into their cosy and cluttered front room, she couldn't hold in the urge to ask any longer.

'Fine,' Grace snapped back.

'Okay, fine. I'm here when you need it. I'm on your side. I can't imagine what you must be going through right now, but I do empathise. I love you.' Chlo's voice trailed off pitifully.

Grace didn't say anything but squeezed both of her fists so

firmly that her nails stabbed the skin on her palms. It was all too painful, and she knew that if she started to speak it would all come pouring out uncontrollably. Years of pain and blame which she hadn't been able to express. Grace couldn't erase the picture from her mind of the woman she had previously called Mum crumpled into a fragile ball of blood and bone. She didn't know if she was angrier at her for the years she had thrown away, or at the cancer which now consumed her. Either way, the only thing she was sure of at that moment was that she was angry and she didn't know where to place it.

Grace's little finger had successfully broken the skin in her palm, releasing a tiny stream of red flowing liquid. She remained silent until Chlo gave up and became preoccupied with a package that had arrived. How could she possibly know what this feels like? Grace wondered. How could she even begin to understand what it feels like to see the woman who rejected you wither away, knowing that there were dozens of transformative moments where her mum had been absent?

Grace sat on their lavish green-velvet sofa, a purchase that Chlo had made on a whim, and that still had another ten months before it would be paid off on finance. Chlo had decided that despite the decrepit nature of their apartment, with its peeling wallpaper and overcrowded use of plants, what it needed was a sofa that was so expensive that neither of them could afford to buy it outright. Grace had never been one to care about lavish furnishings; she'd been more concerned with having a permanent base to reside in, especially after fending for herself from the age of fifteen. She'd lived in all kinds of places up until now. Chlo had a much more impractical taste for the lavish things in life, which Grace was enjoying, provided Chlo didn't expect her to summon up the cash to pay for unnecessary purchases.

She remembered the morning that the sofa had arrived and how the two of them didn't move from it for the rest of the day. They ate on the sofa, fucked on it and then fell asleep. She brushed her hand over the spot where Chlo had left a perfectly circular wet patch, and as she moved her hand from the spot to her thigh, Grace smiled at the memory before heading off to bed.

Grace was curled around her sister in a warm embrace. Their limbs had become interlocked throughout the course of the night making it difficult to identify whose limb belonged to who. Sandra tugged gently at one bony, brown leg that must have corresponded to Maya's body as she started to wriggle loose.

Maya had woken up in a panic again: she frequently woke up in the middle of the night with terrors. Grace would always wake up around the time that her sister did. She'd walk over to her room and hold Maya close until she fell asleep, and this occasion was no different.

Their mum had decided it was vital for them to have their own space to forge their own identity, so she didn't dress them in sickly sweet matching clothes like most parents of twins did during the nineties. When family and friends came bearing adorable little matching sets, Sandra would donate them to charity or give one of them as a present to a mum-to-be at church.

She had read on the BBC that if she wanted her girls to develop their own identities, she should refrain from referring to her twin daughters as 'the twins' in favour of calling them by their names. On top of slightly differing decor and style, they were encouraged to take up different hobbies and make separate groups of friends.

'Why are you here again, Grace?' their mum asked as she poked her head round the door. 'How many times have I told you that you are both big girls and you should sleep in your own rooms? Just because you are twins it doesn't mean that you should be glued to each other, you know.'

The girl's bedrooms had been painted in different colours and dressed with different furniture. When Grace's mum had been informed that she was carrying twins, her friend, Aunty Adaze, had told her that twins had traditionally been seen as a bad omen and that for some Igbo people in south-eastern Nigeria, the presence of twins would be a very stressful burden to bear. Some people viewed twins as having a supernatural ability to manifest unpleasantness and wreak havoc in society. While Grace's mum hadn't believed this in its entirety, she did make a point of treating her children like two different little girls. She had always been slightly superstitious and wanted to cover every eventuality to avoid these omens coming true.

'I'm giving you two minutes,' Sandra said with authority, 'by which point I want to see you getting ready. You need to catch the bus in thirty minutes if you want to be on time for school. Chop-chop.'

'Baby, are you okay?' Chlo had her arms wrapped around Grace. 'You were doing that thing in your sleep again – you were getting really upset and I didn't know how to make it stop.'

Grace was in a dream-like state, dozing in and out of conscious-ness. She hadn't slept through the night, but it was now time to wake up and go to work.

'Oh, don't worry about it,' she whispered to Chlo as she got dressed. 'I'm fine. I'm going to be late so we can talk about this later, okay?' she added, as she headed out through the bedroom door, barely making eye contact.

Chlo followed Grace out of the room, trying and failing to pull her into an embrace.

'I'm not your enemy!' exclaimed Chlo as she continued to try and grasp at Grace, who was washing her face in the bathroom. Chlo couldn't see her face but could feel her growing exasperation. The tiny nature of their flat made it easy to feel claustrophobic.

Chlo started to sob. 'I need you to tell me what's wrong.'

Grace remained with her back turned, looking out of the

bathroom window with vacant, tired eyes. 'Sometimes I just need a minute,' she murmured. 'I'm not used to having someone else in my space all the time, and I'm really going through it at the moment. It's all just a lot.' She turned around to a rather stunned-looking Chlo and pecked her on the cheek as she rushed towards the front door.

Chlo shouted after her, 'I'll pick you up around five. We can head to the hospice then. I've looked it up and visiting hours end at eight most days.' She wasn't sure if she was within hearing distance at that point, and Grace didn't reply.

It was one of the rare days on which Chlo and Grace hadn't been to the hospice. Chlo had planned a romantic night in for them. They watched *Set It Off* for the millionth time and consumed a vat of popcorn, which had been perfectly balanced to have just the right amount of sweetness and saltiness. After polishing off a bottle of rosé, Chlo had wasted no time in leading Grace to the bedroom. Grace got undressed and curled up under the duvet.

'Stay there,' Chlo said softly. 'Just stay there for one minute, you look perfect. I'm coming.'

Grace forced a smile. Almost two months had passed since she had first begun visiting Sandra and opportunities for intimacy had become sparse. Chlo was determined not to let this particular opportunity go to waste. She knew that she had to be careful to avoid upsetting the balance. For the first few weeks she had played it cool, but by the time it got to a month she had taken to mentioning the lack of sex constantly, and when that didn't work she had gone on a charm offensive, busting out the massage oils and flowers whenever she could.

Grace could hear Chlo's footsteps as she ran to the bathroom, brushed her teeth and paced across the creaky floorboards and back to the bedroom. Chlo hopped into the bed so fast that she risked crushing her. She kissed Grace aggressively, as though it was to be their last, her body moaning as she poured every ounce of love into the motion. Grace's lips were tighter than usual and Chlo gently massaged her cheeks to get her to relax. Chlo had stripped down and their naked bodies touched, their legs intertwined, but Grace still felt vacant. Chlo gently worked her tongue into Grace's mouth but it wasn't met with anything and after a few minutes, Chlo rolled over, tried to suppress a sigh – which Grace still heard – and stared blankly out of the window.

Grace got up and walked out of the room. She could barely sleep through the night these days. The skeleton of her mum haunted her as she closed her eyes. Grace thought that part of the reason that Chlo continued to pressure her was because she had never experienced grief or loss. The feeling for Grace was overwhelming as she pictured her mum's skeletal body and confronted the possibility that she would never see her again, and although they had been covering new ground in her hospice visits, she was worried that there was much that would remain untouched. The thing about death is that it is incredibly final.

Chlo and Grace pulled up to the hospice again. Grace headed straight for the ward, and Chlo for the waiting room and Maya – it had become a routine.

'Shall we get out of here?' Chlo asked Maya. 'It's hot. We could go and sit in a park somewhere. You know they'll be talking for hours – they won't even realise we're gone. We must have been through every glossy woman's mag in this waiting room,' she said through a giggle.

Maya didn't hesitate. 'Let's go. I've spent the best part of three months in here. They have an impressive amount of time to catch up on.'

Chlo led Maya out of the hospice and into her car. When they were buckling up, their hands grazed each other, which sent a tingling feeling down Maya's spine. Chlo's naturally whiny disposition was balanced out by the depth in her big brown eyes. Maya found herself drawn to the warmth in her face; Chlo had kind eyes, a beautiful smile, and a pert and peachy bottom. Maya wondered whether Chlo had felt it too.

'I think there are some bottles of Corona in the boot if you want a drink,' offered Chlo.

As they hopped out of the car at Plumstead Common, Maya grabbed two bottles of Corona and popped them open using her teeth.

'Here you go.'

As the two women sat next to each other on the common, lying on a blanket Maya had found in the boot of Chlo's car, Chlo spoke: 'The other day when you asked me how I knew I liked women . . . Well, your sister is the first woman I've been with properly. Aside from the occasional fling or game of spin the bottle, which were orchestrated by the boys in my school.'

Maya was surprised to hear that Chlo wasn't a seasoned lesbian.

'I met your sister at carnival, hit it off and now here we are.' Chlo gulped as she swigged the last few drops of her beer. 'Sometimes I think your sister is getting bored of me though. It isn't exactly how it used to be any more, but I suppose that's what happens when you've been with someone for so long. And don't get me wrong, when we do have sex, it's amazing. It's just so rare.'

Maya loved her sister, but she enjoyed this admission. 'Oh, I see. That's unfortunate.'

Chlo interjected. 'That was probably wildly inappropriate of me, maybe it's the beer. I don't always know who to talk to about it and you seem . . . ' Chlo paused before she finished her sentence, 'so . . . nice.'

They remained on the common for another hour or so in which time they had returned to the car for another beer.

'You're beautiful,' Maya spurted.

'Oh, thanks,' Chlo's eyes lit up as she blushed.

Chlo and Maya were lying side by side under the sun, their little fingers had been interlinked for some time now and soon after these words had left Maya's mouth, Chlo sat up and rolled over so that she was seated firmly on Maya's lap. She bent down and kissed her. Chlo wasn't the most graceful and Maya could feel the entirety of her weight bearing down on her. She could feel the fullness of her body pressed against her and it brought back the feelings Maya had felt aged fourteen for Joanna and suppressed soon after her sister was kicked out of the house. Without hesitation, she kissed her sister's girlfriend back with fervour until Chlo suddenly jumped up.

'Oh no,' she murmured. 'That is not good, that isn't good at all. She can't find out.' Chlo's eyes widened in a state of panic as though she had just realised that she'd kissed her girlfriend's twin. 'Especially not with everything that is going on. This didn't happen,' she continued. 'I'm going to get some water from the shop. I'll meet you in the car.'

When the pair arrived back at the hospice, Grace had just finished with her mother and was waiting for them.

'Oh, there you two are,' Grace said. 'My two favourite girls.'

'We just went for some, er ... fresh air,' announced Chlo with a stutter. Maya didn't say anything; she knew that her twin would become suspicious if she said too much.

'I'm going to stay with Mum for a bit,' said Maya as Chlo sloppily planted a kiss on Grace's lips. Grace could smell the faint scent of wheat on her breath.

'I missed you,' said Chlo as she and Grace headed out of the hospice waiting area.

'Bye, Maya, we'll be back in a couple of days. Don't stay too long,' Grace shouted back to her twin. She lingered in the hallway for a few moments, moving slowly as she considered the fact that her sister had borne the burden of looking after their mum for all this time, watching her grow weaker and less capable. The girl's father had left a long time ago, and their only other living relative was their grandmother who, at eighty-one, wasn't exactly in a position to share in any of the responsibilities of caring for her daughter.

'Come on, let's get out of here,' said Chlo, as she guided Grace, who appeared to be daydreaming, out of the hospice.

The car ride back was filled with a familiar silence, which made Chlo relax. She felt comfortable in the knowledge that if Grace had suspected something, she surely would have mentioned it over the twenty minutes that they had now been in the car. It had become routine for Chlo to ask Grace how everything was with her mother and also routine for Grace to respond with snappy, monosyllabic answers about how they were working through it. Although she tried to understand, in her own way, Chlo was largely unaware of the depths of the trauma Grace was experiencing. Chlo thought it strange that she hadn't cried and she'd taken the fact that there was no outpouring of emotion to mean that she was coping much better than had been expected.

As the pair arrived back at their flat, Grace made a beeline for the shower.

'You know the hospice is probably really clean, Grace, you don't need to shower so often,' Chlo barked after her.

Grace proceeded to lock the door. Their shower was the one thing in their flat which worked without a problem; it was loud and powerful, and as soon as the taps turned on Grace began to sob, letting out so much sorrow that she thought she might drown.

When Grace stepped into their bedroom Chlo was lying there scantily clad. Grace froze.

'Come over here,' said Chlo. 'I want you. I miss you. I need you.'

Grace, still frozen, stared straight through her girlfriend.

'Grace, I'm talking to you. Can't you hear me? Come here, baby, please.'

Grace regained consciousness, stepping out of her haze. 'Babe. I can't right now. I need you to be patient with me. I thought you'd understand, but I don't know what more I can tell you. What I'm going through right now is a lot. I don't know why I expected you to understand. I can't get in that headspace right now. I know that you think I'm someone who is always on, but right now I can't be.'

She could barely finish her sentence before Chlo had interjected. 'This will make you feel better. I promise.'

Grace sighed. It was obvious that Chlo would not be able to understand. Chlo opened the drawer next to the bed and whipped out a vibrator, scowling at Grace as she refused to break eye contact. Grace usually managed to keep her cool, but Chlo's whininess had driven her to the edge.

'Don't hurt yourself,' Grace snapped. She proceeded to pull on some clothes before uttering, 'I'm going out. I don't know when I'll be back. I know that I need some space.'

After twenty minutes had passed, and Chlo had been left to stew, she grabbed her phone from the nightstand and typed:

Hey. How are you feeling today? I hope you didn't have to stay too long at the hospice. Thinking of you xx

She searched for Maya's name and pressed send. Seconds later, Maya replied.

Maya: You're so sweet for checking up on me.

Chlo: I do try.

Maya: I hope that sister of mine isn't giving you too much hassle.

Chlo: She's not giving me any hassle at all, mate, that's the problem.

Maya: Don't mind her. You're beautiful. If she can't see what's right in front of her, she must be mad.

Chlo replied with a blushing face emoji.

Maya: I can't stop thinking about that kiss.

Chlo sent back several blushing faces this time.

Maya: Is that all you can say? Looking forward to seeing that blushing face on Saturday.

Chlo was just about to reply but at that exact moment, Grace walked into the bedroom.

'Who are you texting this time?'

Chlo was a terrible liar and she searched for the most reasonable answer. She knew that Grace wouldn't believe her if she said one of her friends; they were the sort to send constant streams of voice notes rather than text.

'Oh, it's my brother. He's gotten himself into some more mess. Anyway, let's not talk about it. Why don't you get into bed?'

Grace hopped in next to Chlo. Her side of the bed was cold and she could see that the vibrator remained untouched. She looked over at it.

'Didn't fancy her?' asked Grace. Chlo shook her head and snuggled up behind her.

They were back in the playground. Joanna had been off school ill for a few days now, so it was just Maya and Grace this lunchtime. Over the last week, a tension between the two sisters had been brewing. Maya was the passive-aggressive type who would rather bury her feelings than confront them. What she wanted to say was: 'I'm really upset about you and Joanna. I really liked her. She was my friend and you stepped in. I feel like you must have known because you are my twin and you feel ninety per cent of the things I do. You're supposed to know when I'm uncomfortable and unhappy. You are supposed to make it better,' but what she said was, 'How's it going with you and Joanna?'

Grace shrugged at the mention of her name. 'It's all right, I suppose. But do you know who I'm feeling now? Do you know

that girl – Bianca? She's in the year above. She's cool. I heard from
Tracey that she's properly into girls. Not like one of these lipstick
lesbians who opt in and out and are actually afraid of vagina.'
Grace had picked up this way of speaking from watching countless
scripted lesbian dramas on YouTube.

Maya rolled her eyes.

'What was that?' asked Grace. She wasn't looking at her sister
directly, but she could feel her annoyance.

'I think ... I just think that you shouldn't start things up with
people when you don't really like them. There might be other
people who do and they won't stand a chance otherwise.' Maya
still avoided locking eyes with her sister.

'Maya, I knew that's why you were acting all weird. You like
girls too. Damn, Mum's friends at church aren't going to like this
one bit. If you do, I'm happy for you. Be free my sister, free yourself
from the shackles of the patriarchy.'

Maya wanted to roll her eyes again.

'In all seriousness, sis. I could tell that you were getting mad
jealous of what I had going on with Jo. That's why I locked it off
in the first place. Bros before hoes and all that.'

Maya hated the arrogance her sister spouted when it came to
dating. They were only fourteen, but because she'd kissed approx-
imately three girls behind the bike shed and religiously watched
the *L Word* and *Sugar Rush*, Grace had decided that she was an
expert on all things woman related.

'When Grace got kicked out of the house I knew that there was no
way I could tell my mum about who I thought I was. I mean, what
did I even know at that age anyway? It could have been a phase. It's
not like anyone other than our mother took Grace seriously when
she came out. Her sexuality would often garner an unwanted and
perverse reaction when the boys at school got turned on at the
thought of it and asked uninvited questions about the logistics of

lesbian sex. Nobody took my sister seriously. I couldn't risk being forced out of our home like she was when I wasn't sure of who I was. My sister and I balanced each other out and when I lost her, some of my confidence left too. Yeah, I mean, we still kept in touch but there was a deep void that could not be filled in her absence. I missed her presence.' Maya took a deep breath as she struggled to get all her words out at once. Her stream of consciousness continued. 'I love my sister so much even though she can be completely self-centred. She's strong, my sister. I always wished I could be that sure of myself. Anyway, the point is I couldn't function on my own at fifteen – I wasn't independent enough. My mother was twice as hard on me as she was before. I could tell that she was so angry at my sister for what she thought was her choice. A choice that I knew wasn't a choice in the way that she could conceptualise.'

Tears were streaming down Maya's face. Chlo could see that she was in pain and she didn't know how to help. She batted her lashes helplessly and scooted over to comfort her. This was the third of the pair's little escapades out of the hospice. This time, as the sound of rain serenaded them, they had found themselves sitting in Chlo's car talking. It was mainly Maya who was making noise. At that moment, Chlo was what Maya thought she needed. Chlo wiped away her tears and told her that it was all going to be okay, that she had time to figure out who she was. She then proceeded to kiss her on each cheek and finally on her lips. Maya welcomed Chlo's touch without hesitation this time. It had become a routine, never extending further than this. Chlo hopped over her chair, with little care and wound up on Maya's lap once more. Their kiss didn't break. Maya's hands were planted firmly on Chlo's thighs. She ventured higher until she met Chlo's underwear. Chlo took comfort in the fact that this woman looked exactly like her girl-friend, although she did not feel the same. Maya pushed Chlo's thong to one side and entered her, gently. Just as Chlo moaned, lips parted, so did Maya. They stayed here for several minutes until a car beeped at them from behind. Chlo rose slowly as the driver behind continued to beep. As soon as she'd made her way back to the driver seat, she stuck the key in the ignition and drove them back to the hospice at speed.

As they walked through the doors, the freckled receptionist greeted them.

'Oh, thank goodness you're back. I'm afraid your mother passed away about an hour ago. Your sister was trying to call you both, but neither of you were picking up. I'm sorry, loves. Let me know if I can do anything.'

THE DAMPNESS IS SPREADING

Emma Glass

Based on
The Fairy Midwife
WALES

It never stops raining. I almost say it out loud. It never stops. The clouds are low, rolling grey, the sky feels too close, I am suffocating. And when I breathe in, raindrops pelt my lungs. I am drowning, I feel it now, dampness sitting between my skin and bones, mould growing, spores stretching out under my feet, white and green fuzz like mould on unwanted fruit.

I turn my head away from the window but the sound of the rain knocking against the glass draws my eyes back to the water. And beyond the glass, more water, the sea swelling up, a creeping monster reaching. Something outside, something reaching in, clawing through the static, calling to me.

The sound of different liquid brings me back into the room, a gurgling, squelching *POP* and ooze. The head is almost out and I bend my knees, stretch out my arms and reach for the baby.

I watch Rhiannon – she has the woman's hands gripped in hers and they are breathing together, hard, deep breaths in, ragged breaths out. Rhiannon is screaming '*PUSH!*' and the woman is just screaming.

I guide the baby towards the world. Come, little one, come, little baby, but keep those eyes closed tight now, you don't want to see what I see, not just yet. Her eyes are trapped shut, her mouth is round and wide open, singing. I wrap the baby loosely in a towel, I lift her up to her mother's chest. Rhiannon slips behind me to cut the cord with heavy silver scissors. She puts the scissors down on the trolley next to her and handles the afterbirth.

The woman is now a weeping mother. She clutches her baby to her chest in shock, in awe. I help her to bring baby to the breast and hear the almighty shrieking of the tiny pink queen soften to a snuffle as she learns to take air and then milk. The mother cries loudly in pain and in love. I wipe her forehead with a towel but I leave her tears.

'It's okay, it's okay,' I say. 'Look at her, she's perfect, she's an angel, she's a wonder.' The words are wooden.

'Am I doing it right?' asks the mother. I lean in and put my finger between the baby's nose and the mother's breast.

'Yes, yes, but is it hurting?' I ask.

She nods and closes her eyes. 'Everything is hurting. Are you sure it's right?'

Of course I'm sure.

'How does it feel? Tell me. Can you feel her sucking, can you feel milk coming?'

'Yes, but what is it supposed to feel like?'

Oh.

I know what she wants to know. She wants the reassurance of another mother. I've been asked before. Lots of times before. But this is the moment I dread. This is when I know I'm towards the end. Right now, I can avoid the question, I can describe to her the feeling from the books I have read, from the papers I have written, the talks I have given; the catalogue of expert knowledge flips open, I rustle the pages, I can tell her everything, but what I want to do, what I really want to do is slap her and scream '*I DON'T KNOW!*' and take her baby and run. Why does she get to have one and I don't? A perfect one, with fingers and toes and a beating heart. One that will grow outside of her, live beyond her.

She looks up at me, waiting for the words to fall from my lips and wrap her in comfort. My gloved hand is trembling, hovering over her red, sweating forehead.

Rhiannon looks up from between the woman's legs and says, 'Eira, did you weigh the baby?'

I shake my head and move my hands towards the baby, I put my hands around her belly and lift her away; her mother is dazed, a cloud sits over her eyes, steam from the sweat and the screaming.

'Hey! What are you doing?' She snaps away from the haze.

'I'm just weighing her, I won't be a moment.' I am bristling and irritated; the baby wriggles and squirms. I place her in the silver tray; she is sticky and shiny, a yellow crust of dried birthing fluid has formed on her brand-new skin, crystallised. She shines like a sherbet lemon on sweet shop scales.

'Eight pounds exactly. Funny, she looks smaller.'

I am sharp and nasty like the sour grains inside the sherbet lemon. Rhiannon stares at me, confused, mouth askew. I take her back to her mother, I try to take the edge out of my movements, I lay her gently down across her mother's chest.

'Rhiannon, I'm going next door for a minute to check on Mrs B,' I say.

'Yeah, okay, I'll finish off here.' She looks up at me. We both know there is no Mrs B. This is our code for 'I need to go to the toilet, I need to get a glass of water, I need a fucking break.' She mouths w-h-a-t's-w-r-o-n-g. I shake my head and remove my gloves, toss them in the clinical waste bin on top of the purple pearlescent placenta. I wipe my sweaty palms on my uniform.

I step out from behind the curtains. I don't look back. I don't look back at the tiny baby I just helped bring into the world. I don't look at the mother, the woman who has just made a miracle in a breath. I have no gratitude. No softness of feeling. No kindness. No love. I have emptiness in my belly.

I wash my hands in scalding hot water, turning my skin red and puffy, soaping and soaping up to my elbows. I dry my hands and leave the ward.

I stand in the corridor, leaning against the window sill. The rain is really coming down now. The clouds are rumbling, turning, spewing open. I press my palm to the cold glass; I can feel electricity ripping through the clouds, the air is thick like cotton wool. The day is weird. I feel hot. I feel rotten.

The corridor is quiet. It is usually filled with families and helium balloons or pacing men and crying toddlers. There is no one here today. I turn and see my reflection in the stainless-steel doors to the lift. My silver head is creased, distorted by the dents in the door where punches have been pounded, broken knuckles of broken fathers of the babies that didn't arrive, or those that came too quickly, too blue, too perfect for words, too perfect for this world. I have bandaged a bloody fist in this exact spot. I have held men upright as they've crumpled with grief, wailing in the place of their lost babies. I have always been a part of their grief or their joy. I have always been a part of the turning circles of life and I have turned with them, spinning in and spinning out, grateful for the glimpses of joy when they come. But now I am cold and shivering. I try to cough out the dampness. I should have brought a glass of water but oh more wetness, I just want to be out of it.

I look down at my shoes but my eyes fall on my empty belly, my belly which has always been empty. It carried once. Something small, a small apple or a large egg, but I bled. And for years after, something small like a grape and once, a golf ball, but never any bigger and I have always bled.

I wanted to keep them, all of them. Even the tiny ones, even the specks, the tiny droplets of blood. All mine, all a part of me. I wanted to keep them all, tiny matchstick babes in matchstick boxes, in a drawer where I could bring them out from time to time to love and to look at and say once I was more than this husk. Why couldn't I keep them?

I think of him in these moments, so full of loss. His face forms fully in my mind, his soft lips ask me: 'Why can't you, my love? Why can't you grow our babies?' When no answer comes, his face greys and folds with grief, beyond anger, his cold words stick like snow: 'What's *wrong* with you?'

He left me then. He took my soul with him.

I came here searching for life. I have found life but it does not belong to me. It grows all around and I am the dead tree. I'm standing here, stuck in the ground, standing for way too long. I will be here until the end of days, with the rain coming down and then rising up, swelling to my ankles and then my knees, the slowest death, not even by drowning. Here until the water breaks my skin down, until my bones soften and melt. And even then I will not be able to forgive myself.

My head hurts with thirst and splits in two as the lift doors open and a man spills into the corridor. I take a step back as he tumbles forward.

He is bent over and dripping wet. The rainwater runs off the peak of his cap; he is soaked through, squelching against the tiles in sodden holey trainers, his grey tracksuit bottoms have splash marks up to his knees and his thin hooded jacket clings to his thin body. His movements are strange. His knees are bent and he looks like he might keel over. One of his hands is bunched in his pocket, the other is cupped and held out to me, like he is begging on the street.

'Missus, oh missus. Please, missus.'

His slurry voice is close to silence. He stumbles, knees nearly knocking the ground.

'Missus!'

He pitches louder this time, his acrid breath blossoms upwards like a pure methadone mushroom cloud.

'Can I help you? What is it?' I am steady.

'My sister. It's my sister. Her waters have broke, she's gone into labour.' He is swaying.

'Your sister? Where is she?'

He stifles a laugh and then he belches loudly. I turn my head away in disgust, the smell is unreal, the breath that comes out of his mouth is yellow. I look down the corridor towards the ward – there is no one around.

'Missus, please 'elp us, will you? She was trying to walk up the stairs. I'll go an' fetch her.'

He steps backwards towards the lift and presses the button without turning around, or looking; his fingers hit it like he's been here before, like he does this every day. As the doors open behind him, he grins widely at me. His teeth stick upwards and outwards; they are brown, the top front tooth is missing and in that black gap, in that black hole I see down to hell. A shiver smashes over me like an ice-cold wave.

I know this man, I have seen him before.

He steps backwards into the lift, the doors shriek shut.

I know this man.

I knew him as a boy. His teeth were not always brown. But the walls of the house were. Brown with cigarette smoke, with smack smoke. Bare concrete floors, old cardboard boxes flattened and strewn for the little ones to play on. He was ten and his sister was five. I stooped and knelt down on a cardboard box next to her. She had golden curls, real cherub chunky cheeks, unreal because the rest of her was so skinny, skin and bones. She was showing me toys in a catalogue, carefully turning the pages, carefully running her little finger over the print.

'Will you bring me this toy next time? Will you bring me this one, with the ballet shoes?'

'I'll try,' I'd say, lying, feeling the lie sink into the pit of my stomach, sitting heavy.

We were there to weigh the children, fill out forms for the mother to get food vouchers. We were there to make sure the mother was not using again. The walls were brown and gummy, and the children had thin, dirty clothes on, no winter coats, no toys. We were there to try to drag them out of hell. But we did not. We could not. Their mother was stuck. Too deep, too far gone. Too many marks in her arms, too many debts. Her children paid them.

I remember the health visitor telling me in the car on the way back to the surgery that the little boy had his tooth knocked out by the man his mother owed money to. She said that man was likely to have been his father. She told me that he was taken in by an old man in the next street who had caught him knocking on back doors in the middle of the night asking for tinfoil. He sat at the old man's kitchen table eating biscuit after biscuit until his mother came, wrapped her trembling fingers around his arm, drew blood with her dirty fingernails and pulled him back to her.

This was the saddest story I had ever heard. I told everyone about the tinfoil. But in a week I was gone. I was sent to a nursing home to care for the elderly and there were new sad stories there. Sadder because of the love left behind, sadder because they were all so lonely or were incontinent or had to be fed with a spoon.

The images of these two little children crush into my vision, but their names don't come. Their grubby faces and hands. The guilt. How could I have left them? The boy has turned out just like his mother. The poor girl. The tears collect in the corners of my eyes; I blink them hard away and I wait for the lift doors to open.

I keep my back against the wall. The rain continues to fall, the damp air whispers behind me, curling the hairs at the nape of my neck. I hold my breath until those doors open – it feels like for ever. What if she remembers me? What if she is high like her brother? The baby! Oh no, the baby!

And then the lift doors open and the light pours into the corridor, all shining silver and gold. The pouring rain pauses; there is silence. I look into the light: it is so bright, like the doors have opened out on to a mountain close to the sky, with the glorious sun beaming down on me, on my face, the warmth, the light, the pureness. The sickening shiver leaves me. I feel dry for the first time in years, my skin feels warm, I roll my head back and bask. But the sound of rapid breathing breaks my bliss. I blink off the bright light, my held tears escape and I wipe them away quickly. I approach the open doors. There, she stands.

Her face is beautiful. Her skin glistens like it has been dusted with stars, pure and white, glowing as she turns her rose petal cheek towards me. Her eyes are wide, two glimmering orbs, so brown, almost black, lined with endless lashes. Her lips are perfectly pink, slightly parted, letting out little puffs of breath, a sweet sound like angels sighing. Her hair is pure gold, weaved and plaited falling over her shoulder like a rope, down to her waist. She is wearing a plain grey dress with long sleeves; she has no coat, no bag or belongings, but she has a huge round belly, which moves gently up and down with every breath. She can't be more than seventeen, but that can't be right, my mind is cloudy. I would have looked after her more than twenty years ago. I glance into the corners of the lift but her brother is nowhere to be seen.

I go to her with my arms wide open.

'Come, come quickly, tell me your name,' I say.

She sucks in a long slow breath, she smiles and nods and steps forward.

'Where is your brother? He was just here.'

She says nothing but smiles; she takes my arm and looks into my eyes. For a moment, her face is so close to mine, I can almost feel the velvet of her warm cheek.

'How long ago did your waters break? How frequent are your contractions?'

She is still smiling but her eyes roll back in her head, she stumbles back towards the lift, her shoulders hit the metal doors and they clang loudly. I put my hand against her soft cheek and stroke it.

'Can you hear me? Are you all right?' I panic. I won't be able to move her if she collapses.

I slip my arm into the small of her back, I bring her close to me, try to take her weight; she opens her eyes and begins to shuffle forward with me. I bring her close because this could be it. This could be my second chance to save her and she could pull me out of the water, she could pull me out from under.

'What's your name?' I say. 'My name is Eira, I can help you.'

'Eira,' she says gently, the word drifts out of her mouth. 'Snow. Eira means snow,' she says, the words tickling her lips, making them twitch.

We walk slowly towards the ward.

She is not heavy against me – she moves with strange ease for a young woman moments away from giving birth. When we reach the doors, Dr Davies is washing his hands on the other side of the glass. He glances up and hurries to dry his hands and open the doors for us.

'Who is this, Eira? Were we expecting her?' He moves to the other side of her, puts his hand on her shoulder.

'No,' I say, 'she just came up in the lift, her brother was here before. He must be parking the car.' I'm not convinced and I don't sound convincing.

We rush into the nearest bay and help her on to a bed. I pull the curtains around it whilst Dr Davies grabs a silver trolley stocked with a sterile birthing kit.

'Can you tell us your name? How old are you? We need to know so that we can help you,' says Dr Davies. His voice is stern and her eyes widen, her lips tremble. She looks so scared. I rush to her side and take her hand. Her fingers are long and soft and cool. I put my hand to her forehead which is also cool. No sweat, no sweeping redness. She grips my hand and says in a whisper, 'Please save my baby.'

Then she closes her eyes and I feel darkness fall over the world.

I put an oxygen mask over her face and turn the tank up as high as it will go. I watch her chest rise and fall. She looks like she is sleeping. I've never seen anything like this. I touch her neck with my fingers and feel her pulse and it jumps against me; it is strong but not faster and not slower, just pulsing. I look down at Dr Davies. He is examining her with gloved hands. He looks puzzled.

'Eira, I can see the head and she appears to be pushing.' His mouth stays open.

'What do you mean? She has passed out – she can't be pushing.' I move down to the end of the bed and peer between her legs. Her dress ripples, her hips spasm slightly and then stop. The baby's head advances. I have never seen anything like it.

'Stay with her, Eira, you know what to do,' says Dr Davies. 'I need to go and get Dr Matthews. I'll call Rhiannon or one of the other midwives to come and help you.'

The curtain flies open and he is gone.

I am not afraid to be alone. I have had the first touch of hundreds of babies. They come into my hands, not all willing and gladly. These hands, these steady hands, these hands do not fail. But even with a team of ten, with incubators and intubation on stand-by, these hands do not get to choose.

The end is near, I know it's near because when joy swells my heart with every new life, my lungs expand to compete for space in my chest. My lungs are blackened with mildew, with the dampness of death that I have breathed in and in and in. Why am I this cruel creature? Why can I not remember the warmth of life?

I look down at my hands, skin peeling at the knuckles. My hands are as red and white and dry as my hair, once burning red and curling all around, now streaming grey like rain running down the window of a fast car. I tuck a strand behind my ear; the motion catches in my memory. A shiver tingles through me as I feel the bliss of taking down my hair after a long shift. It untangles from the tight bun on top of my head, each strand sighs as it is released back into the wild. I love this part of the day and I think about the steam and heat of the shower running over my head when I get home. But the memory of tucking my hair behind my ear comes with the feeling of grit in my knees and blood on my hands. I am taken back to a time when I delivered a baby to a teenage girl in a car park. She did not want her baby, she was going to pull it out by herself and leave it at the doors of the hospital. I found her in the dark and we did it together, my hair flying about in the breeze, stones cutting through the bare skin on my knees. She loved and kept her little boy because I told her I had recently lost one of mine. I got home that night and took the longest shower. He was still with me then and he held me all night whilst I cried and cried. He tucked the hair behind my ears and kissed me as I lay there in my wetness.

My skin cracks and smarts as I hastily put gloves on and touch the crowning head. Another twitch, a slight movement and it's out, the baby is screaming, I put the tips of my fingers on its shoulders and wait for the next push and when it comes, I pull and the baby comes out. I clamp and cut the cord quickly, I drop the scissors on the tray, kick the trolley out of the way and wrap the baby, rubbing her with a towel, a gorgeous baby girl, a beauty like her mother.

I step to the head of the bed. The woman is still, her face porcelain and peaceful. I gently lift the oxygen mask up off her face and squeeze her shoulder.

'Wake up, wake up, she's here! She needs you.'

Those lashes gently curl and flutter, a thousand yellow butterflies bending their wings. She is awake and she looks first at me and then the baby and whispers, 'Eira.'

I bend to place the baby on her but she quickly crosses her arms over her chest.

'Wait! The placenta, is the placenta out yet?' she hisses, the softness in her voice bubbling, beginning to dissolve.

The placenta? The word oozes into the air, it takes up all of the space between us.

'What? No, not yet, I wanted you to see your daughter,' I say, confused. She won't hold her baby. I place her gently in the empty cot at the side of the bed.

'The placenta!' She reaches down between her legs, her thin fingers stretch out groping sharply like scissors for the purple organ.

'What are you doing?' I say, pushing her hands away. 'I need to get rid of this safely.' I slide it out; it is slimy and dark, covered in clots, it is almost black. Her body tenses.

'Please, please, give it to me!' Her voice is now high pitched and pricked with panic, she pulls her sleeves up, puts her hands down and tries to lift herself off the bed. The baby is crying but she doesn't look towards it, her eyes are wide and fixed on the placenta in my hands. I look around for the waste bin. There isn't one, we didn't set one up in time. I push my head through the gap in the curtain. There is no one else here. The ward is eerily quiet. Where is Dr Davies? Was he ever really here?

I turn back and now she is kneeling on the bed. Her dress is hitched up over her belly, revealing a gruesome, veiny globe, purple as a plum. She is growing out of the bed, she is transforming on her hands and knees. Her face is still beautiful but her eyes are black and her smile is gaping and I do not know what she is becoming. Her face is twisting, she is spitting magic.

'You need to rest,' I say, calmly. But I am scared; I feel devastation rolling in like rain clouds.

'Please,' she hisses. 'Please, please help my baby!' The baby begins to wail.

'Please, put the placenta on her eyes, she can't see! She can't see me!' She has lowered her face, her hair falls forward, she is crying now, her tears drop like twinkling crystals. I feel uneasy but pity sticks in my guts.

'Just wait, I'll bring her to you.'

I don't want to give her the baby. I don't want to put the placenta anywhere near the baby. What witchery is this, what madness? She is silent and stone-still now, her wet eyes are glittering and fixed on the placenta in my hands which drips blood and mulch on the floor, splattering like rain showers.

'Please, please, PLEASE! Touch the placenta, touch her eyes, she can't see, she can't see me,' her voice rides high waves over the baby's cries.

Her howling words cut me right down to my centre, her black eyes burn mine. The placenta squelches between my fingers, I hold it up to the light. It is iridescent, glittering, mesmerising, purple and green and blue. The baby screeches, breaking her heart to be soothed. This is not the welcome into the world she deserves. I pick her up with one arm. I look closely at her eyes. They are jammed shut, puffy and pink.

'Please, please! Do it!'

In the echo of her pleas I hear his slurred words 'Please, missus, please 'elp.'

She is rising up, higher and higher, filling the room with purple veins. She has me rapt. This is madness. I have gone mad. But what if the baby can't see her? What if the baby is in darkness, what if she never sees her mother's face, never sees through the impenetrable clouds? What if this is the only way?

My fingers tingle, I am aching, it is all too much. I place the placenta over the baby's face. Her cries quieten. And then she is silent.

She is silent for too long. Her body is still. Her little fists flop. Oh oh oh, what have I done? What have I done?

I lift the placenta up and the baby isn't breathing. I lie her down on the cot and rub her little body vigorously with the towel. I cover her nose and mouth with my mouth and blow into her. Her tiny lungs inflate with the little puffs.

Please.

Please.

Please.

I watch her chest, lying flat and then fluttering. She breathes and then she cries.

And I cry. I begin to sob. The skin on my face is parched and taut with stress, tears drop and sting my skin. My eye itches so I wipe it. It's gluey and wet. I forget I am still wearing the gloves smothered in blood and ooze from the placenta. Ych. I peel the gloves off and pick up a clean towel and wipe my sticky eye with it.

'Eira.'

My name is whispered closely in my ear. I turn and see her. There she is, peaceful again, surrounded by a golden glow, her hair gently swaying, her eyes glistening, she is cradling her baby, singing, 'Eira, Eira, pure snow.' I am captivated, oh I could cling to this picture for ever, but I must be dreaming because out of my other eye, my untouched eye, I see hell.

She is not sitting in the bed, she is crouching on it on spindly spider legs; there are two, there are four, I feel woozy. She cackles and her dank acidic breath floats towards me. She has two heads and many teeth, some are white and some are brown. Her skin is grey and crispy, her fingernails are dirty and chewed, her arms are pricked all over with needle marks and bruises. She is smiling at me with all her brown teeth. Her eyes are flaming, bloodshot red. The baby wails and wails, untouched by her demonic mother.

'Can you see me? Can you see me?' She laughs, her laugh is choking and cruel. She reaches out with her quick, stick arms and grabs me by the hair, she slams the heel of her hand into my mucky eye. She blots out the image of the beautiful mother and babe for ever.

I call out in horror. I try to pull away from the tight hold I am tangled in. I trip and fall on to the floor, pulling the tray of sterile instruments with me; they clatter and clang on the tiles. She stands over me, blood trickles down her legs and splatters over me. She stoops low, her knees snap, she reaches for my neck.

'Which eye do you see me with, Eira?' Her words are slow and slurred. She is shaking violently. 'You can see it now, can't you? Which eye? WHICH EYE?'

She spits in my face. She loosens her grip on my neck and picks up the scissors. I try to push her away. She plunges the scissors at me, sharp silver slicing through soft flesh. Shining silver is the last thing I see.

I dream about an egg cracking open. The weighty yellow yolk bleeds, pierced by shell shards. I have been dreaming many dreams about eggs cracking, but my hands never break them. One rolls off a wooden table on to kitchen floor tiles. One is chucked high into the air and falls down hard and splatters over a red shiny shoe. In one of my dreams a whole carton of eggs is dropped, carelessly pushed off a supermarket shelf, not pushed by my careless hands, but I am there to bend down and open the carton. I don't want to clean it up but I do want to see the mess. Of the dozen eggs only one survives. It sits proudly in the middle of the row, not a speck of gelatinous white, not a speck of yolk, no shell chips mar the surface of the survivor: its shell is perfectly smooth like the skin of a newborn baby. I reach down and pluck it from the carton and hold it in my palm. It is cool and heavy like a pebble. Before I can slip it into the pocket of my dress I am tapped on the shoulder and I am so startled that I drop the egg. Damn it. The weighty yellow yolk bleeds. Bleeds.

I wake up and I am bleeding. A faint tickle, a faint trickle down my cheek. Like a tear but slower, the liquid is thicker, it creeps over my cheek like the sense of impending doom or fear of the dark. I reach for the little tray tucked over my legs at the end of the bed, I grope for the stack of gauze that has been left for me. I take a piece and swipe it over my cheek wiping away the little stream. It is not blood. It is glistening and yellow like an egg yolk.

It takes me a little while to realise that I am wiping ooze from my own face, to understand that the legs in the bed belong to me, that the blue curtains that are drawn around the bed are drawn around me. There is dim light and quiet voices behind the curtain. They fall silent when the bed squeaks as I reach for a clean piece of gauze. Footsteps approach, the curtain twitches as if the person on the other side is hesitating to open it.

'Who's there?' I ask. My voice is crispy, my throat is dry, I clutch my neck, the confusion chokes me.

I know these curtains, I know this bed, I know the sound of a voice coming from a throat that has had tubes put down it, a voice that has been put to sleep for some time.

When the curtains open and the light comes in, I put my hands over my eyes. My left hand meets a strange, thick fabric. I press down on it and feel pain awakening, seeping through stacks and stacks of cotton wool; my head is full, a pain which was far away and travelling nearer, pushing through the cotton wool and pouring outwards. The trickling fluid flows faster now.

Dr Davies steps through the curtains but stops at the end of the bed; he tilts his head, his face is wrinkled with worry.

'Eira, how are you?' he asks. He is awkward and doesn't know what to do with his hands. He folds his arms, unfolds them, takes his glasses off, then coughs and puts them back on again. He steps closer to the bed, shuffling forward and then says, 'May I sit?'

I nod and he eases himself down on the bed. He reaches for my hand and holds it.

'I heard about what happened to you,' he says. I don't know what he means. He was there.

'You were there, weren't you? You saw her, didn't you?' I whisper. He shakes his head. He looks sad.

'No, Eira, I wasn't there and no one saw you – no one saw what really happened. Everyone is worried about you. All we can see is the footage from the security camera in the corridor and all that shows is you talking to a man in the hat and then helping that woman into the ward.'

'Where is she?' I ask in my crusty voice.

He shrugs. 'The mother is gone. We called the police to go out and look for her but we've heard nothing yet. She left and she left her baby. Why didn't you call for help? You could see she was in a bad way. Did she threaten you? That baby could have been in real trouble, she could have died.' He is telling me she could have died in my hands, could've died at my hands. He is shaking his head, he is shaking it with disappointment and sorrow.

'I didn't know, I couldn't see,' I say. She looked perfect to me. I thought it was safe.

'Is the baby okay?' The words barely make it out of my mouth. I am stopped up with guilt and confusion.

'The baby is here. She's on the ward having treatment. She's sickly now, but she'll be okay. She is suffering. It looks as though her mother was using all through the pregnancy.'

I start to cry. Oh, but it hurts. I want the tears to come and never stop; they dribble pathetically from the eye I have left, but nothing comes from the hole in my head. The tears are dammed up, stopped, stuck, coming from nowhere, flowing from nothing. I put my fist to the dressing and press hard with my knuckles. I ram my fist into the hole, I feel the cotton pressing, pressing in on my brain, pressure, pressure, pressure. I want to scream out, but I only manage a miserable mewl.

Dr Davies grabs my wrist.

'Don't, please. I don't know what to say. I know you were trying to help her. I know you are good, Eira. Please. You'll be okay. I promise,' he tries to soothe.

I'll be okay?

'I'll be okay?' I say. 'I'll be okay? Do you see me, Dr Davies?' I snatch my hand away, and point to where my eye used to be. The exquisite beauty that I saw through this eye, the sublime image of a mother and her babe, the only heaven I saw has been robbed from me. Stripped and sliced. The pain pulsates, it is so palpable I can see it. It is the only thing I will see now through this hole.

'Do you see this? Can you see me?' My voice swells and fills the room; it is layered with her loaded drawl. She speaks with me, she speaks through me. We rise up, we are sirens wailing. Our song is high-pitched and screaming. We scream of the damage done to our frail, broken bodies, of the darkness, of the injustice of our rotting lot. We scream out but nobody hears.

He is looking right at me but he does not see. Nobody sees and nobody hears. All we can hear, all anyone can hear is the pouring, pouring, pouring rain.

THE DROLL OF
THE MERMAID

Natasha Carthew

Based on
The Mermaid and the Man of Cury
CORNWALL

Silent sitting. The boat so still upon the tranquil water, the young man with the weight of the world dragging wondered if he should stand and step off return to shore before it was too late. He rested the oars against his thighs and kept his hands gripped like fists to the handles when the storm finally hit he would be ready for it; the fight fierce within primed for the rip the tide that would lift the shovel and dig him down into stranger ground.

From his vantage he could see the bay loop from bight to bight the cut of cliff perfectly taken the moon peering down into each cave and crease the cove carved as if to resemble his face his forefather's features looking down on him, they shouted out his name from the highest crags, calling him under, *Lowan*.

'Not yet,' he whispered, 'not until the village clock strikes midnight I int ready just yet.' He felt his heart hit hard against his chest and put a hand into his coat told it that time was closing in, that it would soon jump miss a beat and stop complete. A man who knew the extent of death the same way he knew the shortness of life, there was no way out only the letting in of salt water the measured leach and seep beneath his skin.

Above the brae of cliff he could just make out the front stone wall of their cottage all lights out the way he had left it the smoke no longer bothering the flue, he had made sure to leave no trace of himself only a piece of the family name *Pellar* carved high above the door. As a boy Lowan wished he could destroy that name knife it into a deep scar, mark it like a memory of something that in time he would grow up to forget. A curse and then not a curse the rot in the wooden doorframe picked and put back good.

Where the smoke had been twisting a few friendly clouds gathered around, they handed him false hope, optimism that this was just an ordinary evening after all, a perfect night for a young fisherman to go about his work on the eve of his twenty-fifth birthday. It took everything in him not to take up the oars and row to where the warm underwater current hit the cold and set out his nets return home with the sun hitting the breakers the belly of the boat bloated with fresh sea-bream. Shame that wasn't how the story went Lowan's story was built in bricks and brier nothing could change its course it was bolted and bound into bedrock and slate the path he walked on had only one name, fate.

Few minutes to midnight Lowan rotated the boat towards the horizon and put his back into what he knew and loved and set his eyes on the thing he could not explain the Atlantic tide that was circling creeping in on him like crows towards carrion.

'Please god,' was all he had in him he wished there was more detail in words and want than that. If he was a man of hymn and verse he would have sung for his family's protection have them grow old without this weight, float them into the sunset to the tune of their own choosing; death and dying played out on some slow distant beat, not this deafening version of defeat.

'Not long now.' Lowan pulled the oars into the boat and pushed his hands into his coat pockets, there was no need to brace when it finally happened he would go down a proud man. He imagined all the kin men that had gone before sitting with him in the boat, he had hoped the thought would give him comfort but it only took up space the air around him thick with the scent of composting seaweed and salt water catching in his throat he knew that without realising, the transformation had already started to find a way in. Lowan could taste the grains of salt stinging the ridge at the back of his tongue he could smell them as they sifted into his lungs like smoke, his breath short his pulse weak he sipped at the air like it was something he had to ration, to savour.

Beneath him he felt the boat softly turning and knew fate was somewhere close, he could see it sitting up at the helm with a lamp in one hand and a stopwatch in the other, its eyes tangling around his limbs, rope ready, tying him to his past, his future and Lowan let it.

A stranger's push nature's pull, the moon's last wink and the clouds banking up from the west; storm warning rising, lifting from an alien place. Lowan closed his eyes and heard the bell strike out imagined how it stripped the sky of everything that was beautiful. Fading light, there was nothing left to do but bow his head, a minute to midnight.

The final moment in memory he held what was left of breath and returned to his childhood the funeral fire they'd been building burning buried beneath the cliff face, the men's singing circling the surrounding bay. The boy on the beach bewildered, Lowan remembered his confusion clearly it was something that helped him slip into that old skin, young mind wondering about everything.

'I int singin,' he shouted, 'Uncle Luten's dead there int nothin good bout that.' Lowan lifted the bottle of unidentified alcohol to his lips and winced, but when he caught his father's eye he smiled and said something stupid like it tasted good.

'You're a man now, Lowan, you're sixteen got to start actin like one.'

The boy nodded.

'What's that?'

'Yes sir.'

'Your uncle Luten is dead it's your turn to take his place, step up and step forward.'

Lowan took another gulp of the drink to prove whatever it was his father wanted of him swallowed it down with his head back eyes closed to keep his tears in tight.

'Make me proud,' his dad continued, 'make your mother proud god bless her wasteful junkie soul.'

When Lowan was sure he wasn't about to cry or cough or blurt out that it was Dad's fault the way things turned out, he opened his eyes and passed the bottle to his father it was what they did. He knew the man liked to bring up Lowan's mother, he used it as a test, a way to stab at his nerves see what jangled free. Len Pellar had done it his whole life a way to wear his eldest son down and rub the woman that he barely knew from his mind completely.

It wasn't always like this, there were times when he didn't speak about her at all. Some days he went around the village of Cury telling folk that Lowan was his kid with one of his other baby-mamas or he would just plain say he found him in a rock pool like baby Moses, a stranger's baby, told them the kid cried so much for his mother that he thought to return him to the sea in those early days.

Lowan liked that story it made him feel different, special, the kink that was in him was not his fault, it was built into his breath and the way he spoke out and it was in his bones too, how he bent and rebounded when Dad tried to beat it out. The family curse was his curse and the man that sat and sung and swigged beside him was the biggest.

He looked across at him. 'Good stuff?' he asked. In truth it tasted like the gel they used to clean the tar from their hands, maybe it was.

'Good stuff is right, keep drinkin that we'll make a man of you yet, Lowan Pellar.'

Lowan smiled and let the minute moment of belonging warm him whelm him in false love. Some days he almost believed that he belonged to this strange band of kin but most days he did not. Like the times when he heard the cheer go up to welcome in a new bank of fog and watched them scrabble out on to the rocks, lamps in their hands ready to swing the gullible boats around. Safe harbour, loot to the winch and up to the track their ancestors had hacked through the crag, then up to the cliff path, they always left the bodies to go under.

Lowan had yet to be asked to contribute to the family business, he supposed they didn't trust him to follow through; he was fine with that, truth was he didn't trust himself. He doubted if he would ever be like them, no matter how hard he tried to swagger and kick out against his love and curiosity for all the small things; the way the sky crimped with colour before a storm or the smell of wild garlic that curdled and swayed within the pocket of air that fell between spring rain and summer sunshine.

Sixteen and nothing about him that resembled a man, he was too short too weak too naïve, these were his father's words but Lowan heard them so often they had become his own.

No matter how Dad grounded him he didn't like to fight like the men had never wanted to go out into the woods with the women and shoot every other animal that walked the earth. When he was too young to argue he was brought out to hunt with his three aunts, they had thought it a good idea to expose the kids to death. A whole gang of them spent the day chasing after a fox that they'd seen worrying the hens. A day when nothing happened and then everything did and ended when the dogs got involved. Lowan remembered his aunties standing back and letting them snap at the animal's hide, one hip peeled to expose the bone the other dragging under and then the women tugging on their leads telling them to leave a little bit for the kids.

They waited for all the children to gather and told them to circle around, to shut up and watch, keep watching. Lowan remembered all the colours of a sunset merging and moving, the tan of the dogs and the orange of the fox and the red that flashed like summer river, flooding through the patch of stubble ground. The tail severed and dragged through the blood puddle and slapped across each of their faces. The other kids laughed as they took turns to beat each other with the brush, but Lowan ran home, calling for his mother despite knowing she was long gone.

When he heard his father talking he sat up.

'You should get yourself over to the fire, prove all this int a worry to you, sing it out of you.'

Lowan looked towards the fire. He hated the celebration that came with bereavement, never understood why the breadth of their emotion only went one way, had only one dimension.

He wanted to say in a minute, or later, but Dad was telling him to get up, get the hell over there. Lowan got to his feet, the full bottle heavy in his hand heart heavier in his chest. He took his time to make his way across the sand, his boots sinking into the damp silt his eyes on the space in front of him until his feet hit flame. All eyes cross-haired on him, he lifted the bottle to pass around, knowing it would come back dregs, good, he hated the stuff.

The heat rising against his skin his face flushed towards thinking better things the sparks flying him upwards away one minute. He watched the tiny worm things circle the fire catch some word of wind and grow wings and Lowan wished he could go with them. He stepped closer to the flames and let the heat smear his face with all the shades of blood, colours to paint him into a different kind of boy, a boy who wore the heat like a mask. When the men hit the chorus he joined in stamped his feet wide and made himself a moment like them; 'Nine long years and the spell int broken nine long years and the curse int done, nine more years and the mermaid back she'll be sure to take another one.'

It wasn't the song that hit him in the gut it was the cheer that went up at the end of each chorus, the something savage that was on show their voices throwing daggers into the ocean daring it to come and get them.

Song for the forgotten, a few words turned towards the ocean waves the place where the legend began where for some of them it would certainly end.

When the women came forward with their chants of celebration and sorrow Lowan took back his bottle and walked until far enough away so he could tip the last of the liquid into the sand.

'I am a man.' He told it. He didn't need drink or a blade or a billion scars to prove it he was sixteen years of age, he still had some years owed to him and he planned to fill them with beauty. Lowan knew the reaper came round ringing every nine years, come the eve of his twenty-fifth birthday he'd be out there waiting for the wave to rise and pull him under. The olden legend was something to be feared except he'd had the worst of damage and destruction already.

He made a dint in the sand a seat to sit and contemplate, remember the family story the way it was meant without song or drink or stabbing sentiment. The story went way beyond what it was, a legend many hundred years in its creation. Lowan only cared for the detail the facts that nailed their family together in loose fantasy, firm tragedy, every kid's destiny involved some kind of cross.

When he had first heard the tale Lowan had been seven years old. He remembered it as clear as if it were last week sitting up on the cliff precipice with Dad. Same cove same time of year, the wind not yet warm enough, a bit of cold running through the air enough to worry the farmers and the newborn lambs that had been put out into the fields. The winter weather sat at their backs, but only just and the daffodils that had come early to the hedgerows, taken down in bud by the bitching wind.

Back then father and son had settled some way from the singing at the tip of the highest crag and together they had watched the blood red sky that had signalled warning muddy the ocean below them, a little wave stringing through ploughing the plateau into a field. Lowan remembered watching the other kids scavenging the inky shore-line looking for wood to bring to the fire and he wondered why he wasn't allowed to help, why he had to sit with Dad out on the cold headland, his legs itching to run his head on everything but the one thing he knew was coming. He remembered that Dad was drinking from a beer can, must have been before the food trucks stopped coming and they had to brew their own. Lowan could still smell the stench of the cigarette that was a constant smoking at the corner of his mouth, each time he went to speak it tongued to the corner of his mouth rolled back when nothing right came to mind. Lowan's dad was a man of few words, he said more with a look than any word could communicate, it was as if he held his family together with string. Easily pulled easily wrapped around, Lowan didn't know it then but he would spend the next few years unravelling.

He kept his eyes pinned to the horizon, the last of colour a thin thread needling through the cloud and waited for his dad to begin, find the right words but in the end he just jumped in.

'The Droll of the Mermaid' was a story Lowan had learnt from pictures and embroideries that hung in the front room the tale of his ancestor Lutey. To the seven-year-old boy he sounded like a good man unrecognisable from Dad and all the rest, a farmer by hand fisherman in his heart, a man that never asked or looked for anything for himself, that was why he found it one day whilst out walking the shore-line. The story went that one day whilst he was out combing the beach, he saw a woman in distress out on the rocks, a woman who cried so much that Lutey had no option but to go to her. Some folk said she was a mermaid or the devil shape-shifting from out the sand but growing up Lowan thought perhaps she was a guardian angel, or a witch, Dad said there were plenty of them around. The part of the story that caught his interest was that she cried so loudly that the gulls about-turned he'd always thought that something, when he shouted at the birds they ignored him, same as everyone he supposed. Lowan always wondered why even if she was a mermaid that she couldn't have just crawled from the rocks until she found water. Instead she waited for ancestor Lutey to rescue her from drying out like a kipper and return her to the ocean with the promise of three wishes but when the time came for goodbyes she wouldn't let the old bloke go.

Lowan remembered Dad putting down his can and taking out his dagger to flash at him, he said that it had stopped the woman dangling, told his boy that mermaids didn't like silver and to remember that; it was a great family secret, like when he told him to not just put the knife in but up or always sleep on your back in case of attack. When Lowan had asked if mermaids liked gold he was told, 'Of course, all em women gold diggers.'

Legend had it the dagger did the trick, it scared the strange woman enough to go good on her word and she told Lutey he could have three wishes but the family could only remember one, this they called the big one. Old man Lutey had asked for the power to heal and not just for him but for his descendants to inherit the same command and it was true, they all had the healing power, it was something to be shown off, to celebrate, they used it on themselves each and every day. There was only one bit of bad news the mermaid had warned him, every nine years the gift would flip become curse and take one of the family with it.

Age seven, the young Lowan was more interested in the story of the mysterious woman than the curse bestowed upon his family or the dagger Dad had placed into his lap. He looked out over the rocks and tried to imagine what this beautiful woman looked like, tried to imagine her beauty beside all the Pellar women.

The rest of the story, the curse part was just something he had to endure whilst his eyes searched for splendour amongst the debris of their existence. Back then the ocean had taken his grandfather, now nine years on his uncle the first-born son so what? It didn't bother him, as a kid there was nothing for him to hold on to, no way of making sense of past stories future glories for the ones that remained. Bullets dodged but Lowan knew there were more to be fired, his childless uncle sunk at sea it was him that would take the next hit.

This had all been nine years ago, but Dad would tell Lowan all this again tonight. Time was running out, an hourglass in a house of no hands there was nothing to catch his life and turn it.

So many years had passed since ancestor Lutey's encounter, but their power to heal was evident in the way they fought and bled and recovered. No longer selfless they were a gang of many, impossible to defeat. There was nothing Lowan's family wouldn't do to take what wasn't theirs, the collapse in rights and rules had made their lives perfect; wrecking when there were boats to wreck, looting when a low mist peeled off the breakers, pulling in ships that they tricked into safe harbour by precariously placed lamps. It made Lowan's heart ache with the thought of all that could have been made good, if only they followed the path that had been set for them, decency instead of tyranny.

He leant back and watched the sky pitch out and saw the shadow of a flock of shags circle the bay, they knew better than to land. If ever there were good folk living in the village of Cury they were long gone now. He saw the tide complete its retreat and the last leg drag the spirit of the dead man away, pulling the curse from him and returning it to Lowan, jinx. He was only sixteen but could swear he felt hands upon his chest, finding flesh to finger and crack open his ribs, nails going in to score his fate like a brand upon his heart. No more. He got up and ran the length of the bay and the night joined him in pall, drowning him like water the ocean returned.

When his boots hit rock he stood and put out his hands found the grit of cliff and rubbed the sticky silt between his fingers. The only part of home he could understand was that which couldn't be taken away the earth and sand goading his feet to run and the tower of rock that threw down an imaginary rope and told him to climb up. Lowan wasn't like the others, he didn't like to rob folk of their livelihoods, he hated the thought of fighting for the sake of sport the spectacle of healing themselves just because they could was not right, would never be right. Whilst people in the heart of the village struggled to feed their children because of the shortages, his family put up the rent on the fields they owned, the fields that they had acquired through bullying, and they robbed the people of fish, running the harbour through a tax nobody could afford. The Pellars had more spuds and fish than they could wish for, but still they would not share it with anyone other than blood. They were strong, robust, despite the nine-year death thing, the something that was his thing now.

Lowan put his back against the pitted crag and looked for light and saw the concealed funeral fire reflected in the thin-skinned glare of the rocks. Tiny cratered pools where seawater had been caught like stepping stones they set a trail that tiptoed out towards the sea. Something about the way the water captured fire had Lowan transfixed a moment and made him merry with the miracle of nature, he went to it.

The first pool of water made a perfect circle of molten gold like an armlet of good fortune and Lowan put his hand through and felt the liquid curdle around his fingers, sink into the veins on his wrist like new blood the gilt replacing purple and blue. No light but the reflected firelight, he took his time to step across the rocks, all the while his eyes he kept on the path that had been placed for him. The thin strip of light that had been riddling the horizon had gone now and the darkness that surrounded him gave comfort, it always did. At night Lowan was free to do what he wanted, go where his father's eyes couldn't find him. Most Pellars feared the dark, they found the shadows too full of their own reflective mischief, but not him, it was where he found himself happiest where he could throw his imagination wide like a net that stretched across the ocean. Into the net he collected wishes and ways to make the things he didn't understand disappear. He placed plans into his night net like memories yet to have, pictured himself away from kin and the curse that he could feel settling in. If he had one wish it would have been to take the power to heal away, live long enough so he could walk the furthest distance possible to get from water. Live the rest of his life on land, lose the lead that would eventually have its hand in his sinking. Since last night when his uncle died, Lowan could already picture his own drowning; the boat trip before his birthday the midnight mass in the chapel up on the hill. Everyone praying but not for him, it would be their own fate that bowed their heads and held their hands too tight together. Whilst his life washed and bleached into whatever it was that was meant for him buried beneath the ocean floor.

He went on, head down eyes slipping over the rocks and dipping into the handholds of water, it was as if he were looking for something, following the breadcrumb trail until he reached the last.

Lowan stood with the rock pool between his feet, the eye of colour at its centre eclipsing the dark bright brilliance. He bent to one knee and put his hand into the water, stretched against the rock and pushed his arm into its craw. When his fingers found teeth he was quick to snatch the thing and throw it against the rocks. He sat back, eyes on the gold his heart in his mouth.

'Some old comb,' he said to himself, 'some comb looted and left I int seen nothin like it.' He leant forward and was careful to lift the object from the rock and raked it through the surface of the water to clean it. Three strokes to unpick the seaweed from its teeth and Lowan brought the comb into his lap, a moment of luck, he wanted to hold on to this instant.

Across the plateau of rocks he could hear the others singing, the party still rising in them, they had forgotten why they were down here beached in the briny winter night. In the morning they wouldn't remember anything of before, would go on hunting and howling and healing, the weight of kin curse off their minds for another nine years. The hereditary hex was Lowan's to endure alone.

He undid the top buttons of his coat and brought the comb to his chest, a way to keep its light from escaping the gold so bright it was as if the entire world's radiance had been swallowed whole. Each tooth a fine golden fibre, Lowan held its smile in both hands realised that he too beamed out into the world. When he heard cheering he was quick to put the comb into his pocket and step out of its light, have it step out of his. Something strange was happening he could sense it in the air, could smell the salt water no matter how far the tide stretched out he could feel it all around. He pulled his collar to his cheek and turned towards where he thought the shore was and tried to make out the position of the fire but it had disappeared. Only one distant light punctured the dark, it wasn't at the cliff steps where it was meant, but looked to be swinging out to sea. Lowan stood at the gateway between what he knew and what he imagined, felt lost in the spin of land becoming sea and the ocean turning to something other, in any case his curiosity had been stabbed by the comb there was nothing more he could do but go on. Lowan took his time as he moved further out on to the rocks, his eyes on the light like a prize he could not let go, with each step he saw the shape shift its weight like water a constant ebb and flow, it pulled him closer. Warmth when there hadn't been warmth tranquil when there had been a good wind kicking from the south, the air no longer wet with mizzle but parched, like the sun had swung around without him noticing. Everything paused, each known thing in Lowan's world quarter turned towards this new energy the possibility of company outside his deadlock life.

When he was as close to the figure as he dared he put his hands into his pockets to feel the warmth of the comb tangle about his fingers, it gave him strength to be without the rush and run of boyhood. In that moment there was nothing on his tongue to say, nothing to do but wait in the chamber of silence the space he'd been given, allow himself to be taken in with the glow of gold the halo of hair that hid the girl's face.

'You've got something that belongs to me,' she said.

Lowan drew the comb from out his pocket and outstretched his arm it went to her made new light and walked her face from out the shadows. He put his hands to his chest, a way to protect his heart it hit hard with the beat of beauty, destiny. He watched her run the comb through her hair, eyes on him, knowing him. Perhaps they were old souls returned, colliding where the shore-line hit the breakers, grey lives come together in a colourful arch, perfectly aligned.

'What's your name?' he asked.

'Morvena.' She smiled.

Lowan nodded. 'I int afraid of you.' He stepped forward as if to prove a point and made the girl laugh.

'I'm not afraid of you either.' She ran the comb through her hair and the effort pitched stars into the night.

Lowan watched, transfixed.

'You should sit.' She pointed to the rock across from where she sat and Lowan did what he was told. Up close he could see that she had been crying, her eyes moved like pools of distant water that seemed to have washed in by the strange tide.

'You okay?' he asked. It was a stupid thing to say, he thought of something more to add asked if she was lost even though he knew she was, she must have been. He'd never seen her before, despite some deep-rooted feeling that he had known her his entire life. She made him feel at ease, had a way of softening the world's corners with pattern and light, a way of hypnotising him, until Lowan suddenly realised she was talking.

'I came down to the beach to look at the tide,' she said, 'I've never seen it so far out, I just wanted to walk the rocks.' She looked over at Lowan, 'and now I can't get back.' She pointed to where she'd climbed down the cliff a tangle of golden lights threading through the hawthorn bushes, they swung into the caves and made music of the sea.

Lowan could see the tide had returned to that distant part of the bay, it pushed against the cliffs and splashed against the rocks.

'Couldn't you walk back and see what's what?' he asked. 'Maybe it int that bad and you can wade in.'

The girl shook her head and lifted the soles of her feet from out the rock pool where she had been bathing them and Lowan watched as her radiance lit them up, revealing the bloody wounds and skin that peeled away from her like scales.

'That int good.' He looked up at her. 'What the hell you bin doin?'

'I was running and the barnacles cut my feet.'

'You dint realise?'

Morvena looked back out to sea. 'The ocean, I just wanted to see how far it would go out, if it would come back.'

'Don't worry it always comes back.' Lowan stood and ran his gaze along the coastline, saw nothing but unfamiliar shadow, his world picked up and put somewhere other. 'Tide's comin in at all angles right now.' He put his hands into his pockets, pulled them out again, looked down at the girl and sighed.

'Help me please?' she asked. 'I'm not meant on land but over there in the shallows.' She waved towards the largest of the caves.

Lowan looked to where she was pointing and sighed. Anyone could see he wasn't strong his back was fillet thin and his limbs fell from him like loose cord looking to be tied into muscle, maybe one day.

He looked at the girl and nodded. 'Okay, but I int strong,' he told her. 'I'll carry you as far as water, but no further.'

Lowan knelt down to the rock and took his time to put his arms around the girl and carefully lifted her from the rock pool. He told her to hold on to his neck as he took one step forward, and then another. All the while he kept his eyes away from Morvena's blinding light, his mind on his boots each step felt like it might be his last. He went on stepping through masses of newly dumped bladderwrack, his toes kicking at the winkles as he lagged up the rocks and skidded down into pools of dark water. With each step he said a little prayer, nothing much just please don't fall, he asked for his family's strength this one time so he could free the girl, return her to whatever world she had come from.

The closer they got to Morvena's cove the brighter the barnacles that covered the rocks they caught at the corner of Lowan's eye, the limpets that blinked like amber eyes and the tiny strands of serrated wrack bristling and becoming brilliant coral. The sky lit up with glowing embers it was as if all the funeral fires had returned with each spark resembling sea stars and fireflies and tiny seahorses passing by. It made Lowan smile.

'Come with me,' said Morvena when they reached the edge of the last rock. 'Carry me into the water I'll show you my home, it's better than all of this.' She tightened one arm around his neck and the other she gestured towards the coastline.

Lowan tried to ignore her, he had greater things to think about; the effort of carrying had his shoulders anchoring under, the last ridge of rock that stepped down to the water was the worst of all.

'Don't let go,' said Morvena, 'not yet.'

Lowan felt her hands grip his hair as he struggled for air, his lungs stretched to splitting it was as if he were already rudderless beneath the ocean.

'I int goin no further,' he told her when his feet hit lapping water. 'I said I'd help you and I did and I int asked for nothin in return.' He looked at the girl and when her emerald eyes met his he looked away.

'You could come with me,' she repeated. 'You would never have to ask for anything where I'm going.'

'I don't want anythin.'

'You can be whoever you want to be, without anyone telling you who you should be.'

Lowan shook his head. 'This int my time.'

Morvena nodded. 'You're a good lad, Lowan Pellar,' she

whispered and before he could question how she knew his name she asked him if he could have one wish what would it be?

Lowan looked towards the garish cave and noticed that lights he had seen earlier were pearls, they ran through the cliff like seams of flint.

'What if everything you touched turned to gold?' Morvena asked.

Lowan shook his head. 'I wouldn't be able to eat or fish or put on my boots, I'd miss soft things.'

'What if you had magic powers or could live for ever?'

Again Lowan shrugged despite the weight of all the world's water in his arms. 'They'd be no point if the ones I loved died and went on dyin.'

This answer made Morvena smile and she told him that he had the sweetest heart she'd ever known. 'I wish you would come with me, all my people think about is what riches they can steal from the sea.'

Lowan nodded. 'Mine too, a different kind of lootin is all.' He bent to the water and told her it wasn't that deep, that she could wade across the tiny estuary towards home.

'I only got one wish,' he told her as she stepped into the water. 'Promise that all em will stop fightin and stealin and whatever else.' He pointed towards his family home.

'I promise.' Morvena smiled. 'And you, promise me that you will protect your good heart and keep healing through kindness.' She had started to swim away but Lowan called her back.

'What do you mean?' he asked.

'Look.' She flipped her feet towards where he crouched so he could see the soles of her feet.

'They're healed.' She smiled.

Lowan watched her dive beneath the water and speed towards the caves disappearing in a flash of radiant light. He closed his eyes and in the distance he could hear the flurry of a few tuneful notes pitched into the air. A tune he used to know, some childhood lullaby whistling goodbye. Lowan sat and waited for the light to fade and the tune he put into his heart until the dark put its claws into it and ripped it out.

Nine good years Lowan could never say he had less than that. He had found a woman from a neighbouring village to love and marry with no promise of anything other than the moment they found themselves in. They were happy to have their routine, Lowan spending all his time fishing or healing hearts and fixing sentiment until it sat straight in those hearts. Like tiny vessels of love he put hope into the chests of the hopeless and set them free to sail. Cury folk born and raised and folk from all over Cornwall knew the secret of the boy with the healing hands, the more he worked at magic the more his family lost theirs, each one falling to the knife the sword by which they had always lived. In nine years Lowan had fought and won the greatest battle, his family. As each one fell he grew stronger, Lowan Pellar was the legacy now. When his father died he stood at the grave and told him that this was what a man looked like; strength showing in deed and feat, not by the scars that counted kills across his fists.

But despite his success, Lowan knew that to the Pellar born all good things came to an end, nine years since his journey into adulthood begun and here he was at the end, water watching and waiting for the final wave goodbye.

He lifted his head to see the ocean spread out just as he had left it, a table at which he had eaten and loved and lived his life as full as nine years would allow, but he sat alone now.

He turned his ear towards the village and waited for the chapel bell to peal off another round of bullets and with each hammer Lowan felt like it was he that was being struck.

Not long now, it mustn't have been. There was no way he could hold on to midnight no matter how he wished his life in reverse. One more minute with his wife, just one. There was still so much

Lowan wanted to do, so many ways to heal the hearts and minds of the many that came to visit; their prolonged pilgrimage to see the weakest of the Pellars, turned out he was the strongest.

Lowan thought it a shame, both gift and gall his cure and curse curdled and served in equal measure. He leant forward and stretched his arms off the side of the boat and hung his head until his eyes met his own, a tide-washed version emerald in the ebb of flowing water. His face a pretty picture looking up at him, smiling when he didn't think he was. Lowan ran his fingers over the current of the water and through the hair of this other self, he closed his eyes and waited to be pulled from the boat, he knew it wouldn't be long. When the bell started up again he counted the blows and brought the stars down from the sky, placed them on the horizon and told all he loved and knew and those he never got to know that he loved them and that this was where they would find him, in the haze that was neither dusk nor dawn but the yawn of light that simmered between.

He kept his hands sunk in the sorrowful water until he could feel the undercurrent rise and fall between his fingers and he felt something within being taken away and an offering of familiarity put in its place. Lowan ran his nails across the object and listened to the tune that he first heard the night he met Morvena and he remembered that he knew it way before that moment, it was a tune he had carried all the way from childhood. He opened his eyes to see the golden comb, his mother's smile reflecting.

He glanced around. The bell that had been ringing life into death had finished its duty. Lowan sat up, he was not meant to witness the end. If this was the afterlife it mirrored life perfectly. He looked towards the horizon and saw the wide mouth ocean the same as it had been yesterday, not one wave threatening, no whites of its eyes or teeth flashing no horses rolling forward, not even the tiny sea kind.

'Today then,' said Lowan. It was today, his birthday.

He cradled the mermaid's comb in his lap and picked up the oars and pointed the boat towards home. A little dawn light rising in the east, one solitary light glazing the bedroom window; two shadows, the child holding on to his heart, Lowan went to them.

THE HOLLOWAY

Imogen Hermes Gowar

Based on
Old Farmer Mole
SOMERSET

Not long after dawn and Evie is out in her pyjamas. It's going to be a hot day, she can tell, but the grass is cool and wet, and the tree-roofed holloway at the end of the drive is dark as an ink-blot, all heavy with moisture and shadows. She stands in her bare feet by the kitchen door, listening to the silence lying smooth and plush like a field of snow or a sheet of good drawing paper. Of course it's not silence at all, but only an absence of people noises, which makes the animal noises all the crisper. The birds are awake, bubbling and cawing, cooing and squabbling and crowing, veils of song wafting in from the next valley. Sheep are bleating in the fields and on the moors, the cries of lambs not long for slaughter met with the grumbly throat-clearing of their mothers. Evie thinks she even hears the whicker of ponies at the stables up the hill. Mum or Luke or Dad must already be there, shaking pellets into their troughs, perhaps leading them out into the paddock to stretch their legs before the day's work begins.

Evie's right hand is full of blueberries from the fridge. She steps from the gravel on to the damp lawn, and crouches by Mum's favourite tall poppies, their last flowers blood-red and ragged-petalled. Dewdrops darken her pyjama bottoms: she puts her palm to the earth and leans deep into the flower-bed.

'Here,' she says. 'I brought these. I hope you like them.' The berries roll down the leaves and vanish among them. She sits back on her heels and eats the last of them herself, biting them in half to see their pale flesh. There are clover leaves between her toes, and a chenille of moss among the blades of grass.

'Evie?'

It's Mum, standing at the kitchen door with her favourite chicken mug in her hand and her dressing gown wrapped tightly around her. 'What are you up to?' she says.

Evie shrugs.

'I didn't hear you get up, little one, you were quiet as a mouse.' Mum reaches out her arm and Evie runs to her, pressing her cheek into her dressing gown. 'Watch my coffee!' Mum lifts her mug up and away. 'It's hot.'

'I was quieter than a mouse,' says Evie, tipping her face up to Mum's.

'That's true; they made a racket last night. It must have been them – nobody else would do the hundred-yard dash in our attic.'

'House elves, Mum, having a disco. Why aren't you dressed?' Evie glances around her arm into the kitchen. The red quarry-tile floor is mopped clean: no muddy footprints here, no heavy feet. No ketchup-smeared plate on the kitchen island, no toast crumbs scorching on the Aga. She sniffs, but all she smells is something lemony and soapy from the sticks Mum has standing in a bottle.

'Having a disco! Evelyn Grace!' Mum laughs and presses her palm against the back of Evie's head, fingertips burrowing through her hair. Evie wants to snuggle into Mum's arms but somehow her body won't snuggle: she feels as if her limbs are strung on too-tight elastic, and she leans stiffly, plucking at the fluff on Mum's lapel. 'I've got a little morning off,' says Mum. 'Luke's gone to the stables for me, and taken the dog with him. Dad's out too.'

'Out where?'

'Out through the door.'

Evie tuts. Mum makes this joke so often it's like saying 'bless you' or 'excuse me' or 'fine, thanks'. It would be rude not to.

'You know him,' Mum adds. 'He's out and about.' She heads for the lounge, its thick carpet showing the lines of the vacuum cleaner she ran around it yesterday. 'Come and hang out with me, baby, it's never just the two of us.'

They curl up on the sofa and Evie leans her head against Mum's chest. She feels better now. She hadn't exactly noticed the sick little stone of worry in her stomach, but she notices now it's gone. Mum kisses her forehead and Evie closes her eyes, listening to the tiny crackle of Mum's dressing gown rising and falling with her breath, and underneath it the thud of her heart.

'You used to cuddle up like this when you were a little sprout,' says Mum. 'I could hold you in one arm then. I miss our hugs.'

'Yeah. Can I go on your tablet?'

'Oh, Evie.'

From the kitchen, a bang. And barking – Dexter's barking – and the skitter of his claws on the tiles. Mum does not move but her whole body feels different. Her arm around Evie's shoulders grips tighter as noises advance through the house – the door from the kitchen to the hall flung open; footsteps advancing across the tiles.

'Claire!'

Evie can smell horse manure now, and mud and the damp of the outside, but also that sour, pungent, ferret smell that means Dad has not slept all night.

'Stay there,' Mum murmurs to her. She stands up, pulling her dressing gown around her.

'Claire?'

Mum crosses the lounge as if she were answering any knock on the door. 'In here,' she says, smiling.

Dad's face is red and loose, Dad's but not quite. He's wearing the clothes he put on yesterday, lace-up shoes now fat with mud and pony dung. Dexter the spaniel scuttles at his heels, low to the ground, making noises in the back of his throat that are neither growl nor whimper. 'I've just been to the stables,' says Dad. 'I thought you'd be there.'

'Ah! Right.' Mum's smile becomes a bit less rigid. 'Luke said he'd go instead. He *was* there, wasn't he?'

'But you weren't,' says Dad. 'I was worried.'

'Well, that's sweet.' She touches his arm very lightly, as if she isn't sure. 'He just wanted to give me a break.'

Dad bristles. 'Oh, you needed a break? I suppose you think you're the only person who works hard around here.'

'He was being kind.'

'It's really not a big ask, Claire. You should be able to handle it. *I* was there, bright and early.'

Mum's gaze flicks over Dad's raw-looking eyes, his unbuttoned shirt, his dirty lace-ups. It's a quick glance, but not quick enough.

'What's that filthy look for?'

'Nothing.'

'*Nothing, nothing,*' he mimics. 'Princess Claire! Swanning around, so superior. What the fuck do you take me for? What the fuck sort of man doesn't even know where his wife is on a morning? Is that the sort of man you think I am?'

'No, Steve, no. Look,' she adds coaxingly, '*Evie's* here. I was home with *Evie*. And our boy went to muck out.' She speaks low and calm but her eyes are fixed on Dad's face and she stresses 'Evie … *Evie*' urgently as if it were a secret code. Mum wind-whipped on a clifftop, rotating a mirror in her hand so it flashes *Evie, Evie, Evie* into the void, but its light never catches Dad's eye.

'It's seven in the morning,' Mum whispers. 'You're tired. I'll go up right now, get ready for the first lot of punters, okay?'

He stands still, his hands hanging at his sides with the fingers curled loosely. He watches Mum from under his brows, his lips parted so Evie can hear his breath rattling through thick saliva.

'Okay?' whispers Mum, skirting round him. 'I'll just nip upstairs and shower.'

Dexter has curled his tail under his haunches, his spine curved as if he wishes he were a woodlouse and could roll right up. His eyes swivel on their whites to watch Mum go by: Dad watches too. So does Evie. Her chest burns it's so long since she last took a breath.

'*Now* you want to go to the stables,' Dad spits as she puts her foot on the first step.

'Sorry?'

If it was a film he'd have grabbed her throat or wrapped her hair around his fist like a halter – something like that, to show it was serious – but Dad moves slowly and roughly, and maybe he gets Mum's elbow or the big loose sleeve of her dressing gown: she gasps and stumbles at the same time as his feet slither on the tiles, leaving long streaks and gobbets of muck, and Dexter whisks around them, his paws dancing and scratching, uttering high questioning barks until white flecks appear at the corners of his mouth. Dad is shouting 'You want to go *now*. Couldn't be arsed earlier, could you?', but Mum, kneeling on the floor, says nothing, and her face is blank, the thoughts are whirring through her mind so fast she has forgotten to put on any expression at all.

Dad grabs her by the arm and pulls her to her feet. 'Jesus Christ, the laziness of you,' he's growling, 'that's you all over, isn't it?' Evie presses her hands over her face: she doesn't like to see Mum yanked about, with her mouth clamped shut and her head nodding. Sometimes when this happens she urges Mum on in her head, thinks, *Go, run*, imagines Mum twisting free from Dad's hands and racing down the hall to the backdoor, the hem of her dressing gown flapping out of sight. Yet, when Mum says, 'Yes, love, I know. I'm sorry. I'm sorry. I should have gone myself,' she is relieved.

But somebody is running. Not away but towards: through the open window Evie hears the scatter of gravel, and sees her brother Luke, his limbs flying as if he has been thrown. His expression is like Mum's, hawkish but blank, as if he sees every detail but is only looking for one.

'Is he there? Is Dad there? He's proper off on one.'

She can't speak at all. She can't even nod. He doesn't stop anyway, just sprints past the window towards the front of the house. In the hall there is the thud and swing of bodies – Dad snarling through his teeth 'You miserable bitch, you waste of fucking space', Mum gasping, 'Okay, Steve' – but they are out of sight of the door and Evie can't see, won't look, until she hears a new pounding and realises that Luke is at the front door, and it is locked from the inside.

'Evie! *Evie!*' he is yelling. 'Evie, unlock it!'

She gets off the sofa, runs on her tiptoes across the carpet with the vacuum lines Mum likes so much. She freezes on the threshold to the hall where Dad is punching Mum and Luke's palms are slapping against the front door's glass panels, making Mum's keys rattle in the lock where she always leaves them overnight. 'Evie!' Luke calls again, 'I can't get in!'

'The kitchen,' Evie tries to say, but she can't find her voice. She is trapped there, her courage spent, with Dexter cowering behind her legs. Mum is down, slack like a pile of laundry, and Dad gives a sloppy, glancing kick from his muddy brogues.

'Help me out here, Evie!' calls Luke.

'I don't want him to hurt you too,' she wails.

'Fuck's sake. Fuck's *sake*.' He vanishes from the door and his steps recede on the gravel. Then the kitchen door goes bang-*bang* and he flies in, lifting Dad away from Mum as if he weighed nothing. When did Luke get so tall? He was always bigger than Evie but not man-size, not Dad-size. Suddenly it's like something else has entered him and he is not that narrow-chested boy, tripping on his feet and stooping his head – he is six feet tall and fills his body entirely. He actually grabs Dad's shirt and yanks him away so that he lurches and staggers into the wall. 'Don't *do* that to my *mum*,' bellows Luke.

'Luke, no!' Mum's struggling to get up. Her voice is just a croak and her face is swollen and weird, smeared with muck. She crumples back to the floor.

'He doesn't get to do this. I won't let him.'

'Leave it.' Mum lifts herself on her arm again, swallowing hard, her bottom lip trembling so hard she claps her hand to it and lies down again, her cheek to the tile. 'Take Evie and go to the stables. We'll be late to the trek otherwise. We can't keep people waiting.'

'Mum!'

'Go on, both of you,' she says to the floor. 'I'll have my shower. I'll catch up.'

Dad has deflated. He slouches past Evie into the lounge and topples on to the couch like a felled tree. Evie has sniffed Mum's red wine, and the beer Luke opens when he sits out on a sunny evening with his speaker in the grass at his feet, but when they say you can smell the booze on Dad it's not like that at all. It comes from his skin, and it's acrid and greasy like something's gone bad in his veins. That smell stays in the couch cushions for a long time.

When she sees he won't move again, Mum seems to shake something out of herself, and she sits up fluffing her hair and lifting her chin. She grabs the banister and hauls herself to her feet, staggering, cupping her arm around herself as if she expects another blow. 'Awful, the way he gets,' she grimaces. 'Oh – ugh! What's this?'

She's trodden in a puddle of urine: Dexter is curled against the front door, his snout pressed to its hinge, crying. 'Oh, puppy. What a mess. Were you frightened?' She stumbles over to him in a crouch and wraps him in her arms: Evie sees Mum has his ear gently between her finger and thumb and is rubbing it over and over as she gathers him against her and whispers, 'Poor baby. Poor Dex. Don't be scared. We're okay. I'll clean this up.'

Luke and Evie stand there a long time, but Mum doesn't raise her head. 'Come on, then,' Luke says eventually, and he leads Evie away.

He gets a shirt and shorts out of the dryer for her, and while she dresses he fills her flask with water, and lines it up on the side with a tangerine and a cereal bar and a box of raisins. 'You ready?'

he asks, and she nods. She feels numb and rattled, a bit like at the end of a disco, when the music has stopped and the lights are up but your ears are still ringing. Outside, Dad's Land Rover is slewed across the drive, its indicator blinking, the gravel ploughed up under its wheels. The driver's door hangs open and as they pass by Luke hops in to take the keys out of the ignition. He hesitates with them in his hand for a moment; then he puts them on the seat and slams the door. 'C'mon, Evie, let's go.'

They take the sunken lane to the stables. This is an old, old road, Luke always says, a hollow way worn down by many journeys: the banks are high as Evie's nose, only just far enough apart to let a car through, and for every type of plant you find in the hedgerow you can add another hundred years to its age. Evie counts musk mallow and herb Robert, foxglove and chickweed and quickthorn and beech. Sometimes there are little wild orchids like dancing white smocks in the shade, and there are lemony sorrel leaves for snacking, and the blackberries getting fat and heavy on their brambles. The air is clean as a brook, green coins of leaves layering above and around them so that even though it's August, in the holloway it still feels like the dewiest and most luminous day of spring.

'You can't be like that, Evie,' says Luke suddenly. 'You just froze up today.'

'I'm sorry.'

He tightens his hand around hers. 'I won't always be here, that's all. When I start uni . . .'

She can't reply.

'You could still call me,' he says.

There is a rustling in the hedgerow, a thrash of greenery as something bolts away from them. Peering through the hawthorn Evie sees ropes of exposed roots, soil caving away to reveal the warrens beneath. On the other side of the hedge dandelions are blowing, and she hears the shift and chomp of a sheep.

'Luke?'

'Mm?'

She'd meant to ask a question, but when she opens her mouth the answer comes out instead: 'Not everybody's dad is like that.'

They walk on in silence. Luke's face is still and his eyes are raised up to the branches closing above them, where something is hopping and calling, making the boughs waver with an invisible weight. 'A goldfinch, must be,' he says. Then he adds, 'No. Most people's dads don't do that.'

'And it's a secret.'

'*We* keep it a secret. Maybe people know about it.'

'They definitely don't, Luke,' she says earnestly. 'If they knew, they'd do something about it.' Dad has some kind of magic, she thinks, that he does these things and nobody sees them. It even works on Mum. It works on Evie too, kind of, because she keeps quiet without being told.

'Okay,' Luke says. 'But someone round here sees everything.'

'Who?' She knows, but she wants to hear him tell it again.

'The pixies.'

'Nah.'

'Yep. See, a holloway is a barrier between one man's land and the next. It's the most in-between sort of place there can be, so when you're walking here you can be sure you're walking with the pixies. They're tricksy and they're always watching, but if you're good in your heart, they'll be good to you. This is their land before it's ours,' he prompts her,

'And we don't muck about on it,' she finishes. She always walks lightly here, swift and business-like in a way she feels the pixies will approve of, with her head held up and her fists at her sides. She never yanks the nesty roots of plants from the bank, or kicks in the rabbit warrens: in her mind she tells the pixies, *I love this place just like you do* and hopes for a sign of their approval. Dad's magic is strong but the pixies' magic is stronger, she is sure of that. Still, because she's begun to wonder if she's too big for stories, she says, 'I'm not sure.'

'Think what you like. They're out here, and they can see when things aren't right.'

'They haven't done anything about it.'

'Not *yet.*'

The holloway rises up out of the valley, its banks shrinking, the trees opening out into sunshine. In the middle of the road where it crests the hill they see a column of shimmering gold as tall as Luke, which turns to them expectantly as they approach. The dust on the path is all lit up, and the tips of the leaves, and the strands of hair that fall across Evie's face, so she squints and brushes her hand across her eyes. When she looks up again the figure is a trembling cloud, which reaches out its arms and then all of a sudden disperses.

'Midgies,' spits Luke, wafting his hands as he steps through them, and Evie ducks her head and clamps her mouth shut while she does the same. Their wings tickle her bare skin, and she runs to catch up with her brother.

At the stables Luke is in charge of sorting out helmets for the trekkers. Evie goes straight to where the ponies are being tacked up by the summer staff, striding proudly past the little girls her own age who stand bright-eyed with excitement or apprehension. They are holiday-makers, or families from Taunton and Bristol and Exeter on a day out, and it is important to Evie that they see she is set apart, a girl who walks casually among animals and knows the countryside well. She flicks her hair as she rubs the ponies' noses and checks the set of their bridles. 'Don't mess about, Evie,' Luke calls, but she pretends not to hear him, and lets them snuff at her hair with their hot nostrils.

Mum arrives buckling her helmet over her long hair, Dexter at her heels with his plumey tail held high. She's done a good job of sorting herself out: if you didn't know her you wouldn't see that her usual bouncy step is stooped and tentative. The bruises don't show under her loose shirt, and the parts of her face not shaded by her hat and sunglasses are flawless. Mum watches a lot of contouring tutorials.

'Hi, folks!' she chirps. 'What a beautiful day! Welcome, welcome, thanks for joining us!' Evie's heard the chat a thousand times but she always likes to watch Mum deliver it. Even when she starts sluggish, a draught of energy fills up her veins until she's laughing and gesticulating and joking, everybody's friend. She explains that these are gentle ponies and that the trekkers will be in good hands with her and Luke on their ride, that this is a family business with ten years' experience of Exmoor pony trekking, but every day is still a new adventure.

They ride in single file along the holloway, Evie bobbing lightly in her seat with the gentle roil of her favourite pony, Tricks. The animals know the route well, and pace the dappled tarmac in a dark-eyed sort of trance, but when they emerge from that greenlit tree-vaulted tunnel and see the hawthorn give way to gorse, and the cool meadow grass to fuzzy turf, they toss their heads with excitement. There is a skylark overhead shaking its wing-tips like a cheerleader, and the heather is lit up purple, and the patches of long marsh grass are bleached blonde and swishy. Evie feels a rush of giddiness but can't tell if it's hers or Tricks's: she doesn't know if she touches her heels to his belly or if he simply hears her thoughts, but he sets off at a spritely trot and then a canter along the bridle-way.

'Evie,' calls Mum, 'stay in line, baby,' but Evie keeps going. The wind is cooler and brisker up here, and it keens in her face and tugs her hair; the moor spreads around and below her, mottled purple green and gold for miles under the burnished sky, and on the far horizon a smudge of dark sea. From here the holloway is a caterpillar of greenery between the fields, their house a speck with glints for windows, the village a little grey ant's nest, nothing more. *Nothing down there matters*, Evie thinks, and perhaps this is how it feels to be a pixie, to sit up here and gaze upon the silly comings and goings of the people, clearly and coolly and without fear. She is so filled with exuberance and beauty she thinks she might take off flying.

'Evie!' calls Luke, pulling up his pony alongside her. 'We're not insured for your twatting about. Can you come back and set a good example?'

'Yeah, okay,' she says, but doesn't move. She is gazing out across the plain of the world. 'It's lovely, isn't it?'

'It is.'

'Do you *have* to go to university?'

He clonks the top of her helmet affectionately with the palm of his hand. 'Not if I've failed my exams. Results day tomorrow, then we'll see.'

They file on to the stone circle, which really is barely a circle at all, more of a scatter on the shadow-spotted plain. Nobody knows why it's there, this handful of flat seal-grey stones half-hidden in the scrubby grass, freckled with lichen, but it was laid out with purpose and so the riddle of its existence must be taken as an overture from those people of the past. They are reaching into the modern; they wish to be seen. The trekkers dismount and mooch around the stones half-interested, eating snack-size chocolate bars. Mum circulates among them taking their photographs with the ponies. She moves more stiffly than usual, her arms curling defensively around her ribs every now and then, but her laughter still carries across the stones. It's a nice day to be up on the tops: some beardy men in windbreakers stand with their hands on their hips and their binoculars on their chests, squinting across the moor, and a couple in colourful trousers tumble with their toddlers on the scratchy grass.

Evie sits cross-legged by a stone and rests her arm against it conversationally. Its surface is warm and roughish, like an elbow.

She gets out the cereal bar, the tangerine and the raisins: shakes the raisins into her hand and lays them out carefully. She eats the tangerine and the cereal bar but pushes the raisins around on their stone altar until they are all in a straight line.

'Do one thing for me,' she whispers. She does not specify the thing because she's heard that the pixies will twist your meaning, but surely this way they will know what to do.

The trouser family are doing a sort of tai chi, standing with their heads tipped back and their arms outspread. One of the windbreaker men has been digging in his rucksack and now pulls out a shallow drum that he begins to play, a soft tattoo that carries like fingertips on the surface of the air. There are more people there than she had thought, and she realises they are all singing and humming, their eyes closed, their anoraks knotted around their waists, their voices half lost on the wind and not, anyway, for any human person's benefit. The trekkers huddle at a distance, watching with their bodies turned away so as not to betray their curiosity. Evie stretches her legs out before her and bounces her heels in time on the heather.

Luke strolls over and sits down next to her. 'See?' he says. 'It's not just me who believes in the pixies.'

'Is that what you're meant to do?' asks Evie.

'Dunno,' he shrugs. 'They're nutters. What are you doing with those raisins?'

She flattens her hand over them and scowls up at him. 'They're in use.'

He straightens up. On the moor road the other side of the stones a Land Rover is beetling along. 'God, is that Dad? He found the spare keys, then.' He brings both hands up to his head and scrapes his fingers through his hair. 'He's not slept it off.'

Evie jumps to her feet. The Land Rover is Dad's all right: it pulls into the car park and he climbs out. He's holding a bunch of flowers. 'Mum,' says Luke sharply, and Evie sees his hands are balled into fists, which makes her clench her own. They stand on the flat stone, watching as Mum raises her hand and limps towards Dad, and Dad raises his hand and strides towards her. They meet in the middle of the plain, she ducking her head over the flowers and then looking up at him bashfully. He puts his hands on her shoulders and says something, and she says something back, and then they stroll back to the group with their arms around one another, Mum tucked into Dad's armpit like a teenager. 'Evie,' Dad calls, 'how's my girl?' and she goes meekly to him, letting him pull her into a hug with Mum. When she sees Mum smiling she starts to smile too, and reaches up to pat Dad's smooth jowl. 'You shaved,' she says.

'Is that better?'

'Yeah.' She looks around and sees the trekkers watching them, the other mums' faces softening, and is happy not to have to be ashamed. Dad is jostling and tickling her, and Mum is hanging on to her flowers and laughing, and there is for once nothing to worry about. Later, while Mum is getting ready to go to the hospital to have the pain in her ribs checked out, Dad will pursue her around the house hissing, *I saw you up there. Flirting away. You think you're all that. It was embarrassing, did you know that? I was embarrassed. Everybody was embarrassed* until Evie thinks the whispering will be going round and round in her head for ever. But outside, Dad is good at making anybody like him: he scatters high fives and quips, and when he leaves there is a little groan of disappointment. Nobody notices Luke's blank face, and the way Dexter trots watchfully around the perimeter of the stones, tail down, eyes returning to Dad again and again. The trekkers, back on their horses, wave and call to Dad *See you Steve! Bye, Steve! You in the pub later?* Evie, something bitter stuck in her throat, thinks, can he be both of those Dads? What spell has he put on all those people so they can't see that his dog is afraid of him, and his son is angry with him, and his wife is in pain? *Nobody sees,* she thinks. *Why can nobody see?*

She looks back to the raisins she laid out on the stone, but they are gone.

Mum's only cracked a couple of ribs, but the hospital keeps her in overnight. Dad's mad about that, but Luke has whispered to the nurses about what a workaholic Mum is, and how she'll just be out on the ponies tomorrow, and they decide she can stick around so they can get a more conclusive X-ray of her jaw which probably isn't broken but you can't tell with the swelling.

Luke drops Evie at the primary-school holiday club on the way to get his results. 'Good luck,' Evie says as he kisses her goodbye, but he just grimaces. It's scorchy hot, and she stands by the iron railings touching them lightly on and off with the backs of her calves to see how long she can tolerate their heat. She feels very lost and small, but if she lifts her eyes from the playground she can see the moors rippling with sunshine. She wishes she were up there now. She has begun to think, *Can people really not see, or have they just not noticed?* If she, Evie, told somebody, it might become clear to them.

Jess, an activity leader in a baggy green T-shirt, is pacing the playground plopping coloured plastic cones down in a grid pattern, but when she sees Evie she raises her free hand to wave and then beckons her over, screwing up her eyes against the sun. It feels like a sign.

'Hi, Evie! How are you doing?'

Evie takes a breath. 'Not so good.' Her chest feels weird, she puts her hand to the base of her throat but it's like she's shivering inside. She knows she has to say it quickly. 'My mum and dad had like a bit of a fight.'

'Oh, right? Oh dear, Evie, that's a shame.' Jess's brow knits but she looks flustered too, and her eyes flick over to the windows of the school. Evie, however, is vibrating with shock: she has never said anything like that before. It feels like a bomb went off. Her words throb in the air around her, but Jess seems barely to have heard them at all. 'Can you help me put these out?' she says, picking up the stack of cones again. 'If you take the blue ones I'll take the yellow ones.'

'It was really bad,' Evie tries to say, but Jess talks over her:

'Mums and dads do argue sometimes. I know it's not nice. Have they made it up now?'

Evie's face prickles and the tips of her ears are hot. Her palms are damp all of a sudden: she wraps her arms around herself and grabs handfuls of her T-shirt to blot the sweat. She might as well have told her she saw Mum on the toilet or repeated her swearwords, the sort of information an almost-Year-Six knows better than to bring out in public.

She feels trapped like a spider under a tumbler. What now? If she persists, blundering and scrabbling against the smooth glass. If she says, 'No, miss, he hit her and she fell down,' what does she expect to happen? She hasn't thought this through. Looking about herself now she can't imagine it all happening in this playground, this patch of hot asphalt, with Noah and Hayden grappling for possession of the scuffed football and the little kids crouching in a semicircle by the wall to study a beetle. What would Jess say, what would she do? She's not a teacher, she probably doesn't even know the teachers. And then what? Would Evie have to talk to somebody more important? Would heads swivel as she was led out of benchball or finger knitting, would there be whispering as she sat waiting to be seen like a kid who'd misbehaved? Mum and Dad would come in for a meeting, she supposes, and Dad's rage would be terrible. Or what if the police came? Evie doesn't want any of that. But Jess is shading her eyes and looking down the far end of the playground where someone else in a green T-shirt is tapping their wrist.

'Time to ring the bell,' she says, already setting off. Evie, trying to keep pace, lets her steps become bouncy, and she swings her draw-string shoulder bag.

'My dad does get pretty mad,' she says casually, but too quietly, and Jess is already too far ahead to hear her.

In the afternoon when they've had too much sun they watch *Matilda* in the assembly hall. The big room is cool and grey, shot with light when the blinds twist in the breeze. The display boards are bare, pocked with old staples and scraps of coloured paper from where last term's work was torn down. It's strange to be somewhere so familiar but with the rules a bit different: the children sit all mixed up, not in their year groups, and lounge about and pick their bare feet which would never be allowed if school was on. Evie sits up straight even so, and watches the film while her friends braid one another's hair and draw pictures. Matilda gets magical powers because someone needs to sort those grown-ups out, but in the movie she uses them to feed herself cereal and make playing cards dance around her living room. 'That's not in the book,' Evie mutters, but nobody's listening. She puts her legs out in front of her and watches her toes point and flex. When they do meditation, Mrs Brockwell always says, start by scrunching up your toes, and then *relax* them. Now twirl your ankles, and *relax*. And move on all the way up to your head so every bit of you's nice and floppy. But Evie has that feeling again, as if all her bones are threaded too tight, like a necklace that'll just go pop one day. She scrunches her eyes shut and rotates her ankles this way and then that, but it doesn't work.

Jess tiptoes over to her, white plimsolls picking their way between the kids on the mat. 'What's up, Evie?' she whispers in a voice that somehow isn't any quieter than normal talking. 'You look like you're in pain.'

'It's not in the book,' says Evie.

'Hmm?'

'She doesn't do that in the book.'

'Well, books and movies don't have to be exactly the same.'

'But she shouldn't *do* that.' Evie's voice is raised without her meaning it, and becoming shrill. 'That's not what she got the magic for.' She knows people are looking at her – she hears a giggle or two – but she feels as if something has been stolen from her. Her limbs are rattling on their elastic.

'It's just fun,' Jess cajoles. 'It'd be a bit doom and gloom otherwise, wouldn't it?'

Evie scrambles to her feet. 'You don't understand,' she says. She is shaking. 'It's a stupid film. *Stupid.*' And then because she's run out of things to do or say, and because everybody's staring at her, she begins to cry.

'Hey,' says Jess. 'Hey. Come on. No need – just because you don't like the film . . . Come on, Evie. Everyone else is enjoying it. Come and do some colouring.' She takes Evie by the shoulder and steers her to the far end of the room: Evie feels the raised eyebrow Jess shares with the other grown-ups. She thinks she hears the words *temper* and *tantrum* but maybe they're just hanging in the air. Anyway, she doesn't care. She sits cross-legged on the parquet and Jess passes her a tub of felt tips. There's a stack of sugar paper too: Evie lets her hair hang down around her face and chooses a pink pen. She presses its tip to the soft paper and watches the ink bloom out like a rose. She does another. Press, hold, bloom, release. And again.

'Draw properly,' hisses Jess. 'That's just wasting it.'

Evie ignores her. Press, hold, bloom, release. The ink separates into its component colours of red and orange and lilac and blue, so it's sort of a science experiment.

'Evie!'

She picks up another pen and lies down on her belly, her arm crooked around the paper so nobody can see it. She writes, *will you please help me.* Jess is lounging in her chair staring down into her lap: her phone is hidden in her hands but its light shines blue upon her face. Evie folds the note up small and shoves it in her pocket.

*

That night they go out to the nice pub in town that does pizza. Mum wears her black dress with the floaty sleeves and has even put on a little bit of lipstick, although the bruising on her jaw has bloomed since she got out of hospital, and lies like a stain under her make-up. Dad raises his glass to Luke, saying, 'Honestly, mate, I'm chuffed for you. We all knew you could do it.'

Luke presses his lips together. He is staring at his pizza, which sits almost untouched on his plate: Evie wonders if he feels like she does, hollow and bewildered and fearful.

'Our boy, off to Oxford,' Mum is saying with determined brightness. 'I can't believe it.'

'He earned it.' Dad leans over to top up her glass but she shakes her head.

'I'm driving, Steve.'

'Oh, go on. We're celebrating.'

She opens her mouth and then closes it again. Her eyes flick to his face. 'I can't,' she says softly, and he sits back in his chair, arm slung across the back, staring at her as if she is a difficult child.

'Where do you get off?' He spreads his hands, then leans across the table towards her, smiling. 'Your own son's big night and you can't bear to get in the spirit of it. *I'm driving, Steve.* What a martyr! It's not a favour if you go on about it, love. Luke, how's it feel to have a narcissist for a mother?'

'It's fine, Dad. Leave it.'

'You see, Claire? Your kids have learned to placate you.' They are not the only family celebrating tonight. The room is full of chat and laughter, clinking glasses and faces soft with pride and drink. Nobody seems to notice the dangerous mood that has fallen over this table, and Dad is talking on in his low, cruel way, always perfectly pitched to get lost in crowds. 'All that drama after the trek. You *know* they won't do anything for ribs, but you just had to have your moment in A&E.'

'I'm sorry.' She drops her face. 'It really hurt.' She blinks hard. 'It *hurts*.'

'Oh, here we go,' he sighs, pushing his chair out. 'Crying in a restaurant. Sort yourself out.' He saunters off in the direction of the toilets, and they watch his bulk sway between the tables, the flicker of his hand as the other diners call his name.

'Mum,' says Luke gently, and she blots her eyes with the corner of her napkin, glancing around to make sure she hasn't been noticed.

'I'm sorry. I didn't mean to get emotional.' She takes a breath and smiles. 'This dinner's about you. We really are so proud.'

'I'm not going.'

'Oh, Luke, no,' says Mum. 'You're so clever. Don't waste this chance.'

'I'm happy here,' Luke says. 'I like the ponies. And I can get bar shifts.'

'That's not a long-term plan.'

'I could get a deposit together ... '

'You don't want a house at eighteen! You should be free! No responsibilities.'

Luke starts sawing angrily at his pizza, the slices slithering on the plate. 'I don't think that's an option.'

'Evie,' says Mum, 'give your brother's head a wobble. Should he go to *study at Oxford*?'

'Yes!' she cries, doing her special excited-for-university hand wiggle she has been perfecting since Luke sent his forms off and she first felt that stone of worry heavy in her stomach.

Luke looks carefully at her. 'You want me to go away?'

'Don't mind.' She shrugs.

'Oh, go on, Luke, you'd be brilliant,' says Mum. 'Look at your grades! Your teachers love you. Do you know how tiny the chances are of getting in? And you've gone and done it.'

'Mum! I just don't care about it that much.'

Mum presses her palms against the table and breathes in

carefully through her nose. When she speaks again it sounds as if her whole body is trembling. 'I don't want you to get stuck here,' she says. 'You've got to have your life.'

'Can you just shut up?'

'Luke!'

'Really! Leave it!'

'You *need* to get out,' she says.

'And who'll look after you and Evie?'

'I will.'

'But you don't. Seriously, Mum, I had a fucked-up childhood and now you're putting Evie through the exact same thing. I've worked so hard *all* though school and then *all* through college so that one day I can get the fuck away from here, but do you know what? I can't go anywhere. Evie's got nobody else.'

Mum is looking for Dad, but he's leaning at the bar, laughing with some mates. 'Look,' she says, 'I'm sorry that you kids have seen us fighting – you know how much stress Dad's under. He doesn't always handle it right but he loves you. He loves all of us.'

'Mum! Seriously! Leave him!' Luke is rising out of his seat, his face bright and urgent. 'I can help you. People will help. It'll be better.'

'No, Luke.'

'You did it before. It was okay – it was fun! Just you and me in that flat, with friends and movie nights and stuff. Evie, did you know Mum left Dad once?'

Evie shakes her head.

'It was different then,' Mum says. 'We didn't have the stables. We didn't have Evie.'

'But what if—'

She shakes her head. 'No.'

Luke is blinking hard. 'Every time I leave the house I wonder, *Is this the last time I'll see my mum alive?* Can you imagine what that's like?'

They stare at one another for the longest time. Mum's eyes are glistening, tears wobbling right on her lower lashes. Then she straightens her napkin and says, 'Leaving him would not make me any safer.'

Dad is on his way back, taking big jovial strides with a glass of whiskey in each hand. 'That's my boy!' he's announcing to the pub. 'My boy's off to Balliol! Stand up, Luke, let them all see you.'

As Luke half-rises in his seat, an awkward red-faced genuflect, and Dad's mates at the bar cheer, Mum murmurs to him, 'You just need to go, my darling. You mustn't think about us.'

'Have a drink.' Dad slams a whiskey down in front of Luke. 'Don't worry, Claire, I didn't get you anything. I know how you feel about fun.' He rubs his hands together. 'Come on, boy, drink up. Then we'll get out and celebrate properly, you and me.'

'Oh, now, maybe he'll want to meet up with his friends,' flutters Mum, 'it's such a big night,' but Dad turns in his chair so that his back's towards her, and acts as if he can't hear her.

'It's all right, Dad,' Luke says, sipping his drink. 'I'll come out with you. I'd like to.'

It's a warm night, and Evie is bare-shouldered as they leave the restaurant, Dad and Luke striding ahead down the high street while Mum digs out her car keys. The street is full of teenagers, girls walking swiftly arm-in-arm, nails done and eyebrows freshly stencilled; boys bursting into song as they stagger and shake their fists at the sky, which is purpling over the moor but still not quite dark.

'Look!' says Evie. Floating up high is one golden orb, far far away, pulsing like a little heartbeat as it drifts. Then another appears, then a string of them, then a swarm, drifting gently across the sky. Their jellyfish-throb hazes around them, and from somewhere distant and unseen come whoops and cheers. Evie and her family stand gazing, Evie's hand in Mum's, Dad and Luke a little way off.

'Sky lanterns,' says Mum. 'They're letting them off at the stone circle, I think. Not very safe.'

But so pretty, Evie wants to say, but her voice is gone again, and her throat aches with some large emotion she can't begin to name. She makes to lean against Mum's side but remembers about her cracked ribs and pulls away again. Dad and Luke have started walking again, Dad pointing up at the sky where the lanterns are dispersing, some caught up on breezes too high to be felt, some vanishing into the distance until they are lost among the stars.

'Bye, then,' says Mum, but Dad makes like he hasn't heard her, and Luke only spins round on his heel to walk backwards for a step or two.

'I'll not stay out late. Go safe, Mum.'

Mum drives in silence for a long time, and Evie sits in the back leaning her forehead against the window to watch the lanterns' gentle progress over the lanes and the villages. When they enter the holloway the sky is blotted out by leaves and the car is very dark. Hidden in the front seat, Mum says, 'You mustn't worry. Dad won't hurt us.'

'He hurts you.' Evie grips handfuls of her shorts; reaching brambles tap and scrape against her window.

'What's really important, love, is that we *have* to let Luke go. It's not his job to look after us.'

The thought of no Luke feels like having her spine ripped out. Yes, she is frightened of what Dad will do with him gone, but what scares her more is the thought that soon nobody will know the truth but her. Luke will recede into the clean, smiling, safe world out there, and join the ranks of unseeing people who turn their faces from her secrets even when she holds them out to them. Letting Luke go means letting Luke forget, letting him not care. *Nobody sees,* she thinks, *because nobody wants to see.* Even Mum.

'Just stop pretending everything's okay,' Evie says. 'Please.'

The headlights catch a place where the leaves thin, the abrupt turning for their drive. Light catches Mum's cheek but Evie can't see her expression as she flicks the indicator and the car lumbers up the patchy gravel. 'This is us,' she says. When she turns off the engine, the night is extra quiet, a soft dark ground of nothing, shrilling around them as they sit staring ahead. Through the cloth of her shorts Evie can feel something in her pocket. She pulls out a wedge of folded paper enclosing the words *will you please help me.*

'Let's go,' says Mum, and the slam of her door is an imposition upon the silence.

Evie follows her across the gravel until they reach that mysterious point where the light over the kitchen door detects their presence and flicks on to greet them. Inside, Dexter is pacing figures of eight, claws tapping and tail thumping. Mum gets out her house keys but Evie skirts the pool of yellow light and goes instead to the dark flower-beds. She kneels in front of the poppies where the soil is cool and dry and alive-smelling, and reaching through the leaves presses her folded paper into the ground. 'Do this one thing,' she whispers. 'I don't have anything for you. But please, you must see what's happening.'

Then Mum gets the door open, and Dexter plunges out making sneezes and exclamations of joy, corralling Evie and Mum into the light and the house, where the fridge hums and the tiles are mopped and the air smells lemony.

Evie wakes early to the sound of knocking, but can't be sure whether it comes from inside her dream. She lies still listening for Dad's snoring, an angry drone like a wasp at the window, but nothing – only voices downstairs, Mum saying, 'Come through.'

She gets out of bed and tiptoes along the landing so lightly that her pyjamas barely swish. She descends the stairs slowly, pausing on each step so her view of the hall widens in increments between the banisters. The hooks with Mum's coat, and Evie's, and Luke's, but not Dad's. Mum's key in the front door like always. The lounge door, ajar.

'No, I don't think that can be right,' Mum's saying. 'Steve does stop out all night sometimes. It's nothing to worry about.'

'I'm so sorry, Mrs Mole.' This an unfamiliar voice, a woman's. She sounds local. 'Like I say, we found him on the moor this morning. He just lost his footing.'

A little squashed cry. 'No, no. He was in town last night, with Luke. My boy here, Luke, he's got into Oxford. They were celebrating.'

'He must have been so proud,' the voice says warmly. There is the beep and burble of a walkie-talkie. 'God, sorry. I'll turn that off. Luke, you were with your dad? He'd been drinking?'

'We had a few drinks.' Luke's voice is wispy thin, Evie almost cannot hear. 'He wanted to go up on the moor, see the lanterns.'

'And you went with him?'

'I didn't *want* to. I ... I dunno ...'

'Are you all right?'

'Yeah. I just— this is a lot. I'll make us some coffee, okay?'

When he comes out of the lounge his face is grey, his eyes staring almost out of his head as if he has been talking with ghosts. He leans against the wall breathing quick and shallow. Then he spots Evie peering between the banisters. 'Oh my god.' He reaches his hands out to her and she runs to him. 'The police are here,' he whispers, pressing his face into her hair. 'Dad.'

A cold and awful feeling rushes over her, as if she were filling up with sea-water. She is shaking, and Luke clutches her to him so she can feel his chest convulsing, a wheeze of pain in his throat. All the prayers she said, all the offerings she left, the note the police will surely find in the garden if they search it: *will you please help me.* Evie asked the pixies, and the pixies have answered.

'... hit his head ...' they are saying in the other room, '... over in a split-second ...'

'I'm so sorry, Evie,' Luke is saying. 'I didn't want this. I didn't mean ...'

Mum is on her knees on the carpet, keening through clenched teeth.

How badly Evie wants to tell him, *It's my fault. I wished for this. I asked every day.* Is this what she asked for? Had she thought it could really happen? Luke might understand. It was him, after all, who told her all the old stories, about the watchers in the holloway and on the moor who would set justice right if its scales had slipped. He's waited for them twice as long as Evie. But clinging to him she knows she will never breathe a word of her guilt to him or to anyone, and although his arms are wrapped around her she feels as if she's drifting further and further away, like a balloon cut from its tether. She looks through to the lounge, over the heads of Mum and the policewoman, and out of the open window. The hills are bright with sunshine but the holloway is dark and velvety, and from it comes the song of many voices.

THE ORIGINAL TALES

The Green Children of Woolpit[*]

'Another wonderful thing,' says Ralph of Coggeshall, 'happened in Suffolk, at St Mary's of the Wolf-pits. A boy and his sister were found by the inhabitants of that place near the mouth of a pit which is there, who had the form of all their limbs like to those of other men, but they differed in the colour of their skin from all the people of our habitable world; for the whole surface of their skin was tinged of a green colour. No one could understand their speech. When they were brought as curiosities to the house of a certain knight, Sir Richard de Calne, at Wikes, they wept bitterly. Bread and other victuals were set before them, but they would touch none of them, though they were tormented by great hunger, as the girl afterwards acknowledged. At length, when some beans just cut, with their stalks, were brought into the house, they made signs, with great avidity, that they should be given to them. When they were brought, they opened the stalks instead of the pods, thinking the beans were in the hollow of them; but not finding them there, they began to weep anew. When those who were present saw this, they opened the pods, and showed them the naked beans. They fed on these with great delight, and for a long time tasted no other food. The boy, however, was always languid and depressed, and he died within a short time. The girl enjoyed continual good health; and becoming accustomed to various kinds

---

[*] Thomas Keightley, *The Fairy Mythology* (1892), pp. 281–3

of food, lost completely that green colour, and gradually recovered
the sanguine habit of her entire body. She was afterwards regener-
ated by the laver of holy baptism, and lived for many years in the
service of that knight (as I have frequently heard from him and his
family), and was rather loose and wanton in her conduct. Being
frequently asked about the people of her country, she asserted that
the inhabitants, and all they had in that country, were of a green
colour; and that they saw no sun, but enjoyed a degree of light like
what is after sunset. Being asked how she came into this country
with the aforesaid boy, she replied, that as they were following
their flocks, they came to a certain cavern, on entering which they
heard a delightful sound of bells; ravished by whose sweetness,
they went for a long time wandering on through the cavern, until
they came to its mouth. When they came out of it, they were
struck senseless by the excessive light of the sun, and the unusual
temperature of the air; and they thus lay for a long time. Being
terrified by the noise of those who came on them, they wished to
fly, but they could not find the entrance of the cavern before they
were caught.'

Ay, We're Flittin'*

In the house of an honest farmer in Yorkshire, named George Gilbertson, a Boggart had taken up his abode. He here caused a good deal of annoyance, especially by tormenting the children in various ways. Sometimes their bread and butter would be snatched away, or their porringers of bread and milk be capsized by an invisible hand; for the Boggart never let himself be seen; at other times, the curtains of their beds would be shaken backwards and forwards, or a heavy weight would press on and nearly suffocate them. The parents had often, on hearing their cries, to fly to their aid. There was a kind of closet, formed by a wooden partition on the kitchen-stairs, and a large knot having been driven out of one of the deal-boards of which it was made, there remained a hole. Into this one day the farmer's youngest boy stuck the shoe-horn with which he was amusing himself, when immediately it was thrown out again, and struck the boy on the head. The agent was of course the Boggart, and it soon became their sport (which they called *laking with Boggart*) to put the shoe-horn into the hole and have it shot back at them.

The Boggart at length proved such a torment that the farmer and his wife resolved to quit the house and let him have it all to himself. This was put into execution, and the farmer and his family were following the last loads of furniture, when a neighbour named

---

* Thomas Keightley, *The Fairy Mythology* (London, 1892), p. 307

John Marshall came up – 'Well, Georgey,' said he, 'and soa you're leaving t'ould hoose at last?' – 'Heigh, Johnny, my lad, I'm forced tull it; for that damned Boggart torments us soa, we can neither rest neet nor day for't. It seems loike to have such a malice again t'poor bairns, it ommost kills my poor dame here at thoughts on't, and soa, ye see, we're forced to flitt loike.' He scarce had uttered the words when a voice from a deep upright churn cried out, 'Aye, aye, Georgey, we're flitting ye see.' – 'Od damn thee,' cried the poor farmer, 'if I'd known thou'd been there, I wadn't ha' stirred a peg. Nay, nay, it's no use, Mally,' turning to his wife, 'we may as weel turn back again to t'ould hoose as be tormented in another that's not so convenient.'

The Dauntless Girl*

She lived first with a farmer, and he and his friends were a-drinking one night and they ran out of liquor. So the farmer he up and say 'Never you mind, my girl will go down to the public and bring us up another bottle.' But the night was very dark so his friends they say, 'Surelie she'll be afeard to go out such a dark night by herself all alone.' But he say 'No, she won't, for she's afeard of nothing that's alive or dead.' So she went and she brought 'em back their licker, and his friends they say it was a very funny thing she shewd be so bold. But the farmer he say 'That's nuthin at all for she'd go anywhere day or night for she ain't afear of nothing that's alive or dead.' And he offered to bet a gold guinea that none of 'em could name a thing she would not dew. So one of 'em agreed to take the bet and they were to meet the same day as it might be next week and he was to set her a task. Meanwhile he goes to the old passon and he borrows the key of the Church and then he goes to the old sexton and the right-side it with him for the half the guinea to go into the Church and hide himself in the dead house so that he was to frighten the Dauntless Girl when she came.

So when they all met together at the farmer's he say '*This* is what the Dauntless Girl *won't dew* – she won't go into the Church alone at midnight and go to the dead house and bring back a skull bone.' But she made no trouble about it and up and went down to the

* William Rye, *Recreations of a Norfolk Antiquary* (1920), pp. 22–6

Church all along of herself and she opened the door of the dead house and she picked up a skull bone.

Then the old sexton from behind the door he muffled out 'Let that be, that's my mother's skull bone.' So she put it down and picked another. Then the old sexton he muffled out again 'Let that be that's my father's skull bone.' So she put that down tew and took up still another and she say out loud for she'd lost her temper, 'Father or mother, or sister or brother, I *must* hev a skull bone and that's my last word,' and so she up and walked out with it and she locked the door of the dead house behind her and she come home and she put the skull bone on the table and she say 'There's your skull bone, master,' and she was for going back to her work.

But him as had made the bet he up and say 'Didn't yew hear nothing, Mary?' 'Yes,' she say, 'some fule of a ghost called out to me, "Let be that's my father's skull bone and let be that's my mother's skull bone," but I told him right straight "that father or mother, sister or brother, I *must* hev a skull bone," so I tuk it and here t'be and then as I was goin' away arter I had locked the door I heard the old ghost a hallering and shrieking like mad.'

Then him as had made the bet was rarely upset, for he guessed it was the old man sexton a hallerin' about for fear of being locked up all alone in the dead-house. And so it was for when they ran down to let him out they found him lying stone dead on his face a dead-o-fright.

And it sarved him right to try and terrify a poor mawther. But her master he gave her the golden guinea he had won.

A little while after down in Suffolk there was a squire and his mother, a very old lady and she died and was buried. But she would *not* rest and kept on coming into the house 'specially at meals.' Sometimes you could see all of her, sometimes not at a, but you'd see a knife and fork get up off the table and play about where her hands should be. Now this upset the servants so much that they would *not* stop, and the Squire was sadly put to, to know what he should do. One day he heard of the Dauntless Girl, tree villages off, who was feared at nowt. So he rode over and told her all about it, and asked her if she would come as a servant, and she said she paid no regard to ghosts so she would come, but that it ought to be considered in her wages. And so it was and she went back with the Squire. First thing she did was to allus lay a place regular for the ghost at meals and took great care not to put the knife and fork criss cross way. And she used to hand her the vegetables and the rest just as if she were real. And would say 'Peppaw, mum, or salt, mum, as it might be.' This fared to please the old ghost, but nothing come of it till Squire had to go up to London on some law business.

Next day the Dauntless Girl was down on her knees a-cleaning the parlour grate when she noticed a thin thing push in through the door, which was just ajar and open out wide when it got into the room, till she turned out to be the old ghost.

Then the ghost, she up and spoke for the first time and she say 'Mary, are you afeared of me?' and the girl say, 'No, mum, I've no call to be afeared of yew, for *yew* are dead and *I'm* alive,' which clearly flummoxed the old ghost, but she went on and say 'Mary, will yew come down into the cellar along o' me – yew musent bring a light but I'll shine enow to light yew.' So they went down the cellar steps and she shone like an old lantern. And when they got down she pointed out to some loose tiles and said 'Pick yew up those tiles.' So she did and there were tew bags of gold, one a big 'un and one a little 'un, and she said, 'Mary, that big bag's for your master and that little bag's for yew, for you are a dauntless girl and deserve it.' Then off went the old ghost and never was seen no more and the Dauntless Girl she had a main o' trouble to find her way up in the dark out of the cellar.

Then in tree days' time, back there came the Squire and he said 'Morning, Mary, hae yew seen anything of my mother since I've been away?' and she said 'Iss, sir, that I hev, and that if yew ain't afraid of coming down into the cellar along me I'll show yew something.' And he larfed and said *he* wornt afraid if *she* wornt for the Dauntless Girl wor a very pretty girl.

So they lit a candle and went down and she opened up the tiles and she say there are the tew bags of gold, the *little* one is for yew and the big 'un is for *me*. And he say Lor! For he thought his mother might have given *him* the big one (and so she had), but he took what he could. And the Dauntless Girl she ollus afterwards crossed the knives and forks to keep the ghost from telling what she had done. But arter a while the Squire thort it all over and he married the Dauntless Girl, so arter all he got both bags of gold, and he used to stick-lick her whensoever he got drunk. And I think she deserved it for deceiving the old ghost.

The Great Silkie of Sule Skerry[*]

An eartly nourris sits and sing,
And aye she sings, Ba, lily wean!
Little ken I my bairnis father,
Far less the land that he staps in.
Then ane arose at her bed-fit,
An a grumly guest I'm sure was he:
'Here am I, thy bairnis father,
Although that I be not comelie.
I am a man, upo the lan,
An I am a silkie in the sea;
And when I'm far and far frae lan,
My dwelling is in Sule Skerry.'
'It was na weel,' quo the maiden fair,
'It was na weel, indeed,' quo she,
'That the Great Silkie of Sule Skerry
Suld hae come and aught a bairn to me.'
Now he has taen a purse of goud,
And he has pat it upo her knee,
Sayin, Gie to me my little young son,
An tak thee up thy nourris-fee.
An it sall come to pass on a simmer's day,

---

[*] F. J. Child, *The English and Scottish Popular Ballads* (1882–1898). Child, no. 113

When the sin shines het on evera stane,
That I will tak my little young son,
An teach him for to swim the faem.
An thu sall marry a proud gunner,
An a proud gunner I'm sure he'll be,
An the very first schot that ere he schoots,
He'll schoot baith my young son and me.

Chillington House[*]

'That is called Giffard's Cross,' said Father Huddlestone, 'and it was set up in old times by Sir John Giffard. Sir John, who was excessively fond of the chase, kept a collection of wild beasts, and amongst them a very beautiful, but very fierce panther, which he valued more than all the rest. One day, it chanced that this savage animal slipped out of its cage, and escaped into the park. Made aware of what had happened by the cries of his terrified household, Sir John snatched up an arbalest, and rushed out into the park, accompanied by his eldest son. He easily ascertained the direction taken by the panther, for the beast had been seen to skirt the avenue. At that time there were no gates here, and the limits of the park extended far beyond the place where we are now standing. Sir John and his son ran as swiftly as they could, and were still speeding on, when they beheld a young woman and a child coming along the road. At the same moment, they discovered the panther couched amid the fern, evidently waiting for his prey. Sir John and his son had halted, and though the distance was almost too great, the old knight prepared to launch a bolt at the beast. But while he was adjusting his cross-bow, his son remarked that he was out of breath, and fearing he might miss his aim from this cause, called out to him in French, *'Prenez haleine, tirez fort.'* By this

[*] Harrison Ainsworth, *Boscobel* (London: Routledge, 1872), Book IV, Chapter 1

time the poor young woman had perceived her peril, and uttering a loud shriek, clasped her child to her breast, and essayed to fly. It may be by the interposition of holy Hubert,' continued the priest, reverently, 'whose aid Sir John invoked, that she was saved. Just as the panther was about to spring, the bolt flew, and was lodged in the animal's brain. On the spot where the mortally-wounded beast rolled on the ground, this memorial was placed. Thenceforward, also, Sir John Giffard adopted as his motto the words of counsel addressed to him by his son.'

The Tale of Kathleen[*]

A young girl from Innis-Sark had a lover, a fine young fellow, who met his death by an accident, to her great grief and sorrow.

One evening at sunset, as she sat by the roadside. crying her eyes out, a beautiful lady came by all in white, and tapped her on the cheek.

'Don't cry, Kathleen,' she said, 'your lover is safe. Just take this ring of herbs and look through it and you will see him. He is with a grand company, and wears a golden circlet on his head and a scarlet sash round his waist.'

So Kathleen took the ring of herbs and looked through it, and there indeed was her lover in the midst of a great company dancing on the hill; and he was very pale, but handsomer than ever, with the gold circlet round his head, as if they had made him a prince.

'Now,' said the lady, 'here is a larger ring of herbs. Take it, and whenever you want to see your lover, pluck a leaf from it and burn it; and a great smoke will arise, and you will fall into a trance; and in the trance your lover will carry you away to the fairy rath, and there you may dance all night with him on the greensward. But say no prayer, and make no sign of the cross while the smoke is rising, or your lover will disappear for ever.'

From that time a great change came over Kathleen. She said

---

[*] Lady Sperenza Wilde, *Ancient Legends, Mystic Charms and Superstitions of Ireland* (1887)

no prayer, and cared for no priest, and never made the sign of the cross, but every night shut herself up in her room, and burned a leaf of the ring of herbs as she had been told; and when the smoke arose she fell into a deep sleep and knew no more. But in the morning she told her people that, though she seemed to be lying in her bed, she was far away with the fairies on the hill dancing with her lover. And she was very happy in her new life, and wanted no priest nor prayer nor mass any more, and all the dead were there dancing with the rest, all the people she had known; and they welcomed her and gave her wine to drink in little crystal cups, and told her she must soon come and stay with them and with her lover for evermore.

Now Kathleen's mother was a good, honest, religious woman, and she fretted much over her daughter's strange state, for she knew the girl had been fairy-struck. So she determined to watch; and one night when Kathleen went to her bed as usual all alone by herself in the room, for she would allow no one to be with her, the mother crept up and looked through a chink in the door, and then she saw Kathleen take the round ring of herbs from a secret place in the press and pluck a leaf from it and burn it, on which a great smoke arose and the girl fell on her bed in a deep trance.

Now the mother could no longer keep silence, for she saw there was devil's work in it; and she fell on her knees and prayed aloud –

'O Maia, mother, send the evil spirit away from the child!' And she rushed into the room and made the sign of the cross over the sleeping girl, when immediately Kathleen started up and screamed –

'Mother! mother! the dead are coming for me. They are here! they are here!'

And her features looked like one in a fit. Then the poor mother sent for the priest, who came at once, and threw holy water on the girl, and said prayers over her; and he took the ring of herbs that lay beside her and cursed it for evermore, and instantly it fell to powder and lay like grey ashes on the floor. After this Kathleen grew calmer, and the evil spirit seemed to have left her, but she was too weak to move or to speak, or to utter a prayer, and before the clock struck twelve that night she lay dead.

The Brothers*

My dear Friend,
July 17, 1778.

According to your request, I shall give you all the particulars
I have been able to collect concurring the Brothers Steps.
They are situate in the field about half a mile from Montague
House, in a North direction; and the prevailing tradition
concerning them is, that two brothers quarrelled about a
worthless woman, and as it was the fashion of those days, as it
is now, they decided it by a duel. The print of their feet is near
three inches in depth, and remains totally barren, so much
so, that nothing will grow to disfigure them. Their number
I did not reckon, but suppose they may be about 90. A bank
on which the first fell, who was mortally wounded and died
on the spot, retains the form of his agonizing posture by the
curse of the barrenness, while the grass grows round it. A
friend of mine shewed me these steps in the year 1760, when
he could trace them back by old people to the year 1686; but it
was generally supposed to have happened in the early part of
the reign of Charles II. There are people now living who well
remember their being ploughed up, and barley sown, to deface
them; but all was labour in vain; for the prints returned in a

---

* *The Gentleman's Magazine*, Vol. 74, part 2 (1804), p. 1194

short time to their original form. There is one thing I nearly forgot to mention: that a place on the bank is still to be seen, where, Traditions says, the wretched woman sat to see the combat. I am sorry I can throw no more light on the subject; but am convinced in my own opinion that the Almighty has ordered it as a standing monument of his just displeasure of the horrid sin of duelling. I remain your loving friend,

Thos. Smith.

The Fairy Midwife[*]

The old woman of Garth Dorwen was in the habit of putting women to bed, and she was in great request far and wide. Some time after Eilian's escape there came a gentleman on horseback to the door one night when the moon was full, while there was a slight rain and just a little mist, to fetch the old woman to his wife. So she rode off behind the stranger on his horse, and came to Rhos y Cowrt. Now there was at that time, in the centre of the rhos, somewhat of a rising ground that looked like an old fortification, with many big stones on the top, and a large cairn of stones on the northern side: it is to be seen there to this day, and it goes by the name of Bryn y Pibion, but I have never visited the spot. When they reached the spot, they entered a large cave, and they went into a room where the wife lay in her bed; it was the finest place the old woman had seen in her life. When she had successfully brought the wife to bed, she went near the fire to dress the baby; and when she had done, the husband came to the old woman with a bottle of ointment that she might anoint the baby's eyes; but he entreated her not to touch her own eyes with it. Somehow after putting the bottle by, one of the old woman's eyes happened to itch, and she rubbed it with the same finger that she had used to rub the baby's eyes. Then she saw with that eye how the wife lay on a bundle of rushes and withered ferns in a large cave, with big

---

* John Rhys, *Celtic-Folklore: Welsh and Manx*, Vol. 1 (Oxford, 1901), p. 213

stones all round her, and with a little fire in one corner; and she saw also that the lady was only Eilian, her former servant girl, whilst, with the other eye, she beheld the finest place she had ever seen. Not long afterwards the old midwife went to Carnarvon to market, when she saw the husband, and said to him, 'How is Eilian?' 'She is pretty well,' said he to the old woman, 'but with what eye do you see me?' 'With this one,' was the reply; and he took a bulrush and put her eye out at once.

That is exactly the tale, my informant tells me, as he heard it from his mother, who heard it from an old woman who lived at Garth Dorwen when his mother was a girl, about eighty-four years ago, as he guessed it to have been.

The Old Wandering Droll-Teller of the Lizard, and his Story of the Mermaid and the Man of Cury[*]

To you will I give as much of gold
As for more than your life will endure;
And of pearls and precious stones handfuls;
And all shall be so pure.'
Duke Magnus, Duke Magnus, plight thee to me,
I pray you still so freely;
Say me not nay, but yes, yes!
'I am a King's son so good
How can I let you gain me?
You dwell not on land, but in the flood,
Which would not with me agree.

— DUKE MAGNUS AND THE MERMAID

From a period, more remote than is now remembered, to the present time, some members of the family called Lutey, who for the most part, resided in the parish of Cury, or its vicinity, have been noted conjurors or white witches. They have long been known, all

---

* William Bottrell, *Traditions and Hearthside Stories of West Cornwall*, Vol. 1 (1870)

over the west, as the 'Pellar Family'. The word Pellar is probably
an abridgment of repeller, derived from their reputed power in
counteracting the malign influences of sorcery and witchcraft.

According to an oft-told story, the wonderful gifts of this
family were acquired by a fortunate ancestor, who had the luck
to find a mermaid (here by us pronounced meremaid), left high
and dry on a rock by the ebbing tide. Some forty years ago,
uncle Anthony James – an old blind man, belonging to the
neighbourhood of the gifted family – with his dog, and a boy
who led him, used to make their yearly tour of the country as
regularly as the seasons came round. This venerable wanderer, in
his youth, had been a soldier, and had then visited many foreign
lands, about which he had much to tell; but his descriptions of
outlandish people and places were just as much fashioned after
his own imagination, as were the embellishments of the legends
he related, and the airs he composed for many old ballads which
he and his boy sang to the melody of the old droll-teller's crowd
(fiddle). However, in all the farm houses, where this old wanderer
rested on his journey, he and his companions received a hearty
welcome, for the sake of his music and above all for his stories,
the substance of most of which every one knew by heart, yet they
liked to hear these old legends again and again, because he, or
some of his audience, had always something new to add, by way
of fashioning out the droll, or to display their inventive powers.
Uncle Anthony had much to tell about ghosts, witchcraft, and
conjuration; curious traditions connected with some old families formed the substance of many strange tales; he had always
something new to relate concerning the extraordinary powers of
his neighbours, the white-witches of Cury, and of many other
things which were equally wonderful and fraught with interest
to us simple folks at the Land's-End.

Among all the favourite legends, related by this humble relic of
our old bards, none were oftener told, or more varied in the telling,

by adding to the story whatever struck his fancy at the moment, than the following.

Droll of the Mermaid

Hundreds of years ago, there lived somewhere near the Lizard Point a man called Lutey or Luty, who farmed a few acres of ground near the seashore, and followed fishing and smuggling as well, when it suited the time. One summer's evening, seeing from the cliff, where he had just finished his day's work of cutting turf, that the tide was far out, he sauntered down over the sands, near his dwelling, in search of any wreck which might have been cast ashore by the flood; at the same time he was cursing the bad luck, and murmuring because a god-send worth securing hadn't been sent to the Lizard cliffs for a long while.

Finding nothing on the sands worth picking up, Lutey turned to go home, when he heard a plaintive sound, like the wailing of a woman or the crying of a child, which seemed to come from seaward; going in the direction of the cry, he came near some rocks which were covered by the sea at high water, but now, about half ebb and being spring tides, the waves were a furlong or more distant from them. Passing round to the seaward side of these rocks, he saw what appeared to him a fairer woman than he had ever beheld before. As yet, he perceived little more than her head and shoulders, because all the lower part of her figure was hidden by the ore-weed (sea-weed; query, is *ore* a corruption of *mor*, sea?) which grew out from the rocks, and spread around the fair one in the pullan (pool) of sea-water that yet remained in a hollow at the foot of the rocks. Her golden-coloured hair, falling over her shoulders and floating on the water, shone like the sunbeams on the sea. The little he saw of her skin showed that it was smooth and clear as a polished shell. As the comely creature, still making a mournful wail, looked intently on the distant and ebbing sea, Lutey remained some minutes, admiring her unperceived. He longed to assuage her grief, but, not knowing how to comfort her, and afraid of frightening her into fits by coming too suddenly on her, he coughed and ahem'd to call her attention before he approached any nearer.

Looking round and catching a glimpse of the man, she uttered a more unearthly yell than ever, and then gliding down from the ledge, on which she reclined, into the pullan, all but her beautiful head and swan-like neck was hidden under the water and the ore-weed.

'My dear creature,' says Lutey, 'don't 'e be afraid of me, for I'm a sober and staid married man, near thirty years of age. Have 'e lost your clothes? I don't see any, anywhere! Now, what shall I do to comfort 'e? My turtle-dove, I wouldn't hurt 'e for the world,' says Lutey, as he edged a little nearer. He couldn't take his eyes from the beautiful creature for the life of him. The fair one, too, on hearing his soothing words, stayed her crying, and, when she looked on him, her eyes shone like the brightest of stars on a dark night. Lutey drew near the edge of the pullan and, looking into the water, he discovered the fan of a fish's tail quivering and shaking amongst the floating ore-weed: then, he knew that the fair one was a mermaid. He never had so near a view of one before, though he had often seen them, and heard them singing, of moonlight nights, at a distance, over the water.

'Now my lovely maid of the waves,' said he, 'what shall I do for 'e? Speak but the word; or give me a sign, if you don't know our Cornish tongue.'

'Kind good man,' she replied, 'we people of the ocean understand all sorts of tongues, as we visit the shores of every country, and all the tribes of earth pass over our domain; besides, our hearing is so good that we catch what is said on the land when we are miles away over the flood. You may be scared, perhaps,' she continued, 'to see me simply dressed, like naked truth, because your females are always covered with such things as would sadly hinder our sporting in the waves.'

'No, my darling, I am'at the least bit frightened to see 'e without your dress and petticoats on,' Luty replied, as he still drew nearer, and continued as kindly as possible to say, 'now my dear, dont 'e hide your handsome figure in the pullan any longer, but sit up and tell me what makes 'e grieve so?'

The mermaid rose out of the water, seated herself on a ledge of the rock, combed back her golden ringlets from her face, and then Lutey observed that her hair was so abundant that it fell around and covered her figure like an ample robe of glittering gold. When this simple toilette was settled, she sighed and said, 'Oh! unlucky mermaid that I am; know, good man, that only three hours ago I left my husband soundly sleeping on a bed of soft and sweet sea-flowers, with our children sporting round him. I charged the eldest to be sure and keep the shrimps and sea-fleas, that they mightn't get into their daddy's ears and nose to disturb his rest. "Now take care," I told them, "that the crabs don't pinch your dad's tail and wake hint up, whilst I'm away to get 'e something nice for supper, and if you be good children I'll bring 'e home some pretty young dolphins and sea-devils for 'e to play with." Yet noble youth of the land,' she went on to say, 'with all my care I very much fear my merman may wake up and want something to eat before I get home. I ought to know when the tide leaves every rock on the coast, yet I was so stupid as to remain here looking at myself in the pullan as I combed the broken ore-weed, shrimps, crabs, and sea-fleas out of my hair, without observing, till a few minutes since, that the sea had gone out so far as to leave a bar of dry sand between me and the waves.'

'Yet why should 'e be in such trouble, my heart's own dear?' Lutey asked, 'Can't 'e wait here, and I'll bear ye company till the tide comes in, when you may swim away home at your ease?'

'Oh, no, I want to get back before the turn of the tide; because, then, my husband and all the rest of the mermen are sure to wake up hungry and look for their suppers; an, can 'e believe it of my monster (he looks a monster indeed compared with you), that if I am not then at hand with half-a-dozen fine mullets, a few scores of mackerel, or something else equally nice to suit his dainty stomach, when he awakes with the appetite of a shark, he's sure to eat some of our pretty children. Mermen and maidens would be as plenty in the sea as herrings if their gluttons of fathers didn't gobble up the tender babes. Score of my dear ones have gone through his ugly jaws, never to come out alive.'

'I'm very sorry for your sad bereavements,' said Lutey. 'Yet why don't the young fry start off on their own hook?'

'Ah! my dear,' said she, 'they love their pa, and don't think, poor simple innocents, when they hear him whistling a lively tune, that it's only to decoy them around him, and they, so fond of music, get close about his face, rest their ears on his lips, then he opens his great mouth like a cod's, and into the trap they go. If you have the natural feelings of a tender parent you can understand,' she said, after sobbing as if her heart were ready to burst, 'that, for my dear children's sakes, I'm anxious to get home in an hour or so, by which time it will be near low water; else, I should be delighted to stay here all night, and have a chat with you, for I have often wished, and wished in vain, that the powers had made for me a husband, with two tails, like you, or with a tail split into what you call your legs; they are so handy for passing over dry land! Ah,' she sighed, 'what wouldn't I give to have a pair of tails like unto you, that I might come on the land and examine, at my ease, all the strange and beautiful creatures which we view from the waves. If you will,' she continued, 'but serve me now, for ten minutes only, by taking me over the sands to the sea, I'll grant to you and yours any three wishes you may desire; but there's no time to spare – no, not a minute,' said she, in taking from her hair a golden comb in a handle of pearl, which she gave to Lutey, saying, 'Here, my dear, keep this as a token of my faith; I'd give 'e my glass, too, had I not left that at home to make my monster think that I didn't intend to swim far away. Now mind,' she said, as Lutey put the comb into his pocket, 'whenever you wish me to direct you, in any difficulty, you have only to pass that comb through the sea three times, calling me as often, and I'll come to ye on the next flood tide. My name is Morvena, which, in the language of this part of the world, at the time I was named, meant sea-woman. You can't forget it, because you have still many names much like it among ye.'

Lutey was so charmed with the dulcet melody of the mermaid's voice that he remained listening to her flutelike tones, and, looking into her languishing sea-green eyes till he was like one enchanted, and ready to do everything she desired; so stopping down, he took the mermaid in his arms, that he might carry her out to sea.

Lutey being a powerful fellow, he bore the mermaid easily on his left arm, she encircling his neck with her right. They proceeded thus, over the sands, some minutes before he made up his mind what to wish for. He had heard of a man who, meeting with similar luck, wished that all he touched might turn to gold, and knew the fatal result of his thoughtless wish, and of the bad luck which happened to several others whose selfish desires were gratified. As all the wishes he could remember ended badly, he puzzled his head to think of something new, and, long before he came to any conclusion, the mermaid said,

'Come, my good man, lose no more time, but tell me for what three things do ye wish? Will you have long life, strength, and riches?'

'No,' says he, 'I only wish for the power to do good to my neighbours – first that I may be able to break the spells of witchcraft; secondly that I may have such power over familiar spirits as to compel them to inform me of all I desire to know for the benefit of others; thirdly, that these good gifts may continue in my family for ever.'

The mermaid promised that he and his should ever possess these rare endowments, and that, for the sake of his unselfish desires, none of his posterity should ever come to want. They had still a long way to go before they reached the sea. As they went slowly along, the mermaid told him of their beautiful dwellings, and of the pleasant life they led beneath the flood. 'In our cool caverns we have everything one needs,' said she, 'and much more. The walls of our abodes are encrusted with coral and amber, entwined with sea-flowers of every hue, and their floors are all strewn with pearls. The roof sparkles of diamonds, and other gems of such brightness that their rays make our deep grots in the ocean hillsides, as light as day.' Then, embracing Lutey with both her arms round his neck, she continued, 'Come with me, love, and see the beauty of the mermaid's dwellings. Yet the ornaments, with which we take the most delight to embellish our halls and chambers, are the noble sons and fair daughters of earth, whom the wind and waves send in foundered ships to our abodes. Come, I will show you thousands of handsome bodies so embalmed, in a way only known to ourselves, with choice salts and rare spices, that they look more beautiful than when they breathed, as you will say when you see them reposing on beds of amber, coral, and pearl, decked with rich stuffs, and surrounded by heaps of silver and gold for which they ventured to traverse our domain. Aye, and when you see their limbs all adorned with glistening gems, move gracefully to and fro with the motion of the waves, you will think they still live.'

'Perhaps I should think them all very fine,' Lutey replied, 'yet faix (faith) I'd rather find in your dwellings, a few of the puncheons of rum that must often come down to ye in the holds of sunken ships, and one would think you'd be glad to get them in such a cold wet place as you live in! What may 'e do with all the good liquor, tobacco, and other nice things that find their way down below?'

'Yes indeed,' she answered, 'it would do your heart good to see the casks of brandy, kegs of Hollands, pipes of wine, and puncheons of rum that come to our territory. We take a shellful now and then to warm our stomachs, but there's any quantity below for you, so come along, come.'

'I would like to go very well,' says Lutey, 'but surely I should be drowned, or smothered, under the water.'

'Don't 'e believe it,' said she, 'you know that we women of the sea can do wonders. I can fashion 'e a pair of gills; yes, in less than five minutes I'll make you such a pair as will enable 'e to live in the water as much at your ease as a cod or a conger. The beauty of your handsome face will not be injured, because your beard and whiskers will hide the small slits required to be made under your chin. Besides, when you have seen all you would like to see, or get tired of my company and life in the water, you can return to land and bring back with you as much of our treasures as you like, so come along, love.'

'To be sure,' said Lutey, 'your company, the liquor, and riches below are very tempting; yet I can't quite make up my mind.'

The time passed in this kind of talk till Lutey, wading through the sea (now above his knees), brought her near the breakers, and he felt so charmed with the mermaid's beauty and enchanted by the music of her voice that he was inclined to plunge with her into the waves. One can't, now, tell the half of what she said to allure the man to her home beneath the flood. The mermaid's sea-green eyes sparkled as she saw the man was all but in her power. Then, just in the nick of time, his dog, which had followed unnoticed, barked and howled so loud, that the charmed man looked round, and, when he saw the smoke curling up from his chimney, the cows in the fields, and everything looking so beautiful on the green land, the spell of the mermaid's song was broken. He tried long in vain to free himself from her close embrace, for he now looked with loathing on her fishy tail, scaly body, and sea-green eyes, till he roared out in agony, 'Good Lord deliver me from this devil of a fish!' Then, rousing from his stupor, with his right hand he snatched his knife from his girdle, and, flashing the bright steel before the mermaid's eyes, 'By God,' said he, 'I'll cut your throat and rip out your heart if you don't unclasp your arms from my neck, and uncoil your conger-tail from my legs.'

Lutey's prayer was heard, and the sight of the bright steel (which, they say, has power against enchantments and over evil beings), made the mermaid drop from his neck into the sea. Still looking towards him, she swam away, singing in her plaintive tone, 'Farewell my sweet, for nine long years, then I'll come for thee my love.'

Lutey had barely the strength to wade out of the sea, and reach, before dark, a sown (cavern) in the cliff, where he usually kept a few tubs of liquor, buried in the sand, under any lumber of wreck, secured there above high-water mark. The weary and bewildered man took a gimlet from his pocket, spiled an anker of brandy, fixed a quill in the hole, and sucked a little of the liquor to refresh himself; then lay down among some old sails and was soon asleep.

In the meantime, dame Lutey passed rather an anxious time, because her husband hadn't been home to supper, which the good man never missed, though he often remained out all night on the sands to look after wreck, or with smugglers or customers in the 'sown' and on the water. So, as there was neither sight nor sign of him when breakfast was ready, she went down to the 'sown' and there she found her man fast asleep.

'Come! wake up,' said she; 'and what made thee stay down here without thy supper? Thee hast had a drop too much I expect!'

'No by gamblers,' said he, rising up and staring round, 'but am I here in the "sown" or am I in a cavern at the bottom of the sea? And are you my dear Morvena? Ef you are, give me a hornful of rum, do; but you don't look like her.'

'No indeed,' said the wife, 'they cale me An Betty Lutey,

and, what's more, I never heard tell of the lass thee art dreaman about before.'

'Well then, of thee art my old woman, thee hast had a narrow escape, I can tell thee, of being left as bad as a widow and the poor children orphans, this very night.'

Then on the way home, he related how he found a stranded mermaid; that for taking her out to sea, she had promised to grant his three wishes, and given him the comb (which he showed his wife) as a token; 'but,' said he, 'if it hadn't been for the howling of our dog Venture, to rouse me out of the trance, and make me see how far I was from land, as sure as a gun I should now be with the mermaidens drinkan rum or huntan sharks at the bottom of the sea.'

When Lutey had related all particulars, he charged his wife not to say anything about it to the neighbours, as some of them, perhaps, wouldn't credit his strange adventure; but she, unable to rest with such a burden on her mind, as soon as her husband went away to his work, she trotted round half the parish to tell the story, as a great secret, to all the courtseying old women she could find, and showed them what Lutey gave her as the mermaid's comb, to make the story good. The wonder (always told by the old gossips as a great secret) was talked of far and near in the course of a few weeks, and very soon folks, who were bewitched or otherwise afflicted, came in crowds to be helped by the new pellar or conjuror. Although Luty had parted from the mermaid in a very ungracious manner, yet he found that she was true to her promise. It was also soon discovered that he was endowed with far more than the ordinary white-witch's skill. Yet the pellar dearly purchased the sea-woman's favours. Nine years after, to the day on which Lutey bore her to the water, he and a comrade were out fishing one clear moonlight night; though the weather was calm and the water smooth as a glass, about midnight the sea suddenly arose around their boat, and in the foam of the curling waves they saw a mermaid approach them, with all her body, above the waist, out of the water, and her golden hair floating behind and around her.

'My hour is come,' said Lutey, the moment he saw her; and, rising like one distraught, he plunged into the sea, swam with the mermaid a little way, then they both sunk, and the sea became as smooth as ever.

Lutey's body was never found, and, in spite of every precaution, once in nine years, some of his descendants find a grave in the sea.

Here ends the droll-teller's story.

Old Farmer Mole*

They'll tell 'ee three things 'bout an Exmoor Pony 'can climb a cleeve, carry a drunky, and zee a pixy'. And that's what old Varmer Mole's pony do.

Old Varmer Mole were a drunken old toad as lived out over to Hangley Cleave way and he gived his poor dear wife and liddle children a shocking life of it. He never come back from market till his pockets were empty and he was zo vull of zider he'd zit on pony 'hind-zide afore' a zingin' and zwearin' till her rolled into ditch and slept the night there – but if his poor missus didn't zit up all night vor'n he'd baste her and the children wicked.

Now the pixies they did mind'n and they went to mend his ways. 'Twad'n no manner of use to try and frighten pony – he were that foot-sure and way-wise he'd brought Varmer safe whoame drunk or asleep vor years, wheresoever the vule tried to ride'n tew.

This foggy night the old veller were wicked drunk and a-waving his gad and reckoning how he'd drub his missus when he gets to shoame when her zee a light in the mist. 'Woah, tha vule!' says he, 'Us be to whoame, Dang'n vor lighting a girt candle like thic. I'll warm her zides for it!'

But pony he wouldn' stop. He could a-zee the pixy holdin' thic

* *Somerset Folklore* by Routh Tongue, ed. K. M. Briggs (London: Folklore Society, 1965), pp. 115–6

light and 'twere over the blackest, deepest bog this zide of the Chains – zuck a pony down in a minute 'twould, rider and all.

But the old man keeps on shouting, 'Whoa, fule, us be tew woahme!' And rode straight for the bog – but pony dug in his vor liddle veet 'n her stood!

Varmer gets off'n and catches'n a crack on the head and walks on to light. He hadn' goed two steps when the bog took and swallowed 'n!

Zo old pony trots woahme. And when they zee'd 'n come alone with peat-muck on his leg they knowed what did come to Varmer – and they did light every candle in the house and *dancey*!

After that Missus left a pail of clean water out at night vor pixy babies to wash in, pretty dears, and swept hearth vor pixies to dancey on and vorm prospered wondervul, and old pony grew zo fat as a pig.

About the Authors

Naomi Booth is a writer and academic from Bradford. Her novel *The Lost Art of Sinking* won the Saboteur Award for best novella, while *Sealed* was shortlisted for the *Guardian* 'Not the Booker' Prize. She now lives in York with her partner and daughter.

Natasha Carthew is a nature and country writer who has previously been published as a poet and YA writer. Her books include *All Rivers Run Free, Only the Ocean, The Light That Gets Lost* and *Winter Damage*. Many of these have been nominated for national awards including the Branford Boase and Carnegie Awards. She was born in Cornwall where she spends much of her time outdoors as a survival expert and teaches Wild Writing workshops.

Emma Glass was born in Swansea. Her debut novel, *Peach*, was longlisted for the International Dylan Thomas Prize. She lives in south London as a research nurse specialist. *Rest and Be Thankful* is her second novel.

Imogen Hermes Gowar studied Archaeology, Anthropology and Art Studies before working at a museum. She used the artefacts in the museum to inspire her writing, and her first novel *The Mermaid and Mrs Hancock* was a *Sunday Times* bestseller and won the Betty Trask Award, along with multiple shortlistings. Imogen lives and writes in Bristol.

Daisy Johnson is the author of *Fen*, *Everything Under* and *Sisters*. She has been shortlisted for the Man Booker Prize and won the *Harper's Bazaar* Short Story Prize, the A. M. Heath Prize and the Edge Hill Short Story Prize. She grew up in the fens and lives in Oxford.

Liv Little is the founding editor-in-chief of *gal-dem* magazine – an online and print magazine run by women of colour to share stories by women and non-binary people of colour. She was raised in south-east London.

Kirsty Logan is the author of five books, including *The Gracekeeper*, *Things We Say in the Dark*, *A Portable Shelter* and *The Rental Heart & Other Fairytales*. She regularly performs at events and festivals throughout the UK and Europe. Logan currently lives in Glasgow with her wife and their dog.

Eimear McBride is an Irish novelist who won the inaugural Goldsmiths Prize and the Baileys Women's Prize for Fiction for her debut novel, *A Girl Is a Half-formed Thing*. Her second novel, *The Lesser Bohemians*, has also been shortlisted for and won prizes. Her third novel is *Strange Hotel*. McBride was born in Liverpool but lived in Ireland, Norwich, Cork and Saint Petersburg before settling in London.

Irenosen Okojie is a Nigerian-born writer who grew up in Norfolk before moving to east London. Her first novel, *Butterfly Fish*, won the Betty Trask Award. Her short story collection, *Speak Gigantular*, was shortlisted for the inaugural Jhalak Prize and the Edge Hill Short Story Prize. Her new collection of short stories, *Nudibranch*, was longlisted for the Jhalak Prize and a novel, *Curandera*, is forthcoming from Dialogue Books. She won the AKO Caine Prize for her short story *Grace Jones*.

Mahsuda Snaith is a writer of novels and short stories. She was the winner of the SI Leeds Literary Prize and Bristol Short Story Prize in 2014. She was named an *Observer* 'New Face of Fiction' for her debut novel, *Things We Thought We Knew*. She currently lives in Leicester.